# EXERCISE
# IN
# TERROR

## Books by Stuart Kaminsky

*Down for the Count*
*The Fala Factor*
*When the Dark Man Calls*
*He Done Her Wrong*
*Catch a Falling Clown*
*High Midnight*
*Death of a Dissident*
*Basic Filmmaking*
*Coop: The Life and Legend of Gary Cooper*
*Never Cross a Vampire*
*The Howard Hughes Affair*
*Bullet for a Star*

# EXERCISE IN TERROR

a novel by

**Stuart M. Kaminsky**

ST. MARTIN'S PRESS • NEW YORK

Design by Paolo Pepe

Library of Congress Cataloging in Publication Data

Kaminsky, Stuart M.
    Exercise in terror.

    I. Title.
PS3561.A43E9  1985   813'.54     85–11732
ISBN 0-312-27480-7

First Edition

10  9  8  7  6  5  4  3  2  1

*For  Merle*

*Old Acquaintance we'll renew*
*Prospero had One Caliban & I have Two*

——William Blake
dedication to the painting of
*Satan Calling up His Legions*

# EXERCISE
## IN
## TERROR

# 1

## August 1, 1975, 7:35 P.M., Chicago

There were two plates of glass between Maureen and David. First there was the windshield of their Chevy, sprayed with dozens of circles of dirt that were outlined by the lights from Bittie's hot dog stand. Beyond the windshield was the window of Bittie's, almost covered by painted announcements of specials: $1.15 for a Bittie's Burger and Fries, $1.25 for a Bittie's Special Hot Dog. A painted cartoon figure looking something like Elmer Fudd stood in the middle of the window clutching an oversize and not particularly appetizing hot dog sandwich with drops of mustard and ketchup spraying out.

Over the shoulder of the cartoon figure she could see David in line, partly obscured by a big man in a blue denim shirt. The big, youngish man was wearing a purple baseball cap with something written on it that Maureen couldn't read at this distance. The big man was standing next to a smaller, slightly older man, who was talking to the girl behind the counter. Both men were smiling, and the girl looked as if she were wearily humoring them. They were the same two men Maureen had seen that afternoon at the A & P, the ones who had followed her. It was probably a coincidence that the two men had come to Bittie's. It was far from the A & P, far from their neighborhood, but Bittie's was well known.

David glanced toward her and their eyes met. It was a clothes-sticking, hot, wet night. He tossed his head back, nodded at the two men in front of him, and shrugged a what-can-I-do shrug. She knew he wanted to be home by eight to watch "The Rockford Files." She wanted to get the baby in bed and the air conditioner on. She shrugged back. Something caught the eye of the big man in the purple baseball cap, who looked past the cartoon of Elmer Fudd directly at Maureen, something that made it clear that coincidence wasn't involved in his being there. The man's face was round and pink. He touched the shoulder of his smaller companion, said something, and both looked toward Maureen.

"Mom," Miles whined at her side.

She turned away from the stares of the two men.

Maureen, Miles, and the baby, strapped firmly into her Baby-Tight seat, were in the back seat of the car waiting for their hot dogs. Bittie's was a favorite for all of them, with its white tile exterior, its miniature castle facade; it had probably gone through a dozen owners. Until last year, when Miles turned eight, they had fooled him by telling him that they were going to Bittie's McDonald. Now, Miles, a skinny, bespectacled version of David, accepted Bittie's. The real McDonald's didn't have hot dogs.

"Mom," Miles repeated, adjusting his glasses by twitching his nose. "I want a big fries for myself. Daddy doesn't know it. I want to go tell him."

Maureen looked up again to see David, still stalled in line by the two men, talking to an old couple waiting behind him. The old man, his white hair combed straight back, was looking angrily at the big man with the baseball cap, who was holding up the line. The girl behind the counter had her hands on her hips and was saying something to the smaller of the two men in front of her. The girl looked dry and pale, young but not pretty.

"Mom," Miles whined again. "I got to tell him."

"You mean you *have* to tell him," she said. "And you don't have to tell him, Daddy will remember. You can take your seat belt off till he gets back."

"Why is it taking so long?" Miles said, angrily folding his hands in his lap and pushing back against the seat. "And Nancy can't have any of my fries."

Miles looked at his little sister, who blinked back at him sleepily as she clutched the black imitation leather of her baby seat.

"She can have my fries," Maureen said, wishing that David would forget the order and come out, so she could tell him about the two men. It was too hot to sit here waiting for a beautifully greasy Bittie Dog and Fries. She looked up, pushed her long, straight blond hair back over her shoulders, licked the line of sweat on her upper lip, and glanced over at Dave, hoping to catch his eye so she could signal for him to give it up. She didn't think he would, but with the two oafs holding up the line, he might. She considered getting out, waving to him, but she didn't want to leave the children.

The bigger man was taking off his cap and wiping his sweaty forehead. His mouth was open in a smile showing large teeth. At this distance and with two windows in the way, Maureen couldn't tell if the teeth were straight or not. She bet they were not. She could feel the moisture under her arms and barely controlled herself when Miles grunted in a near-cry. "Daddy will be right out," she said.

Beyond the Elmer Fudd, she could see David shifting his feet and trying to ignore the line of chatter between the big man and the old man, who was obviously angry and shouting. The old man's wife was trying to pull her husband away, and the big man with the baseball cap was grinning at the old man's anger. In the line beyond, Maureen could now see a young couple, maybe in their twenties, also attempting to ignore the argument in front of them.

"David, come out of there," she said softly.

"He can't hear you," Miles said.

"I know he can't hear me," she said. "I'm trying magic."

"You don't know magic," Miles said.

"Sure I do," Maureen said, wiping the moisture from her upper lip. "Just ask Nancy."

"Nancy can't talk," Miles said. "Mom."

"I'm just making a joke, Miles," Maureen said irritably, out of patience. This was supposed to be a pleasant end to the weekly night out. First, they had gone to Indian Boundary Park, where Miles had waded in the pool and Nancy had crawled on the blanket, watching people wander by. David had talked about the possibility of applying for a job he knew was open at Roosevelt University. At thirty-five, he was at the point where he had to make a move or settle for what he had. What he had was a job teaching history at Oakton Community College. He wasn't unhappy, but he didn't want to stop there. He knew he could do better. Money was no problem. With Maureen bringing in more than a hundred a week from her twenty hours as a substitute in the Chicago suburban schools, they were doing all right. If Maureen's mother, Darla, ever got tired of baby-sitting, things might change, but they were getting by.

David was talking to the big man in the baseball cap and his companion. He had stepped between them and the red-faced old man. She couldn't see much of David, who was blotted out by the big man, but she could see his right arm, palm out and up in a peacemaking gesture. David was not a big man, but he was well constructed. He liked playing Sunday softball and ran two or three miles every other day.

"Oh, Dave," she sighed.

She wasn't sure if it was something that David said next or something one of the two men in front of him said, but both of the men holding up the line looked out of the window toward her again. She now saw the smaller man's face clearly for the first time. He was dark with a look of dirty amusement on his face. He started to say something as she looked past him for David.

"What's wrong, Mom?" Miles asked. Nancy stirred at her side and seemed about to cry.

"Nothing, guys," she said, reaching over to touch Miles's cheek. "I'm just a little tired and I want to get home, take a bath, and take it easy. It's been a long day."

"All days are the same in longness," Miles corrected. "All the days are twenty-four hours. Mrs. Laynie said."

"Right again, Miles," she agreed.

Nancy had found her thumb and was sucking away with a dreamy look on her face.

When Maureen looked up this time, a tough-looking man in his fifties was standing next to the girl behind the counter. He was wearing a chef's apron and demanding the attention of the two men.

Maureen recognized him. His name was Paretti or Parenti—Lou Parenti. They had exchanged hellos a few times and had told him how much they liked Bittie's. Bittie, he had told her, had been his father's nickname. He didn't know why. Everyone called him Bittie, too, and he had accepted his father's nickname just as his son, who also worked in the place on weekends, would one day probably adopt it.

The two men were leaning threateningly in Bittie's direction, but it wasn't working. Bittie said something between his teeth. The smaller of the two men cocked his head and looked as if he was going to say something, but he couldn't hold Bittie's stare. He broke away, slapped the big man with the baseball cap on the arm, and headed for the door.

"Mom," Miles cried.

"In a minute," Maureen said, holding her hand up to quiet him.

The big man was standing in the door, and the smaller man had turned to shout something back at Bittie, David, the old man and woman, the young couple, and maybe at Maureen. He shouted so loud that Maureen could hear his croaking voice but not make out the words. Then the man went out the door, followed by his hulking shadow. Maureen was suddenly afraid that the two men would come in her direction; surely they would if they had a car and had parked it in the small lot. She reached over and pushed down the lock buttons of the Chevy. Then she closed the open windows.

"Mom, what are you doing?" Miles cried. "It's hot in here. What are you doing? I'm going to tell Dad. He doesn't like the windows closed."

The two men appeared around the corner of the building.

"Quiet, Miles," she said in a loud whisper. "Quiet or I'll . . . if you're quiet, I'll let you stay up late tonight."

She leaned back into what she hoped was the darkness of the rear seat and looked over at the two men. The smaller man, who she could now see was not small at all but only smaller than the hulk at his side, stopped and rapped on Bittie's window. The window rattled as his knuckles landed firmly on the hot dog in Elmer Fudd's hand.

"I'll see you with one of your fuckin' hot dogs up your ass," the man shouted at Bittie. Inside the shop, Bittie just glared and reached for his telephone.

"We'd better get out of here, Cal," the big man said, tugging at his baseball cap.

"He's not callin' no cops, that chicken shit," the smaller man said, moving toward a gray pickup truck parked a few spaces from Maureen. There were no cars between. She prayed that they wouldn't look in her direction.

"Mom." Miles wept.

Maureen's hand went out to cover his mouth, but he shook her off. Nancy began to cry.

The smaller man looked at her and then both men piled into their peeling gray truck, with the smaller man behind the wheel. He raced the engine, hit his horn, and backed up with a screech. Maureen could see something bulky in the rear of the small truck, pieces of machinery or something covered with a cloth.

She held her breath as the truck leapt out onto Diversey, barely missing a red Volkswagen Beetle. Only when she heard the truck screeching in the distance did Maureen let her breath out.

Both children were crying.

"I'm sorry, Miles," she said. "I'll make it up to you."

She soothed him with her hand, pulling his reluctant head to her breast and kissing his straight, dark hair. He smelled of park sand and sweat and, she told herself, he needed a shampoo. Nancy was told "Everything's fine, baby," as Maureen leaned forward to open the windows again. Settling back to the smell of wet, sweet air, she looked into Bittie's and saw that David was getting his order: two white bags, one with sandwiches and fries, the other with the drinks. He was looking over at her with a reassuring smile.

"Daddy's coming with the sandwiches," she said in relief.

"And fries," Miles added.

"And fries," she said, reminding herself to clean Miles's glasses tonight after he was tucked into bed.

"Did you see that?" Dave shrugged as he approached the car and nodded toward Bittie's.

Maureen leaned forward to take one of the bags. David's blue short-sleeved pullover was dotted with sweat and his glasses were slightly fogged.

"Maybe we should take it home?" she said.

"It'll be cold by the time we get back," he said.

"David, those two men in there. I saw them this afternoon at the A and P. I think they followed me—us—here," she said.

"I don't want to wait till we get home," Miles whimpered.

David handed Miles a plastic cup of Coke, smiled, and said, "Come on, Mo, the heat's getting to you. It was just two hamheads with a few beers in them. They're gone."

"Get in and eat," Maureen said. She found the fries and handed one to Nancy, who reached out eagerly over the protective top of her baby seat and took it.

"She must be sticky in that thing," David said, leaning through the window for a hot dog. Maureen handed him one.

"That was one of my fries," Miles said.

"I'll give you three of mine if you finish yours," David countered.

"Get in and eat," Maureen repeated, still feeling the tension created by the two men. She looked through the window past David to assure herself that they were gone. The patches of sweat under her arms stung slightly and she decided to stop shaving there till fall or winter.

"I'll eat one out here," David said. "It was hot in there. That fan doesn't do much." He unwrapped the hot dog, put some french fries on his sandwich as he always did. Miles did the same.

"What was that all about?" Maureen said, finding a hot dog for herself and carefully checking to be sure Bittie hadn't accidentally put hot peppers on it.

"Your fugitives from *The Texas Chain Saw Massacre* were putting on a comedy act," David said.

"I'm glad they didn't have a punch line," Maureen said. "David, I wish you'd get in. I'm telling you, I saw those two at—"

"Maybe they're the ones who got Jimmy Hoffa this morning and they're taking a break before they dump the body." David cut her off, talking around a bit of sandwich. Inside Bittie's the old couple were getting their order and an older black man had joined the line behind the young couple.

A car pulled into the parking lot behind them, but Maureen didn't look back. Nancy had cried for another fry, and Maureen had juggled her sandwich to plunk one into the outstretched hand.

Maureen felt something wrong before she actually saw anything. The sensation made her look up at David, who had adjusted his glasses and was looking beyond the car. Maureen turned, rubbing her moist lip, and glanced through the rear window. The pickup truck was a few feet away. It had not pulled into a space.

There was no time to react. The two men were out of the pickup. She could see that they had left the doors open. Both men, the big and the smaller, were coming toward the car.

"Roll the windows up," David said quickly to Maureen, and then he turned to the men, saying, "Look you two . . ."

"David," she screamed, dropping her hot dog; but as she screamed she leaned forward to do what he had said, to roll the windows closed again.

"Mommy, Mommy," cried the terrified Miles. He looked like a frightened baby. Maureen turned toward the window of Bittie's. The girl behind the counter was looking out at the parking lot scene with the other customers. Bittie wasn't there, probably back in the kitchen. Maureen shouted "Help" through the closed windows as she turned her eyes toward David. Hand out, like a traffic cop, he tried to halt the two men.

Something came out from the smaller man's side. It was in his hand and swept toward Dave, hitting his outstretched hand. The remnant of David's hot dog plopped against the side window of the car. Ketchup, relish, mustard, and soggy fries dripped down. A small piece of hot dog clung to the bottom of the window.

"Hold it," David shouted, throwing a hand toward the face of the advancing man. His fist struck, and the smaller man, who was about the same size as Maureen, stepped back. The dark man's free hand went up to his face and blood came down.

David looked at her, and she could see that his left hand

was limp from where he had been hit. He seemed to hesitate for a second, undecided about whether he should run or protect his family. The hesitation gave the big man with the baseball cap enough time to lurch forward and swing a flat piece of metal at him.

Maureen clutched Miles and pushed his head down as the metal struck with a plumping sound against her husband's head. David's hand went up to protect himself, but it was too late. He fell backward, below the line of her vision. Both men stepped forward and the smaller man lifted the object in his two hands. She could see now that it was a black baseball bat.

"No, no, no!" she screamed.

He brought the bat down twice and then looked at her with a dark wild grin. He swung the bat once more, but this time it was at the car. The bat thudded against the window and crashed through it, inches away from where Miles's head had been an instant before.

"Bastard, bastard, bastard!" she shouted. "Get out of here."

The smaller man with the baseball bat turned to look at her. Their eyes met, and he looked at her as if she were a surprise, a curious, familiar surprise.

Then his hand came through the broken window, grasping, grabbing at Maureen. Miles leaned into her in terror and the dark hand clutched her hair.

"Hurry up," the big man shouted from outside.

The world had changed in those few seconds. It was there and not there. Her body was present and she was still part of it, but she was beyond it too. The man was panting, trying to open the locked door with his free hand as he pulled her toward him, toward the jagged broken window. She clutched, scratched at his hand, digging her nails into his wrists. He let go with an animal yelp and then reached in again, to grab her again, but she pulled back against Nancy, tugging the screaming Miles to her. The enraged man thrust his bat through the broken window, jabbing savagely at Maureen. She covered Miles and the baby as the thudding blows hit her arm and chest. She could hear the man panting as he jabbed, and she fought to keep from passing out.

She sensed, rather than saw, the bigger man outside nodding toward Bittie's, and she felt the smaller man reluctantly withdraw when he nodded. Maureen looked with them. Bittie and the black man in overalls were coming around the side of the building. Bittie had a knife in his hand.

"Cal," shouted the big man, "let's go."

The smaller man, Cal, looked at her once more, his body heaving as he whispered, "We'll be back, bitch."

Cal threw his bat at the advancing Bittie and the black man. It thudded against the sidewalk, skittered toward the two advancing men, making them step back. The two attackers jumped into their truck and pulled away, closing their doors as they screeched in a circle and over the sidewalk into the night.

Bittie and the black man hurried forward and stopped next to the car, looking down at where David had fallen. Bittie's face went white. The black man covered his mouth. Maureen saw all this through the shattered window.

"Mommy, Mommy, what happened?" Miles cried. "You're hurting . . ."

She let him go and looked at him. Her frantic hug had pushed the boy's glasses down. His ear was bent back comically. The baby was sitting openmouthed and confused, her mouth filled with pulpy potatoes.

Maureen wanted to sit up and look down at David, to see what had happened, but she knew from the faces of the two men outside the car what had happened, and the pain in her arm and side was real, pounding and insistent. The black man moved around the car to the far side and rapped gently at the window.

"Better come on out, missus, you and the children," he said gently. There was something in his face that made her think that he had seen all this before.

"No," she said, squeezing Miles's hand.

"Missus," the man repeated. "Come on out here where we can give you some help."

"We're covered with Coke and . . . and hot dogs and fries," she said absently. "And they're coming back."

"We'll clean you up inside," said the man. "They're not coming back."

From the corner of her eye she could see the girl in the dirty white-tile castle, her eyes wide, screaming something into the telephone. Bittie appeared behind the black man and she heard the black man say, "She won't come out."

Bittie was biting his lower lip, his eyes filled with tears of rage. "Those sons of bitches," he hissed, throwing the knife in his hand on the driveway.

"Let's help them," said the black man. Bittie nodded, wiping his hands on his apron, and turned to Maureen, who closed her eyes, closed Bittie and the black man out, closed out what she knew had happened to David, even closed out Miles and the baby.

And that was how the police and the ambulance found her when they arrived exactly six minutes and forty seconds later.

"Self-defense," Cal said, crossing his arms and slumping down in the seat, his eyes fixed beyond the horizon of I-57.

Marty wanted to stop for a 7-Up or something. His rear was sticking to the seat of the truck, and his underwear was wet and itchy. He kept shifting as he drove, adjusting his purple cap to keep out the sun.

"I know that," said Marty. "You want to stop for something? There's a Stuckey's just past Kalamazoo. Saw a sign a few miles back."

Cal didn't say yes and he didn't say no. Everyone figured Cal was the smart one, but Marty knew it wasn't so. His cousin was fast and talked a lot, but the real thinking had to be done by

Marty. Just because he was the big one, they figured he was the dumb one. It was always like that, since they were kids, but it wasn't so.

"He hit me," Cal said finally. "I thought there for a minute my nose might be broken."

"I know, Cal," Marty said, scanning the right side of the road for the Stuckey's sign. The truck hit something in the road, maybe a dead raccoon, and bounced. The pinball machine in the flatbed rocked up and slid back against the closed tailgate with a scrape and a bump.

"Watch it, Marty, for chrissake," Cal said.

"I'm watchin'," Marty sighed. "I need a toilet."

"Then find one," Cal grunted, still looking ahead as a green Honda scooted past them. Marty could see a pretty girl driving, her red hair tied back. There were clothes piled in the back seat. She was probably going back to some college early. She glanced up at Marty, who looked down at her. She turned back to the road and sped on. He considered tailgating her for a few miles, maybe touching the front bumper of his pickup to her little green rear. He sped up and could see her frightened eyes in her rearview mirror. The Honda didn't have the guts for the run.

"Self-defense," Cal repeated.

Marty slowed down, grunted agreement, and let the Honda push ahead and get smaller in the hot night haze of the highway.

"If they catch up with us, we tell 'em," Cal said. "We weren't planning any harm. We never touched her. And that guy got what he was asking for."

"Just what he was asking for," Marty agreed. He thought he could see a Stuckey's sign in the distance. Maybe the college girl in the Honda had pulled over and they could talk to her. Cal could talk to her and Marty could listen, but Cal wasn't in the mood.

"They're never gonna find us," Cal said, his arms still folded. Marty glanced at his cousin. Cal needed a shave. Cal always needed a shave. Cal was almost thirty-five, but to Marty he looked pretty much the way he had back in high school in Chester. He even dressed the same, talked the same, acted the same. The only difference was that while Cal had stayed the same, Marty had continued to grow and grow and grow.

"That bitch in the car," Marty said through closed teeth.

"Yeah," said Cal. "She could work you up a sweat. Maybe we should catch up with her?"

"Don't be a damned fool. We're not going back to Chicago," Marty shouted. "Not now."

"I thought you meant . . ."

"The one in the car with the kids. She remembered us," Marty said, reliving the moment when her eyes had locked with his, cursing, fearing, hating him. "We should have dragged her in the truck this morning and stuck it to her after we saw her at the damned A and P. We owe her, Cal. We owe her."

## August 1, 1983, Afternoon, Evanston, Illinois

"You're not trying, ladies," Miles squealed, his hands up in the air. "You'll never get rid of those hips if you keep moving your lips. Now, let's exercise."

Maureen stood, hands folded, watching her son and trying to keep the critical look on her face from turning to a smile. Miles's imitation of Richard Simmons was energetic, savage, and, as far as she was concerned, on the mark.

Miles had come in from playing basketball in the park, his short-sleeved gray sweatshirt heavy with perspiration, his brown straight hair moist on his forehead. He was wearing an old pair of shorts that said BRADLEY UNIVERSITY on them. He had picked up the shorts at the Salvation Army store on Dempster.

Miles's goal was to make the Northwestern University track team as a walk-on when he entered as a freshman in a year. He was pushing himself hard, and his leg muscles were showing the effort. The problem was his upper body. Miles was a slow developer, and his chest and arms just weren't ready for the muscular development he was trying to force on them. Maureen could have told him, *had* in some ways told him, but he would have to find out for himself.

They were standing in the basement, which Maureen had converted into an exercise room five years earlier. The small tape recorder on the table softly played a cassette of Bach three-part piano inventions as background to Miles's act. The walls were paneled with dark pine. Lights were covered under a suspended ceiling high enough to allow jumping, and blue mats on the floor circled the room. An exercise bench and light weights rested on racks in a corner. A mirror stood near the door. Maureen had been looking at herself critically in the full-length mirror when Miles came down the stairs.

It wasn't her body that Maureen was concerned about. She knew that she was taut, muscular, comfortable. She did worry about her face though. At thirty-eight, she could see changes in the mirror, a settling of her features, a fixing of the face rather than a flexibility. It wasn't vanity exactly that made her look. She knew that she was still considered pretty. In fact she knew that she looked better at thirty-eight than she had at thirty. There was a curiosity in examining that face in the mirror, a calm handsome face with long yellow hair pulled back and tied with a red ribbon. But Miles had caught her looking and would not let up till she gave in.

"I used to be a fat, fat, fatty," Miles said, taking off his glasses and pointing to his chest. "Can you believe that? Well, ladies, it is true. I ate, ate, ate like Jumbo the elephant. I ate anything that could be put between two giant Dunkin' Donuts chocolate chip cookies. I ate chocolate chip hamburgers, chocolate chip hot dogs, chocolate chip bacon, lettuce, and tomato sandwiches with gobs of Miracle Whip. Yum, yum."

"I'm not laughing, Miles," Maureen said, leaning back against the wall. She was wearing her blue sweatsuit, which fit snuggly but not tightly. She had not yet worked up a sweat in the cool room when Miles had entered, but she planned to.

"Laugh?" Miles said, opening his eyes in surprise. He put

both hands to his head. "Do you hear that ladies, laugh? There's nothing funny in fat. Do we like fat, ladies?"

"Miles," she said, smiling.

"Do we like fat?" he repeated, cocking his head to one side, reminding her of how he'd looked when he was a little boy.

"We do not like fat," Maureen said, giving in.

"What do we like, ladies?" Miles said. Before she could answer, he bounced up and down doing jumping jacks and said, "We like raw string beans and name-brand health food and woks that I endorse."

"I give up," Maureen said, unfolding her arms and holding up a hand to the deadpan Miles. "Your Richard Simmons deserves an Emmy."

"And a low-cal yummy," Miles added. "I was doing Eddie Murphy doing Richard Simmons. Where's Princess Daisy and how much time have I got before we eat?"

Miles had moved to the corner and was curling the 120-pound weight.

"Nancy is next door playing with Paulette, and I thought we'd go for a pizza at Barnaby's," she said.

"It's only Wednesday," he puffed, glasses slipping down his perspiring nose. "I thought Thursday was our night out."

"Special celebration," Maureen said, watching him. "Billy called. We have a contract to do another videotape."

"No shit?" said Miles, pausing. "Enough for us to visit Grandma in L.A.?"

Maureen had given up exercising for the moment. She sat on the mat, crossed her legs, straightened her back, and leaned forward, stretching as far as she could. "Could be," she answered slowly. "Depends on how soon Billy can get an advance. Even if it comes, I've got two more weeks of classes at the Y and it would mean leaving Lucy in charge at the studio. . . ."

Miles let the weight drop to the blue mat. It bounced once

with a clang, and he straightened up to take off his glasses and wipe his moist face with his sweatshirt. "Does that mean no, maybe, or yes?" he asked.

"It means a strong maybe," Maureen replied, straightening up. The loft she had rented on Elmwood, just outside of the downtown area of Evanston, had changed during her five-year tenancy. From a dimly lit, brick-walled area above a job printer, it had evolved into a busy, bright, wood-paneled fitness center with a growing reputation. Two years earlier it had turned a respectable profit and Maureen was thinking very seriously about opening a second Dietz Fitness Center in Highland Park. "I'll give you a 'for sure' either way by next week."

"You know what just hit me?" Miles said, plopping down on the mat and resting on his elbow. "You might just get famous enough to really meet Richard Simmons. Then you can tell him that you were a fat, fat, fatty. I'll videotape the meeting for 'Saturday Night Live.'"

"Give me about twenty minutes," Maureen said, leaning forward.

Miles recognized the tone and nodded in respect. The jokes stopped when Maureen indicated that she was seriously exercising. She knew that there were people who ridiculed her, and that there would be more if the second videotape caught on and the public speaking and personal appearances Billy was trying for came to pass. But there was a growing number of those who respected and embraced what Maureen had discovered.

It had taken her from the depths of depression and brought her to self-sufficiency and self-respect. It was ironic, an irony that David would have appreciated, though she was having increasing difficulty in remembering what David had really looked like. A few times after they had first married Maureen had commented that her husband looked a little like the actor Tom Skerritt. Now, eight years after his death, whenever she tried to imagine him, a vague image came that was far closer to Tom Skerritt than to the

David who appeared in the photo album on the shelf in her bedroom.

Her discovery was simple. Exercise should not be a means to an end. Exercise could be its own end. Exercise could be for others what it had been for her, a meditation, a relaxation, a means of actually letting go of one's total being while the body absorbed energy and became stronger, more supple. She attacked the exercise programs and the gurus who thrived on fear and pain, who claimed that people should exercise because it might make them look younger for a few more years, exercise because it might give them a few more years of life. For them, exercise was a penalty, a price to be paid, an investment in the possibility of more time or attention. Most exercise programs were, as far as Maureen was concerned, part of the cultural obsession with staying young.

The truth, as Maureen saw it, was that proper exercise relaxed the mind, made the exerciser less ego-bound, freer of the constraints of the fragile body each human carried. Exercise produced body chemicals that attacked depression. Blood carried more oxygen to the brain during a real, sweat-pulling workout, and the brain felt vital, alert, confident.

"The joy of exercise" was the way one interviewer had put it for a neighborhood newspaper. That wasn't quite it, but it was close enough to suit Maureen. Maureen rolled over on her stomach and straightened her body. She moved into push-up position, went down touching her chin and pushed up quickly to clap before landing on her hands. She could feel that her body was straight. She repeated ten clapping push-ups before moving to the overhead leg touches.

When she had begun exercising in the hospital following David's murder, it had come to her as a strange salvation that she wanted to share with others. At first the light therapy had been prescribed to get her arm and shoulder functioning normally again. Erika, her nurse, had said that exercising was a very good idea, frequently prescribed for depressed patients; but she'd said that Maureen also had to work things out more consciously. "Don't hide in jumping jacks and push-ups," Erika had said, after Maureen had read the five books in the hospital library on physical fitness.

"There isn't any place to hide," Maureen had said. "I'm just trying to find someplace to take a breath."

Erika had stood next to her in the small hospital gym, watching Maureen run in place. "That won't save your life," Erika had said.

"Whose side are you on?" Maureen had come back, panting. "Two weeks ago I wanted to jump into a dark closet in my head and stay there. Now I'm talking, moving. I'm alive. I'm glad I'm alive."

"You've jumped from one obsession to another," Erika had said. Maureen thought the other woman had stifled a yawn. Erika had been doing double shifts and had a dozen or more patients plus the case load of a social worker who had quit in protest over salary cutbacks.

"I'm on your side," Erika'd said. "I'm not trying to stop you from this. Dr. Ledebur isn't trying to stop you. Has anyone ordered you to stop? Has anyone told your mother not to bring you more books?"

"Nope," Maureen had said, moving to knee bends. Those first weeks her knees had groaned, her stomach had folded forward over her waist, and she had almost toppled in dizziness when she did a few bends.

"But you've avoided talking about what happened, Maureen," Erika had said, glancing past her at a pair of patients lazily hitting a volleyball back and forth over a low net.

"That's in the past," Maureen had puffed. "I'm not going to hold on to the past. And I'm not going to reach for the future. There's just now. I'm not going to take any more photographs. No more family albums. No more nostalgia. There is just now."

The volleyball had come flying between them and bounded off the nearby wall, hitting Maureen in the face. "Look out," a male voice behind them had called, seconds after the damage had been done. Maureen had wiped away the tears that came into her eyes from the pain of the ball as well as from the surge of unbidden memory that Erika had recalled. "I'm sorry, I'm so sorry," the oafish young man had said, ambling over to retrieve the ball. "I didn't mean to hurt you. I really didn't . . ."

"It's all right," Maureen had said, ignoring the young man. "It's all right. Just a touch of irony, a small added joke." The young man had shuffled away, clutching the volleyball to his chest. "See," Maureen had said to Erika, resuming her knee bends. "It's past."

Erika had reached for her pocket to pull out a cigarette. "It might be easier if you didn't just let it pass," she'd said, searching for matches. "It's not passing. You're moving away, but those memories, even a little one like this, hold on with elastic fingers, stretching, stretching, and never breaking till they're pulled so far that they snap and bring you back to that past you never really dealt with."

"Colorful," Maureen had said.

Erika had struck the match, lit the cigarette, and inhaled as she put the matches carefully back into her pocket.

"I read it somewhere," Erika had admitted with a small smile, "but it's true. What do you say we talk about it this afternoon?"

"All right," Maureen had agreed, her body sagging, her cheek stinging and red from the bruise of the volleyball. She would talk but they weren't going to talk her out of leaving. The rule had been that she had to give five days' notice before she left the hospital. They could appeal her decision, but there had been no indication they would do so.

Maureen had been anxious to put the memory of David's murder behind her. She hadn't wanted to talk about it, face it, deal with it. Erika's image of elastic fingers of the past had been countered by an image that had come to Maureen of a massive internal scab. Leave it alone and it will clear up and go away. The body, a healthy body, will take care of it, heal it. Pick at the scab and it will never heal.

That afternoon Maureen had proposed a deal with Erika: If Erika would stop smoking, she would spend an hour talking about David's murder. Erika had instead spent the hour urging Maureen to talk about why she wanted to make such a deal. "You can't save me or anyone else from themselves," Erika had said. "All you can do is work at saving yourself. It's my job to help you do that. It's not your job to help me."

Erika had said it without anger, quite matter-of-factly, and Maureen had found something interesting and meaningful in the answer. There had been nothing wrong with this overworked woman trying to help her, simply because it was her job and she either accepted or enjoyed her job. In a strange way it had relieved Maureen of some nagging concern she'd had for the nurse. They'd talked for the rest of the hour about Maureen's identification with Erika and thereby never got to talk about the murder. It had not been Maureen's goal, but she hadn't minded the result.

Four days later, her mother and brother Ralph, who had driven in from Pittsburgh, had picked her up at the hospital and been amazed by her attitude and energy. Maureen had been anxious to go see Miles and Nancy at her mother's apartment.

Erika had made it a point to be present when Ralph picked up Maureen's small suitcase. "How are you?" Erika had said, pulling out her cigarettes and lighting one.

"Fine," Maureen had said, pushing her hair from her face.

"Good," Erika had sighed. "Give a call if you want the name of a good analyst."

The drive to her mother's had been relatively quiet. Ralph had made small talk about his wife, his young son, his job. He'd said that Maureen looked fine. He'd avoided talking about David and the children.

"I was in the hospital for more than two months," Maureen had said, interrupting him.

"I know," he'd said, pulling into another northbound lane on the Edens Expressway.

"Why didn't you come to see me?" she'd asked, ignoring her mother's gesture to drop the subject.

"You know how I feel about hospitals," he'd said. "Ever since I was a kid——"

"No one in his right mind likes going to hospitals," Maureen had said. "You do it in spite of your feelings because someone needs you."

"Maureen," her mother had whispered protectively.

"I'm sorry," Maureen had said, sitting back and essentially deciding to write her brother out of her life, but realizing deep inside that she was being unfair, that he owed her nothing. "It doesn't matter."

After the hospital, the insurance money had taken her and the children through a little more than a year. Her mother had stayed with her for the year, helping to take care of Miles and Nancy in the new, less expensive apartment on the far north side in Rogers Park. The children's need had been clear, especially Nancy's. Just a baby, she'd clung to Maureen and feared letting her out of her sight. Miles had been nine when Maureen came out of the hospital, and much harder to figure out. At first he'd been resentful and had clearly thought that Maureen had abandoned them. At nine, he'd been unable to put the feelings into words, but Maureen had decided that he was filled with anger because his mother had left him and his sister by giving in to injury and depression. But as that, too, had passed, Maureen found herself showing great patience with both children. Before David's death and her move to the hospital, she had never been able to give sincere attention to her children, had always seemed to look forward to a future time whan she would have less responsibility for them, when they would be more independent. But when she'd come back from the hospital, she'd found delight in simply and placidly watching them, absorbing their moves, words.

During that first year, while working as a substitute teacher in Evanston and Skokie, she had gone to various exercise classes, looked for a guru of exercise, someone who could articulate what she felt. There had been a few who almost did, but there was always the further goal for them. One quite popular woman, Jene Bartlett, had come close, but Maureen had decided that Jene, who was in her fifties when Maureen had first gone to her class, was an exercise maniac. She had to exercise all of the time or she would have guilt and withdrawal symptoms. She played loud, beating disco as a kind of background metronome always driving for speed and pain. Jene Bartlett had talked of nothing else, thought of nothing else but the body. Jene Bartlett had been a fine-tuned, highly nervous steel straw.

One Wednesday morning in December, the instructor at the YMCA did not show up for one of Maureen's exercise classes. The snow had kept her locked in on Chicago's West Side. Actually, only four women had made it for the session, and one of them suggested that Maureen take over and lead them through the routine.

Maureen had agreed and put them through the already established routine of dance and exercise to records played on an old Webcor in the small gym, which seemed cavernous for four straining bodies. They'd pulsed to the beat of Fleetwood Mac, Eddie Rabbit, and Irene Cara. On Friday, the instructor failed to show up again, and the Y athletic director, an efficient woman named Barrie, had taken over, but no one in the group had liked her pace or relative lack of enthusiasm.

When Barrie showed up on Monday and announced that

she would now be the regular instructor, two of the women in the group had suggested that they would just as soon go on with Maureen leading them. Barrie, instead of being hurt, had leapt on the idea and even agreed to pay Maureen the remainder of the instructor's salary.

That was how it had started. Maureen had finished the six-week program following the traditional aerobic routine. The four other women in the group had urged her to do a second session in the spring, and Barrie had agreed, saying that more bodies would be needed to make it a paying program. A few other women were recruited and Maureen began to insert some of her own ideas into the program, and to change to the non-driving music of Bach, Vivaldi, Mozart, Handel, Cooperin. Some of her notions were too much for one of the regulars, who'd told her after a session that she had joined an exercise class "for my health, not for philosophy lectures."

That had almost ended the whole thing. Maureen came close to quitting, but she decided to do one more class and then one more after that, gradually admitting that leading the class had given a dimension of meaning to her life she didn't want to give up.

A summer course by Maureen drew fourteen people to the Y, many of whom came because they'd heard about her unusual attitude. Surprised by the increase in numbers, Barrie had increased her modest salary for the class. Two years later Maureen was still teaching a class for the Y but had gone on her own, opening the fitness center in the loft, and after the first modest success, quit substitute teaching. The rent on the loft had been gradually rising, but there weren't too many businesses that wanted to be at the top of thirty-three wooden stairs in a building without an elevator. For Maureen, the stair climb was part of the program. She'd written a pamphlet, begun speaking before north suburban groups, and gotten a modest contract to conduct a noon exercise program in her center for Harless Manufacturing Company, a local computer parts company.

With the Harless contract, Maureen found herself making a comfortable living and was able to move with the kids into a rented house just south of Main Street in Evanston. At that point, she had been out of the hospital less than three years.

Six years after David was murdered, Maureen found herself making more money each year than David had, though as Miles pointed out, the figure had to be adjusted for inflation.

Once, she found herself actually thinking that none of this would have happened if David had lived. She would never have known what she could be if he had not been murdered. The night after she had these thoughts was filled with bad dreams and the return of the old nightmare of the man with the baseball bat. She had awakened in her bed, screaming, and Miles, who was fifteen, had come running in terror and held her. When she had stopped shaking, she'd found that he was crying, and she'd held him. They'd stayed up the rest of the night playing Scrabble and Miles had stayed home from school the next day.

Maureen finished her basement exercise, took a deep breath, and let herself come back. It had, she decided, been an unsuccessful workout. Billy's news about the new videotape contract had seduced her into thoughts about the past, let her sink back and away from the present. But it wasn't just Billy. Recently, it had become more and more difficult to lose herself in the routine, to hold out the everyday events and relationships and even the thoughts and images of the past.

If she had been one of her own students, she would have issued the suggestion that the person wait a few hours and try again, concentrating on the body, the motion, sinking into the act so that the individual and the act became the same thing. But there was no time now. She had to get ready for dinner, call Nancy in. She opened her eyes and saw Miles looking at her through his round glasses.

"You all right?" he said.

"I'm all right, Muggs," she said, reaching up to turn off the tape. "Don't worry about me so much."

He shrugged and announced that he would take a quick shower before they went out for dinner, and ran up the basement stairs before Maureen could say anything more. The more that she wanted to say was that Mike would be joining them for dinner. Mike was a presence who, as far as Miles was concerned, needed some preparation for, and, Maureen acknowledged, a presence that increasingly questioned the world she had built for herself and her family.

"Sorry I'm late," Mike said, sitting down next to Maureen in the booth at Barnaby's.

"Paulette's mom had a baby," was Nancy's response. She was daintily finishing her order of cole slaw. Her long dark hair was dangling close to the paper cup.

"Nan," Maureen said, pushing the remaining six pieces of sausage-and-onion pizza with extra sauce in front of Mike. "This week we are going to get your hair cut. There isn't any sense in having long hair in this weather."

"Your hair is long, Mom," Nancy whined.

"I hate that whining," Maureen said with a small sigh.

"Let's back up, okay?" Miles said, making it clear he was holding in his temper. Maureen knew he was also annoyed because he recognized a girl who was in his high school class sitting four tables away. The place was crowded and she probably hadn't seen him. Miles was a holdout against dating and girls. Maureen could see that his body responded to the feminine, but something within him kept him clinging to boyhood. As far as she was concerned, that was all right. It would pass, she was sure, with a sudden initiation or a series of tentative touches. Meanwhile, he could only squirm in the knowledge that the girl, whose name Maureen couldn't quite remember, was not far away across a crowded room. "Do you want to tell us why you were late?" Miles said, reaching for one of the six pieces of tepid pizza and putting it on the paper plate in front of him.

Mike nodded, swallowed the bit of pizza, and washed it down with a drink of root beer. He looked vaguely like George Kennedy, the actor. He was about fifty and constantly booming with energy. Miles respected the fact that Mike had played college football at Miami of Ohio and had actually had a tryout with the Chicago Bears. Mike had even given the opinion that if the United States Football League had existed back in 1968, he would have had a pro career as a tackle or guard. As it was he had managed to lease a reasonable lot in life as a football coach at Saint Jerome's College in Skokie. He had also managed to marry, father two girls—Ginny and Carol, who were now married— and divorce his wife Janet, who took her law degree to Michigan, where she now lived and partnered with her second husband. Both of Mike's daughters lived near San Diego.

"Recruiting," Mike said, his tongue probing his large teeth for an elusive onion. "Good kid from Niles North. Grades a little down. He was hoping some big school would pick him up, but with low grades and weight at about one eighty-nine, he doesn't figure to make it on the line for a Division One school; but I see something there. A year on the weights and a good tutorial program, and he could be a winner. Name's Tyler, Daryll Tyler. Heard of him?"

"I've heard of him," Miles said.

Maureen touched Mike's hand, and he turned to her with a smile. "How've you been?" Mike said, patting her hand back.

"Great," Maureen answered, "if the videotape contract doesn't fall through."

Some men at the next table, wearing black-and-white baseball uniforms, began to laugh, drowning out the end of Maureen's comments.

"That's dirty laughing," Nancy said, pushing her hair back

from her face solemnly. "Like when Sharril and Joyce call me a humky."

"That's *honkey*," corrected Miles.

"That's what brown people call white people," Nancy explained to Mike, who nodded and wrinkled his brow. He was overdoing it a bit, Maureen thought. Nancy was smart enough to know when she was being humored, but she accepted it.

"If they call you a honkey," said Miles, turning to face her, "you just call them—"

"Miles," Maureen interrupted.

"Dumb-dumbs," finished Miles. "Don't worry, Mom, I don't want Princess Daisy stomped."

Miles and Mike reached for pizza at the same time and backed away to defer to the other. Mike had told Maureen that he was never clear about where he stood with Miles. He had spent most of his life working with boys Miles's age, but Mike wasn't comfortable with Miles's sarcasm and spectacle-covered probing eyes.

Maureen had met Mike Rothman at a sports fitness seminar at the Skokie Hilton a year ago. They had been at the same table for lunch and he had seemed genuinely interested in her ideas for fitness. They coincided with his own ideas that college sports should be an end in themselves and not a stepping stone to something else. He'd also made it quite clear that he found some of her ideas verging on the mystical, but a little mysticism or religion was fine with him. He had invited her to give a few training sessions for St. Jerome's football team. The players had started by thinking the idea was a joke and ended by being exhausted by Maureen's one-hour session. It wasn't until Mike and Maureen had known each other for two months that Mike gave even the slightest acknowledgment of sexual interest. It was as if he didn't know how to treat her, what would please or offend her.

It had started with her initiating a good-night kiss on the

cheek and ended by her having to seduce him in his Skokie town house one afternoon. Mike had proved to be, in spite of his bulk and teddy bear appearance, a remarkably gentle lover.

Maureen had had relatively little sexual experience in the eight years since David had died. Before David she had slept with only one person, Casey Brumarik, whom she'd met the summer she graduated from Mather High School in Chicago. Casey had been a North Avenue beach bum for the summer. He had been a strutting, stupid, good-looking hulk in his early twenties, who worked in a mail order house. He was, she had decided, worth the initiation and the six weeks.

Since David's death, she had been to bed with only three men, not counting Mike. She had also almost gone to bed with a married woman named Ann Seaburg, who had taken two classes Maureen taught the year before last. Ann Seaburg had been about forty at the time, tall, very dark, and worldly. Maureen had been surprised that she'd been tempted, but when the moment had come to make a decision as they were having coffee in the Y cafeteria, Maureen had politely backed away. Ann Seaburg had shrugged and taken it well and finished the course, though she didn't return.

The men had been varied and far between. The first had been an intern, about five years younger than she. His name was Al Porter, and she had met him when she attended the group therapy sessions just after she got out of the hospital following David's death. He had seemed like a child at first and looked like a student in one of David's freshman history classes. At first she had thought that his sexual suggestions were a joke, but he'd made it clear that he wasn't joking. She supposed that she had accepted him because he was so childlike. She hadn't wanted to be dependent then, and she didn't want to now. Al Porter hadn't lasted long. He had gone on to residency in psychiatry at Maimondes Hospital and had stopped writing to her after a year.

The other two men over the eight years had been even

more casual and meaningless. She'd let her cousin's friend, who was visiting from out of town, take her to his hotel after dinner at her cousin's house. He'd been a movie producer, a little flashy, a little phony, a little too sincere, but fine for flattery and reasonable in bed. The only other experience had been with the same cousin's husband, who'd been neither flashy, phony, nor sincere. Mal had found out about one of his wife's affairs and Maureen had found herself comforting him, though Mal had never been considered by himself or the rest of the world as attractive.

Mike had proved to be the only durable male in her sexual life, and she doubted he would be permanent, though she was surely not tiring of him and knew he was not tiring of her. On the contrary, Mike had recently been making it clear that he wanted to raise the emotional ante, to push for a commitment.

"Paulette's baby," Miles said, catching her eye. "Nancy said Paulette had a baby."

"Paulette's nine," Nancy said, putting her hands on her hips.

"So?" said Miles, straight-faced.

"You're funning me, Miles," Nancy wailed, her voice rising.

A few people, including some of the baseball players, looked at her. Miles plunged into his pizza, not looking toward the table of the girls he went to school with. Maureen handed her daughter a napkin and indicated that she should wipe her mouth. "Keep it down, Daisy," she said softly.

"Mom," Nancy whined.

They had begun calling her Daisy, though she didn't like it and complained every time. Maureen had vowed to stop but found herself doing it automatically although it brought up images of Daisy Duck. The image of Daisy Duck was somehow uncomfortable for Maureen. There was something unpleasant to her about the idea of a cartoon image, though she was drawn to it and often watched Saturday morning cartoons with Nancy.

"Paulette's mother had the baby," Nancy explained.

"Who is Paulette?" asked Miles quietly.

"You know," Nancy said in exasperation. "She lives next door. You're teasing again."

Miles crossed his eyes and said, "Cross my eyes and hope to die, I forgot Paulette lives next door."

"Mom," Nancy whined.

"Okay, Miles, enough is too much," Maureen said, noticing that one of the baseball players was looking at her. It made her uncomfortable, and she turned to give him a cold stare. Instead of turning away, he smiled softly. She turned back to Nancy as Mike turned his head to see who or what had drawn Maureen's look.

"Something wrong?" he said to her.

Maureen shook her head, indicating that nothing was wrong.

"Anyone want another pizza?" Mike said with a grin, taking them all in.

"I've had enough," Miles said, pouring himself the last of the root beer from the pitcher.

"No more for me," said Maureen.

"Nancy?" Mike said hopefully.

"Pizza is yuckie," she said with a pout.

"You're yuckie," Miles said.

"I am not yuckie," Nancy moaned. "Mom."

"You are not yuckie," Maureen agreed. "Mike, are you sure you want to have anything to do with the Dietz clan?"

"How about if I get a hot beef sandwich and another pitcher of root beer?" Mike answered. "I can think better on a full stomach. Just kidding. The Dietz experience should be required for every man considering a family. I'll be right back."

"What did he mean by that?" Miles said, removing his glasses and rubbing his nose.

"Just talk," said Maureen, nibbling at a crumb of pizza she

really didn't want, to keep her fingers busy and her eyes from having to meet those of Miles.

A baby cried above the voices and an announcement came over the loudspeaker that sandwich order number thirty-four and pizza six were ready to be picked up.

"Maureen Dietz," came the voice.

She had been concentrating on the crumb to keep from looking at Miles and hadn't seen the man approach their table. The voice was tentative and, cutting through the many voices of the large room, it caught her by surprise. She turned suddenly, her elbow catching her glass of watery root beer, which she managed to catch before it tipped. In the brownish amber light she saw the man in the baseball uniform standing over her, the same man who had caught her eye.

"Yes?" she said cautiously, her eye catching Miles's face. Miles looked wary and protective.

"I'm Roger Simcox," the man said. He had long straight hair that came down over his forehead, and a bushy mustache. Up close he looked older than he did across two tables.

"Roger . . ." she began, searching her memory.

"My wife Allie and I were . . ." he began, the smile fading, embarrassed about what he was going to say next but unable to stop. He glanced at Miles and Nancy, who looked up at him with suspicion. "We were in Bittie's the night you . . . remember."

Maureen remembered him now. He was the young man who had been behind David in line the night David was murdered. Under the mustache the face was the same, a bit older.

"I remember," Maureen said, holding out her hand. He took it and shook it once awkwardly. "How are you?"

"Fine, okay," he said. "We've got two girls."

"Hey, Roger," someone called from the group of baseball players. "Let's settle up here."

"Right there," said Simcox, rubbing his hands on his pants.

—— 33 ——

"I'm just in from out of town for a few days. I . . . these your kids, right? They look fine." He held out his hand to Miles, who took it reluctantly. "Good to meet you." Miles nodded sullenly, putting his glasses back on and saying nothing. "Well, I guess that's all I had to say," Simcox said, taking a step back and almost bumping into Mike, who was returning with a pitcher of root beer in one hand and a sandwich basket in the other. "Sorry."

"No harm," said Mike, putting the pitcher down.

"No foul," Simcox added with a nervous grin before going back to his companions.

"Friends?" Mike said, settling back with a grunt.

"No," Maureen said, trying to hide her feelings with a small smile and a touch of Mike's hand.

"Someone want some hot beef, here? I got it cut in half and I can't eat it all," said Mike.

"Force yourself," Nancy said seriously, holding her glass out for a root beer refill.

The baseball players eased past toward the exit, with Simcox making sure he didn't glance at the Dietzes before he left. He seemed to be hiding behind the crowd, regretting the impulse that had made him reach out and touch the past.

"He was there when my father was murdered," Miles said, watching Mike's face. Mike had the sandwich almost to his open mouth. He closed his mouth and looked at Miles.

"Miles, let's just put it away," Maureen said, her hands folded in her lap to keep them from trembling. She looked at Nancy to see how much of this she was taking in. Nancy seemed to have no memory of the death of her father. She had only been an infant. Erika back at the hospital, her own mother, and a variety of others including the young intern Al Porter had suggested that the memory might well be there to emerge painfully in the future, but Maureen wasn't at all sure and wanted references kept in the past. Nancy looked at her seriously and then at

Miles, as if this were an important moment and it was her brother's turn to make a revelation.

"How do you feel about seeing him, Miles?" Mike asked.

"I thought I said . . ." Maureen began, but neither Mike nor Miles was looking at her. The question would have to be answered, but Maureen didn't like losing control.

"He's a jerk," said Miles. "He watched while some Neanderthal beat my father's brains in."

Nancy gave a small sound, and Maureen reached for her. "That's it," Maureen said firmly. "Drop it."

Nancy was crying now. Mike stepped out in the aisle to let her get to the girl, and Miles moved to give her room. Nancy had her arms out to let her mother take her.

"She's a little old for that baby stuff, don't you think?" Miles said.

Maureen considered saying something, but she held back. She had embarrassed him once before in public, when he was twelve. It had had something to do with complaining about a decision she had made concerning how much television Miles could watch. She had slapped him in the park and he had cried. She'd vowed never to hit him again and never, if she could help it, to embarrass him in public.

"Take the car and go home, Miles," she said softly. "Mike will drive Nancy and me."

"What did I do?" Miles demanded, plunking down his glass. "I told the truth. Okay. Forget it. I'm going."

He got up and stalked to the exit before Maureen could say anything. She held Nancy's sobbing face to her breast.

"Sure you don't want half of this sandwich?" Mike said, his eyes on Maureen as he took a bite.

"No thanks," she said a bit sharply, patting Nancy's head.

"If he keeps it bottled up," Mike said, "it explodes. Let him get it out."

"How about letting me decide that?" Maureen said, looking at him with a small but distinct challenge in her eyes.

The girl who had graduated with Miles walked by, holding the hand of an overly clean-cut young man obviously several years older. The girl was pretty, green T-shirted, and smiling.

"Hi," she said as she went past.

"Hi," Maureen said, and then she turned to Mike again to say, "Coach, are you sure you want to get involved with this team?"

"Give me a couple of seasons and I'll have this franchise turned around." He grinned. "We'll have you in the playoffs. All we've got to do is keep Miles from holding the offensive line."

"You're pushing it a little, Coach," she said as Nancy sat up and reached for her root beer.

Mike shrugged; after finishing a massive bite of sandwich he said, accusing, desperate, "'I suddenly felt shaken in a way which I had never experienced before.'"

"Shakespeare," Maureen guessed.

"Ingmar Bergman, *Wild Strawberries,*" said Mike with a smile. "'An idle mind is the devil's playground.'"

"That sounds like the Bible," she tried, wiping Nancy's tears.

"*The Music Man,*" said Mike. "'Trouble in River City.'"

It was after ten when they got to her house. They had stopped at the Dairy Queen for Nancy's favorite, chocolate dipped cones. Nancy had had a big day and didn't complain about Mike's offer to carry her in. Maureen suspected her daughter was putting on the sleep act to get a little attention and to play baby, to be held in the arms of a big man.

The house was on a reasonably quiet residential street in south Evanston. The neighborhood was firmly middle class and mostly black. During the day the sounds of children were powerful. At night, except for a very rare Saturday night party, the street was quiet.

Maureen opened the door with her key and stepped back to let Mike carry Nancy in. "Miles?" she called as they stepped in. The lights were on as they always were when Miles was home alone. The car had been parked in the driveway and there was nowhere he liked to walk at night. Even if he had wanted to wander over to the park to watch one of the night softball games, he would take the car if she didn't object. "Miles?" she repeated. "Nancy, go get your pajamas on. I'll be in to bring you a drink of water and say good night."

"Mom," Nancy said sleepily. "Can't I stay up late?"

"Camp tomorrow," Maureen said, giving her a kiss on the cheek. Nancy pouted but didn't argue. The air-conditioning was on. Maureen didn't like air-conditioning, but Miles did and she took it as a small sign of protest that he had turned it on without permission, that and the fact that he wouldn't answer her.

"Miles," she shouted, looking at Mike for some kind of comment or argument. He held up his hands and moved toward the kitchen, just off the living room.

"What is it?" Miles shouted down from his loft room above the second floor.

"Nothing, just wanted to know if you were lurking," she said. "Anybody call?"

"Some woman," he said. "Said you should call her again in the morning. I left her number near the kitchen phone. Her name was . . . is . . . let's see. Helen Katz."

"Katz?" Maureen called back. "I don't know any Helen Katz."

"I think it's the Salvation Army or something looking for a donation," Miles shouted down. "She said she was a sergeant."

And Maureen remembered.

Maureen had met Helen Katz in the hospital a few days after David was murdered. It had been morning. The sun had been coming in the wire mesh-covered window, and Maureen

—— 37 ——

had been tired, more tired than she had ever been; more tired than the day she and David had been on the rubber raft and gotten lost downstream in Wisconsin for a few hours; more tired than when they had shared driving non-stop from Los Angeles so David could interview for a job even though it cut off the only real vacation they had ever had; more tired than after the nineteen hours of labor before Dr. Whatever-his-name-was with the Hitler mustache decided to take Nancy out by cesarean section.

"Some policeman wants to see you," said the thin, black nurse who had told Maureen her name. The name had been printed on a white plastic tag on her pocket, but Maureen hadn't looked at it.

Maureen had sat in bed wearing some clothes her mother had brought. Her arm and shoulder were in a cast held up by a rope and pully. The throbbing in her chest, the inability to catch her breath, the feeling of fear had drained all of her energy like a parasite.

On the closet door in the room children's drawings had been put up by an unseen roommate or a previous patient. The only other decoration in the clean, white room had come from the shadow of the steel mesh of the window.

"I'll bring them in," the nurse had said, touching Maureen's shoulder.

Maureen didn't move. The nurse had gone out of the door at the left. The door at the right, Maureen decided, must lead to a bathroom, and there might be a mirror in the bathroom. She hadn't wanted a mirror. The thought of a mirror made the sucking in her chest increase, and she gasped for breath as a man and a woman came through the door in front of the black nurse.

The man and woman were white. He was about fifty-five, the age her own father would have been were he alive. He had thin, gray-white hair, and wore a rumpled suit. He looked a little like Lee J. Cobb, even down to the large lower lip. The woman wore an all-business skirt and blouse with a matching vest. Her

dark hair was pulled back behind her ears and she looked efficient, cool, and somewhere in her mid-twenties.

"My name is Barelli," the man had said, holding open his
wallet to show his star. "Lieutenant Barelli. This," he'd said, nodding at the woman, "is Officer Katz. We'd like, if we may, to ask
you a few questions."

Maureen had looked at them and said nothing.

"I'll be at the nursing station if you need me," the black
nurse had said, then left, closing the door behind her. Lieutenant
Barelli had sat on the bed with a weary huff, and Officer Katz
had leaned against the wall, taking out a small notebook.

"It might hit ninety out there today," Barelli had said,
pointing to the window. "They've got good air-conditioning in
the hospital. Mrs. Dietz, we've got to ask you a few questions."

Maureen had looked at him without responding. All she'd
heard was the pounding of her heart, the insistent sucking of the
pump that wouldn't stop.

"Mrs. Dietz," the woman had said, leaning against the wall.
Her voice had sounded rough, a smoker's voice like her father's,
but why think about her father? Richard Foran had been dead
almost five years. David had been dead only . . . how long? A
day? Two?

"Mrs. Dietz," the woman had repeated.

Maureen's left hand had gripped the sheet. She'd had a
sudden urge to get up and measure the room with her hand,
spreading her fingers; first the chair, then the walls, then the bed.

"Mrs. Dietz—Maureen—we've got to ask you some questions about what happened," the woman had said.

Maureen had looked at the man on the bed. He'd nodded at
Maureen sadly, agreeing that questions had to be asked.

"Maybe we should catch up for you first," the man had said
softly. "We've got descriptions of the two men. One big man,
very big wearing a blue shirt and a purple baseball cap. You
remember that, Mrs. Dietz?"

Maureen had looked at him a long time and nodded. His eyes had been a watery blue and seemed quite sympathetic. She'd had the feeling that he had been drinking even though it was early in the morning. There had also been something there that told her that he had seen horror, that he did know what had touched her.

"Mrs. Dietz," the woman at the wall had said gently, taking her cue from the lieutenant named Barelli, "the shorter man wore faded denims, was dark, needed a shave. They were in a pickup truck. Can you tell us anything about the truck? Any numbers in the license? The color of the license? Anything?" Maureen had turned her head to try to listen to the woman over the sound of her pumping chest.

"We got the bat," Barelli had said, his eyes fixed on hers. "Handle was taped. No prints. We got witnesses all over the place. The guy who owns the hot dog stand, girl who works for him, an old couple, but no details."

"The black man," Maureen had said.

Barelli had stood up slowly and held out his hand to keep Officer Katz from moving, pouncing, asking. Maureen had seen her.

"We couldn't find him," Barelli had said. "He took off just before we got there. You don't know his name, do you?"

"Did you notice anything, Maureen, anything? Did you hear anything?" Officer Katz had asked.

"I told that policeman the other night that they were after me, that I had seen them at the A and P on Howard that afternoon. They were after me." She had seen by their faces that the two detectives didn't believe her.

"Mrs. Dietz," Barelli had said gently. "We know how you feel, but this looks like a random incident. There's no evidence here of anyone following you. You've been through a hell of a lot and—"

"They were after me," Maureen had said, almost whispered. "David got in the way."

"Okay," Barelli had sighed, getting off the bed. "We'll check it out."

Maureen had closed her eyes and begun shaking.

"I'll get the nurse," Officer Katz had said.

She had felt the rough hand of Barelli taking her own. "Cal," she'd said. "The big one called the other one Cal. And, and, oh my God, my God, they had something in the back of their truck, a machine with a face, a mirror." She'd squeezed his hand and kept her eyes closed a few beats. Maureen had opened her eyes, trembling violently. The door to the room had popped open, and the black nurse had come in firmly, not running.

"I think that will have to be it for now," the nurse had declared.

"Sure," Barelli had agreed. "We'll be in touch. Take care, Mrs. Dietz, and if you remember anything else . . ."

Barelli had disappeared through the door without finishing. The black nurse had leaned forward, taking Maureen's wet, trembling hand.

Then, two years ago, the past had screamed at Maureen again as she came out of a movie with Miles, a James Bond thing with Roger Moore. They had been to the Old Orchard Theater Number One in Skokie. It had been winter, a very snowy but not terribly cold night. Miles had been talking animatedly as they stepped into the parking lot whiteness, saying that Sean Connery was a better James Bond.

"He's not joking about things all the time, you know what I mean?" Miles had said, peering over the top of his glasses. He was wearing his fur-lined denim jacket and a blue knit hat, the same jacket and hat he still wore.

"I know what you mean," Maureen had agreed, trying to

remember how far down the car was and in which aisle. Not too many people were coming out of the theater. The weather was bad, the picture no longer new, and *The Empire Strikes Back,* which was playing in Theater Two, was clearly much more popular.

"Can we stop at Poppin' Fresh?" Miles had asked as wind and snow swirled up in the space between cars and took Maureen's breath. She had wanted to get back home and relieve the baby-sitter, but Nancy would have been asleep by then and Miles had seldom shown enthusiasm so openly.

"Sure, Double-O Seven, we can get a few slices of humble pie."

"I'd rather have a key lime," he'd said.

"That was your father's favorite," she'd said, almost wishing she hadn't, but it had come out before she could stop.

"I know," Miles had said. She'd looked at his suddenly solemn face and reached out to touch his shoulder as they walked. As she'd reached out, she had glanced back toward the theater and saw the man. He'd been simply standing there, a shadow with his hands in his pockets, no hat on his head; a wild black cutout with wisps of hair dancing in the neon backlight of the theater. And, Maureen had been sure, he'd been looking at her.

"Let's hurry," she'd said, turning away from the man and urging Miles toward the car. "It's damn cold."

"I wonder why James Bond never gets cold," Miles had pondered.

"He certainly gets hot," she'd thrown in, wondering then where the hell the car was. She hadn't wanted to glance back at the man, but she had. He had begun walking toward her and Miles.

"Mom, come on, that's a cheap shot."

Miles didn't like sex jokes, even mild ones, but Maureen hadn't really been thinking about Miles's feelings. She had been thinking about that man, thinking that there was something familiar about him, a familiarity that had made her feel as if she might lose her breath.

"Bond is cool, not hot," Miles had continued. "At least Sean Connery is cool. He was even cool when he was playing that Arab."

The far reaches of the sizeable parking lot had not been included in the light from the lamps mounted on tall metal poles, at least not on a night like that. Maureen had remembered where the car was, in one almost dark corner. She'd looked back. The man had definitely been walking toward them, not hurrying but moving, slouching really, reminding her of the resolute mummy in films that had frightened her as a child. She'd remembered her brother Ralph, with one hand out, dragging his leg behind him, pursuing her through their small house.

"Let's put a move on, sport, the key lime is waiting," she'd urged.

"Hey," Miles had shouted, "take it easy. You're the one who runs two miles in the snow. I'm—"

"I know," she had said, trying to keep it light, "Mr. Feet-don't-touch-the-ground."

They'd found the car and Maureen had remembered that she had locked it. Before David had died he had never locked the car in the winter, claiming the locks might freeze shut, but since that night Maureen had made it a habit to lock the car even if it was in the garage. She'd fumbled for the key buried deep in the pocket of her blue denim jacket.

"Damn keys," she'd whispered, glancing back at the man. He had still been a black silhouette, but a much larger one with each second. Miles had caught her fear.

"Mom, what's wrong?"

He had looked at her face, saw the direction of her eyes, and turned to look at the man. She had tried not to look at either of them as she had pulled the keys out and searched on the jangling ring for the right one. She had sensed Miles's fear next to her, his questioning.

"Mom, who . . . ?"

She hadn't dropped the keys, had found the right one, put it in and opened the door, urging Miles to slide in. She'd been about to get in herself and slam the door shut when she'd sensed the man near her, and then heard his labored breathing.

"Maureen Dietz," he'd said, his voice disoriented, rasping, familiar—and terrible.

"No," she'd said, turning to face him, catching a glimpse of a frightened Miles, sitting in the same position as he had that awful night.

"I couldn't forget you," the man had said, stepping forward and putting out a hand to clutch the car door. He'd been at her side. She had smelled the alcohol on his breath and clothes. His coat had been open in spite of the cold. There'd been no one in the parking lot to call, and the cars had sloshed by darkly on Skokie Boulevard a few dozen yards away.

"Get back," she'd said, trying to be firm, to keep the old fear from coming. In the time between breaths she'd ordered herself to regain control, to take charge and not be taken charge of.

"I've got something for you," he'd said. His hand had clutched her sleeve.

"Let her go," Miles had shouted, starting to slide out of the car.

"No, Miles," she'd said as evenly as she could. "Stay there."

"I . . ." the man had begun as the beam of a U-turning car's headlight caught his face and she'd recognized him. "I haven't forgotten. I saw you."

It had been a distorted mask, the mask of the policeman who had visited her in the hospital after David's murder.

"I don't want it," she'd said. Images of what "it" could be had flashed through her mind, the baseball bat that had killed

David or some . . . He was a policeman, he had followed her. Maybe Nancy had been hurt.

She'd pushed at his arm and forced her way past him into the driver's seat. Her right hip had hit the steering wheel hard, but she had ignored the pain and inserted the key into the ignition. The man, whose name she couldn't remember, had been holding on to the car door, keeping the interior light on. His face had been inches from her.

"We can't let it go," he'd said. "I can't let it go. You were right. They might be back any time."

"Shut up," she'd said.

The car engine had turned over and she'd looked quickly at Miles, who had no longer looked frightened. He'd been staring at the drunken policeman, examining his face with awe.

She'd pushed at him and her elbow had hit the horn, sending a shrill electronic scream into the swirling snow. He had staggered back a step, just enough for her to close the door. She'd known he was standing there talking, imploring. From the corner of her eye she'd seen his hands on the frosted window, spread out as if trying to force it open. She'd thrown the car into reverse and skidded back, scratching against the bumper of a VW on the right.

The man had been in front of her then, in front of the car, a ghastly figure in the snow, the headlights of her car painting him white like a figure in a horror movie. He'd been talking, shaking his head.

"Something for you," he'd shouted. The few hairs on his head had danced wildly. She'd looked back over her shoulder as she backed out, telling herself to be calm, not to flood the engine. When she'd been far enough back, she'd let herself look out the side window, fearing that he would have his face pressed grotesquely against the glass, but he hadn't moved. He still stood in the vacant parking space in the snow between the two deep tracks made by her tires, his arms at his sides. He simply had looked at her and Miles as she'd driven away.

"Who was that?" Miles had asked, looking back over the seat toward the man.

"A policeman," Maureen had answered. "He was drunk."

"But he said he had something for you?"

"Whatever he had I don't need," she had said. She'd inched away from her door as she drove, trying not to touch the window where handprints showed clearly in the frost.

Miles had changed his mind about stopping for pie but she had insisted that she was hungry and when they had gotten to an almost empty Poppin' Fresh he had eaten and she had forced herself to get down a piece of blueberry pie.

For the rest of that winter and early into March she had expected a call or an appearance at the front door. She'd even had a few dreams, not exactly nightmares, of the man with the drunken breath and wispy flying hair appearing suddenly before her, urging her to take something he hid behind his back. By spring she had been involved with renovations on the studio, Nancy's ear infection and operation, and normal day-to-day work. The incident in the snow had blurred in the past. She and Miles never discussed it.

Carla Arlette Lahue's eyes opened in terror. Her mouth went slack and her cheeks flushed crimson. She looked as if she were about to collapse.

"Carla," Maureen said softly, moving to her side. Around them thirty-two women and four men worked out to the soft tape of Glenn Gould playing the Bach Goldberg variations.

Carla looked at Maureen with pleading eyes. Maureen had read that look many times. It said, let me go. Let me out of here. Let me save some face if I can't lose some weight before I have a heart attack.

Maureen looked at the chunky woman evenly, no smile but

no threat, no sign of disappointment. There was a moment of relative quiet except for Carla's heavy breathing, the precise music, and the beat-beat of a single runner on the overhead track that circled the YMCA gym. Maureen knew that most runners moved outside in the summer. She preferred no distractions, but she could never get the athletic director to close down the track during her class. The class always began with a one-mile run on the track or outdoors, but after that she wanted them to concentrate on their workout without being disturbed.

"Mrs. Dietz," Carla said, a sad sagging figure in an oversize blue jogging suit that must have set her back a few hundred dollars. Maureen hated to lose someone, especially someone she knew could be helped. If Carla Lahue, forty-five and baby-faced, could stick it out, she'd be on the way to a new self-image. She had come in hoping that this program would be the one to help her shed pounds, but Maureen was less interested in her shedding pounds than in shedding her poor self-image, her little-girl-helpless self-image.

"If you quit now," Maureen said softly so that the kneebenders around her couldn't hear, "you'll hate yourself, me, and the world. If you stay with it, there's a new woman waiting in your mirror."

"I just can't," Carla panted, rubbing her sweating brow with her blue sleeve.

"You can," said Maureen. "You're thinking too much about yourself, your image, Carla Lahue with a capital *I*. Carla Lahue who feels pain when she does six knee bends. Carla Lahue who has always walked away from the game instead of playing it. Will you try? I'm not begging, simply asking. There's nothing to be embarrassed about."

"I'll try," Carla Lahue said, holding her right hand to her chest, where she obviously thought her heart was. It wasn't exactly a commitment chiseled in marble, but it was a step.

"Now stand straight and do a bend," Maureen said. "Look at the person in front of you to get into the flow, the pattern."

Carla bent tentatively with a groan and a little-girl look at Maureen.

"Don't look at me," Maureen said softly. "Just bend. Stretch and breathe. Good air in, used air out at the peak." The music was there, not demanding, asking for the beat to be followed. Music had its own consciousness. If you listened to the beat of the music, you sank into it. She had accumulated several dozen tapes of Glenn Gould and E. Power Biggs playing Bach and lost herself in them whenever she turned on the tape player.

"Miles loves rock and Mom loves Bach," was Nancy's chant. Nancy, on the other hand, at the age of eight loved *Grease* and *Grease II* and played the records, particularly the track of Olivia Newton-John singing "Hopelessly Devoted," over and over and over, driving Miles to ever-renewed despair.

"That's good, Carla," Maureen said, doing the knee bends alongside of the panting woman. "Now let it go. Stop thinking about the pain, being tired, your children, husband, father, mother, the groceries, the body of the man in the next row."

Carla looked at her in panic. "You're thinking about yourself," Maureen said. "Just bend with the group. Let go. If thoughts come, let them go and imagine the movement of your body as one with everyone else. You are part of a movement, a flow and energy. Your body is part of it and inseparable from you. It is the present. Your mind can relax, let go of tension, thoughts, images. Imagine only that light, no people, no Carla, just a light. Let time pass. Stay with the present. There's no hurry, nowhere to go. There's always now. Push. Push ahead. That's it. That's it."

Maureen backed away slowly, watching them work out. Carla Lahue was still panting, probably wouldn't make it, probably wouldn't show up on Friday, but she might. Beyond the bulk of Carla Lahue, Maureen could see the woman who had come to see her. Since Carla was at the rear of the second row, the woman had been within hearing distance of the conversation. The woman was dressed in a black skirt, white blouse, and carried an oversize blue denim bag over her shoulder. Her hair was dark and pinned up. It looked long, and the woman, at this distance, looked somewhere in her mid-thirties, calm, dark, and seriously good-looking. There was something about her bearing as she sat on a rolled-up gym mat that gave Maureen the impression that the woman was in good physical condition. Part of the impression may have been because Maureen knew the woman's profession, but most of it was a result of almost eight years of experience in watching bodies change, take on confidence.

Maureen moved back to the front of the group, rubbed her hands on her black tights, adjusted the sweatband on her head, and softly said, "Change," to the group before her. They looked up and watched Maureen lean forward, almost touching her head to her knees without bending her legs. She began a slow clockwise movement of her upper body, leaning back as she rose, approaching nine o'clock. "Into the circle, the movement," she said. "Be it, go with it, into it. Stretch and breathe. Be a clock without hands, without time. Turning, turning."

The rest of the session took about twenty more minutes and ended with a final quarter-mile run around the track. The earlier lone runner had departed. The group, including Carla Lahue, ran, keeping pace with Maureen. Their steps shook the small track. Maureen didn't bother to speak, knowing that her voice would not be heard above the striking of feet. She let herself be taken up by the movement. The only bad part of the classes was that someone had to lead, to be aware of real time, not body time. It had become a lower-level ability of hers and she handled it well, though there were times when she would have preferred to abandon even that level. The music helped her sense time, know when to come out of the workout.

When she came back down the stairs, she told various people that she would see them on Wednesday. She considered a special word for Carla Lahue but decided against it. The woman would have to make her own way.

Maureen went back into the gym to face the woman waiting for her. Maureen walked toward her and held out her still perspiring hand. The woman stood with a small smile and shook the offered hand.

"I'm Helen Katz, Sergeant Helen Katz. You remember me?"

"University of Illinois Hospital, eight years ago, you came with another police officer. He had been drinking," Maureen said. There was a slight echo in the gym now that it was empty. Some of the windows were open, letting in sun and a little breeze. A wisp of warm August air touched the perspiration on Maureen's brow.

"What do you think of the class?" Maureen went on.

Helen Katz was a good-looking woman of no more than thirty-five, but there was something firm in her face that made her seem older, as if she had seen too much and had thought about it for too many hours. Maureen had seen that look in others. Her own face had managed to avoid it, but this woman might be bringing back something to change that.

"I liked the guy in the front row," Helen Katz said. "Particular friend of yours?"

There was no challenge in the question, no hostility, just curiosity, open and clear. Maureen liked it and answered. "James Martin," she said. "You did mean that black one?"

"You know I did," said Helen Katz, removing the heavy blue bag from her shoulder.

"He's a police officer, like you. Evanston. No particular friend."

"He may be a police officer," said Helen Katz, "but he is definitely not like me." There was a pause and Helen Katz sighed. "You want to get down to business, don't you?"

"I do," said Maureen, shrugging her shoulders to loosen them.

"You aren't going to start exercising while I talk, are you?"

"No," Maureen said. "I wasn't planning to."

"Good, I don't mind meeting in your territory, but—"

"My territory," Maureen interrupted gently.

Helen Katz rubbed her upper lip to remove the moisture and said, "You think I'm bringing you news you're going to have trouble dealing with, don't you?"

Maureen folded her arms, still standing, let the surge of anger pass, and decided that the woman was right on target. "You went to psychiatrist school?" Maureen asked.

Helen laughed. "No, I got my degree in on-the-job cop school. I don't know if my news is good, bad, or nothing, but I had to come to you with it. It was Barelli's idea."

"The policeman who came with you to see me in the hospital," Maureen said.

"We thought you were out of the conscious world that day. You remember it at all?"

"Vaguely." Maureen shrugged. "I don't much like the past, but I can't deny it. Why didn't Barelli come with you, aren't you working together?"

Helen Katz went to her denim bag, looking for something. Maureen was afraid she was going to try to smoke and that she would have to stop her, which would have been most awkward. Instead Helen Katz pulled out a battered manila file folder with scribbling all over it. Some of the scribbling was in pencil, some in black ink.

"Most police officers would say that Eugene Barelli ate his gun," said Helen Katz, shifting on the rolled mat and pointing with the folder to a spot next to her where Maureen could sit. Maureen sat looking at the folder. "Barelli shot himself," Helen said. "He retired five years ago. His liver was being eroded by

Scotch. When there was only a little piece of it left, he took a last drink and shot himself. His wife called me last week just after he did it and told me he had left this, with a note to give it to you."

Maureen had a sudden chilling vision of the man in the theater parking lot trying to tell her he had something for her. This was the something.

Maureen took the folder, which was bulging with pieces of paper.

"I don't think I want it," she said.

"Suit yourself," Helen Katz said with a shrug, reaching into her huge purse again and pulling out a green package of Certs, which she offered to Maureen, who refused, before taking one herself.

"What else do you have in there?" Maureen said with a nervous smile.

"A pistol," Helen Katz said seriously. "A pair of handcuffs, a ratty paperback of *North and South,* and my lint collection. You want to know what's in the folder? I read it."

"No," sighed Maureen, "but it looks like I can't walk away from it."

"Or do jumping jacks till it goes away," said Helen Katz, sucking on a Certs. "No, I take that back. It's a hot day and I'm just feeling a little bitchy."

"It's okay," said Maureen, looking down at the folder and trying to make some minimal sense of the words written on it.

Across the gym and through the door the sound of heavy metal bouncing on a mat came to them followed by a male voice saying, "Shit."

"Someone dropped a weight," Maureen said.

"He needs a spotter," Helen Katz said.

"You lift weights?" Maureen said. The woman did look as if she was in shape.

"Not much. I used to when I had a husband," said Helen

with a grin. "Now I just run and do some working out, primarily to stay in shape, not for a mystic high."

"That a shot at me?" Maureen said, starting to rise again.

"I'm feeling hot and bitchy, remember," said Helen. "And you are giving me a lot of fuel by avoiding that folder and not asking me what the hell is going on."

"Your husband is dead too, or are you divorced?" Maureen said.

Helen Katz folded her arms in front of her and gave Maureen a look, making it clear she saw the question as another stall. "Howard Bruckner is alive," she said. "At least he walks around, eats as much as he can, sleeps a little, consumes remarkable quantities of Michelob Light—though he is far from a winner—and when he is capable, he picks up women, girls, and others of the female gender in bars that you would prefer not to think exist. Howard is a cop. We are still married. We share the same apartment, have no kids . . . now can we get to it? I've got a stop to make. I'm on my own time."

"I'm sorry," said Maureen, but she wasn't sure that she was sorry. She was quite interested in Helen Katz's tale.

"The truth is that after we interviewed you in that hospital," Katz said, "we started a file and began checking. It got nowhere. You'd think with seven witnesses, eight including you, nine including your son, we'd nail those guys. They hadn't covered their faces, hidden their names, masked their license plate. But it happens. We couldn't get anywhere. We got reasonable descriptions, probably decent artist renderings of them in the newspapers, but no plate number. The guy who owned the hot dog stand—"

"Lou," Maureen supplied.

"Lou," agreed Helen. "Louis Parenti. He thought they had an Illinois plate. The color was right, but none of the witnesses had ever seen either one of the men before. We went over it with them but their memories were, as usual, awful."

"The black man," Maureen said, seeing the sudden flash of the man with the kind face, the man wearing the overalls. "The black man was closest," Maureen went on. "He was calm, would—"

"Couldn't find him," said Helen Katz. "He split before the first squad arrived. According to the witnesses, he helped you in, talked to your kids, made sure you were taken care of, and disappeared, didn't want any part of it. It happens all the time. We tried to find him, but Parenti and the girl working there hadn't seen him before. Dead end, and to tell the truth we were on five cases with more coming in. There was a big fuss for a week or two and then it was just Barelli and me when we could find the time. No good leads. Then, after a while, it was just Barelli, mostly on his own time. I wrote it off."

"And," added Maureen, "you wrote me off."

"You've got it, lady," agreed Helen Katz, taking another Certs and raising her eyebrows. "I stopped smoking three years ago but I still need these things to suck on. Habits."

"Now the file," said Maureen.

"The file," agreed Helen. "When Barelli retired, he copied the file and kept working on the case. Something about you got to him. But, I'll cut it short. Barelli traced the baseball bat. No one in his right mind would have done it. A baseball bat is a baseball bat, right?" Maureen said nothing, so the policewoman went on. "Right. Even if he could find out where it was sold, it could have gone through five or six people, been stolen, anything, but he went to the manufacturer, got lists of every store in Illinois where the bat was retailed. The lists are on file. He traveled to every one of them, checked sales slips where he could find them, spent the best part of his pension on gas and the worst on cheap Scotch. And do you know what he found?"

"No," Maureen said.

"Nothing," Helen Katz said, drawing an imaginary zero in the air. "Then he tried pickup trucks. He had started that while he was still working on the bats. Same procedure. Insane, a drop in your hot tub, but he had a plan. Check every damn dealership in the state that handles pickup trucks, new and used, and describe the men who killed your husband, hoping the name Cal cropped up. There are names associated with car sales, unlike those baseball bats. Barelli traveled from Cairo to Rockford, from Macomb to Antioch, checking leads, memories, descriptions. And you know what he found?"

"Nothing," Maureen guessed.

"Wrong," said Helen Katz. "He thought he found your husband's killers."

A memory—pain, feeling in the chest, anxiety—tapped at Maureen and asked to get in. She wanted to run, escape into some mental exercise, but she held fast and listened.

"It wasn't much," Helen Katz said with a shrug. "It's in the file. All unofficial. He must have seen two hundred big men who bought new or used pickup trucks. But one man matched too well. A man Martin Vanbeeber, a big man who had purchased a 1974 Ford pickup in East St. Louis. Vanbeeber had paid cash for the used truck, but he had left an address with the dealer with the limited warranty agreement. Barelli checked the lead out as he had maybe hundreds of others, but this time he struck—"

"Blood," said Maureen.

"If you want to put it that way," allowed Helen Katz, pushing the last bit of Certs into her right cheek. "He went down to a town called Chester, showed the sheriff the drawing, gave Vanbeeber's name, and got a positive identification. Neighbors agreed. Problem was the Vanbeebers, Martin and his cousin—"

"Cal," Maureen supplied, feeling the pain in her chest coming back.

"Cal is right," said Helen. "Martin and Cal had left the area, leaving no forwarding address, about five years ago. The sheriff said it had something to do with a local tavern owner named Bay Carter who was into shady deals. They'd had an argument with him, and the tavern owner had sent someone after them and they ran for their lives."

"And . . ." Maureen said.

"Not much more," said Helen Katz. "I don't know what he would have done if he had found them, shoot them maybe. It would have ended whatever meaning he had in his life. Maybe he could have gone out feeling as if he had accomplished something, but he didn't."

"They haven't been caught, have they?" Maureen said.

Helen shrugged again and shook her head. "Who knows where they are? No one is even looking for them and as far as the department is concerned the case is long closed. They probably changed their names, moved to Arizona or Vermont or Florida. Maybe they're both dead. The only fingerprints Barelli could find were Cal's. FBI had them. He served a year in the National Guard during Korea. Then they booted him out. Fingerprints haven't done much good. My boss wants me to go on to other things, leave the file on active, hope Cal gets picked up some time for some crime and the file at the FBI gives a reference to us as we requested. It happens sometimes. Truth is there's no real hard evidence here."

"You don't have much faith in it, do you?" Maureen said, sensing that there was something that the woman wanted her to do, to say, but she wasn't quite sure what it was.

"Not much," agreed Helen. "No one is very interested in an eight-year-old murder. There are plenty of fresh, bizarre ones. I could tell you about some sick . . . forget it. Barelli went to their families, school friends, yearbooks, and came up with photographs. The photographs are lousy, high school yearbook blow-ups, old pictures in family albums. Martin finished school, reasonably good student. Calvin was not considered to be too bright."

"What do you want me to do with this?" Maureen finally

asked, holding up the file. Far behind them male voices could be heard laughing, coming closer.

"Nothing," Helen said. "I made a delivery for my ex-partner. You can burn it or dump it in the garbage."

Or in the snow, Maureen thought.

Two men burst into the gym. They were both in their early thirties, wearing shorts, basketball shirts. The shorter of the two was dark and had a mustache. He dribbled the ball a few times and looked over at the two women. They looked back at him, appraising him as he was appraising them. His bigger friend glanced at them and turned away.

Helen gave Maureen a look designed to say that she found neither of the two men interesting enough to look at further. Maureen nodded in agreement. They had effectively beaten the men to either a move, comment, or reaction. The smaller man turned and drove to the basket at the far end of the gym, missing an easy lay-up.

"I want all that in the past," Maureen finally said, looking away. She took a deep breath and decided to tell Helen Katz about the night she had driven away from Barelli in the snow. The policewoman listened without reaction. The pounding of the basketball punctuated Maureen's words. The two men were playing one-on-one, probably showing off a little.

Helen Katz stood up, smoothing her skirt, which was wrinkled and moist. "You got to him. It happens to cops. They keep it all away until one gets through to them. Then they do some strange things or they get a handle on it. Eugene lost the handle."

Maureen held out her hand to shake that of the policewoman and end the conversation. The basketball escaped from the men and bounded in their direction. Helen stepped out and grabbed it and threw it back to the smaller one, who was running after it.

"Thanks," he said with a smile, hesitating for just a beat as if considering pursuing the matter.

"Look at the file," said Helen, hoisting the bag to her shoulder. "Then do what you think best."

The woman took a few steps toward the doorway before Maureen called. "Sergeant," she said. The two men paused at the far end and looked at them.

"Helen," Helen said, turning back.

"How would you like to come to my place for dinner tomorrow night? Meet the kids. Maybe we can . . . talk about it?"

"What time?" said the woman.

"I'm giving a class at my center till five. Let's make it six-thirty. My house is—"

"I know where it is," said the woman. "I'm a cop, remember? Six-thirty will be fine."

The two men resumed their game and the policewoman left. Maureen stood holding the file. She didn't want to open it, not yet. Instead she went down to her locker, tucked it on the upper shelf, and went back up to the track to do another half mile before going home. The half mile worked. She lost the past, but at some level she knew it would be back. It was the past that had been gnawing at her workouts, the past and Mike's attempts to get her to make a comitment to a man, a man she might lose as suddenly as she had lost David. And then Simcox had appeared at Barnaby's, and now this policewoman. The past was scribbled on the file in her locker and it would have to be opened and looked at at some point.

The rest of the day went badly. She went through her routines at her center, got home in time to make meatball sandwiches and listen to Nancy's plans for a school of Barbie dolls.

"If Barbie dolls were a penny each," she asked, playing with a tepid meatball with a fork, "could I have twenty of them?"

"Sure," Maureen agreed. She would have said "sure" to almost anything short of a suggestion that the house be dynamited. Her mind was on the file, the file lying on the desk in her room upstairs. Maureen ate and cleaned up, but Nancy, who had eaten almost nothing, persisted.

"Lesser Barbies cost only a dollar at Cut Rate," she said.

"Lesser Barbies?" Maureen said, clearing the table.

"Barbies that cost less than the real ones," Miles explained. "Fake Barbies, imitation Barbies, ones that you can see through, made of paper in Taiwan."

"They are not made in Taiwan," Nancy insisted. "Are they made in Taiwan, Mom?"

"I don't know," Maureen said. She stacked dishes slowly in the sink, not looking at her daughter. It would take only four or five minutes to put the dishes in the washer and the rest of the evening was ahead of her. A game of Uno with Nancy, maybe a talk with Miles about school plans, and a television show, but the file folder had to be faced. When she put the last glass in the dishwasher, the thought came but it was more of an insight than a clear thought in words. The file had come to her when she was ready for it, when her body and mind had told her that the past had to be faced. She had not been ready two years ago when Barelli had found her in the parking lot with Miles. She had run, run as she had been doing for almost eight years, often literally running five miles a day. Just how she was going to face the past was not completely clear, but it would have to be faced some-how. She was on the verge of breaking through to real success in her life, the videotapes, the likelihood of another studio; but she felt—knew—it wouldn't work, not until those men, the ones who had killed David, were dealt with—faced—at least in her mind. Maybe they wouldn't be caught. She couldn't live out Barelli's dream, but she might be able to put her own nightmare to rest.

It was almost midnight when she called Billy, who answered without a trace of tiredness in his voice.

"Billy," she said. "It's me, Maureen."

"I'll be cordial," he answered. "You have luck on your side. I was up watching the Blitz game. If I had been in bed, cordial would not be what you would get. If the Blitz were losing, you wouldn't get cordiality either, but I . . . is something wrong?"

"Something is wrong," she sighed.

As concisely as she could she told Billy what she wanted and why. She spoke quickly so he couldn't interrupt her with reasonable arguments. She told him that she didn't know if she could go on with the idea of a new workout tape without facing this.

"Well," he groaned. "I know some people at Channel Nine. You got an interesting story and, what the hell, it might drum up some publicity, interest. . . . You don't mind my talking, you know, about using this?"

"I mind, Billy, but I know you can't help it any more than I can help wanting to do this. If you can set it up, please do it quickly before I change my mind."

"Okay," Billy said. "I'll try for tomorrow, maybe six o'clock. Newspapers might pick it up. It's a good story. If not, I got some favors I can call in, particularly at the *Sun-Times*. You mind before we hang up if I get a little philosophical on you?"

"A little philosophy can't hurt," she said, running her finger along the edge of Barelli's file folder.

"We're walking on the outside of a smooth, white egg. One bad step and we break through the shell and find out it's rotten inside. Better to walk lightly on the outside of the shell."

"I can't, Billy."

"You know what can come through that hole in the egg?" he went on.

"You mean *who* can come through it," she corrected. "You don't have to scare me, Billy. I'm scared enough on my own. I've been scared for a long time, but I didn't want to face it."

"And with good goddamn reason," he said. "You stay scared and you live longer."

"Maybe," she agreed, "but the problem is you stay scared."

"There's a quarter left of the Blitz game," he said. "I'm going to watch. I'll get back to you in the morning."

"Thanks, Billy," she said sincerely.

"The way I see it is I'm not doing you a favor," he concluded. "I'm giving in to pressure. Hey, I'm hanging up."

"Okay, Billy," she said. "Good-bye."

"Maybe I shouldn't have done it," Maureen said. They were sitting in the living room watching the tape of the interview with her on the ten o'clock news the next night. She was next to Miles, and Mike was on the brown leather reclining chair her father had given her sixteen years ago as a wedding present. Nancy was in bed and hopefully asleep upstairs.

"Are you asking for a vote?" said Mike.

"No," she sighed, clutching her Like cola in two hands and enjoying the cold against her palms.

# 3

Sitting at the bar, Marty tried vaguely to place the face on the television, but it wouldn't come. He looked across into the dark mirror at his own face. It had changed over the years. He was still a big man, but he had cut his hair and grown a big walrus of a mustache. He was wearing a St. Louis Cardinals T-shirt with the number 23 on it. He had picked up the shirt at a flea market in Belleville and found that people figured he was a retired Cardinal. Marty thought football was a shit game for guys who wanted to make people think they were tough. Horse shit. They played it safe—rules, a uniform and helmet, referees to get in the way.

"Let's see one of them million-dollar babies face up one-on-one with ax handles," he had told Cal, and Cal agreed. Marty's daydream was that some hard-ass college Cardinal would call him out in a bar, say he was no goddamn footballer. Marty would like that. He'd squash that hard-ass good.

Something pulled him out of the thought. The bartender, an almost bald guy in a flannel shirt, passed in front of the mirror with three schooners of amber beer in his hands and he heard a name, his name. "Martin Vanbeeber," said the voice, a woman's voice. Marty turned fast on the stool. He and Cal had not used their real names in years, not since the trouble in Chester with Bay Carter, but someone had called his name. He swiveled, ready, and bumped into the woman next to him.

"Hey," she said, dropping her cigarette on the bar, "watch what the fuck you're doin'." She was skinny and two-in-the-afternoon drunk.

Marty gave her a dirty look, and the guy who had been talking with her, a broomstick of a rummy, turned away.

There was no one there calling his name, but he heard the voice again and turned toward it. It was a woman on the television screen, right up there over the bar on Channel 9 out of Chicago. She was looking out at him, and he was sure she had said his name. He looked over at Cal, but his cousin was in deep talk with the old whore and sipping at his glass. Cal looked old, though he was only forty. His short hair had a bit of gray and his nose was smashed flat in his face from too many fights in too many bars with people like that Indian Billy Bear.

Marty strained to hear what the woman on television was saying, but it was hard with the dozen or so people in the bar talking. The woman was honey-haired, pretty, and serious, and she was saying something and holding up a photograph. The camera kept moving in to the picture, and when it was close enough to see clearly, it hit Marty, and his mouth dropped open. His hand went up to worry his mustache, and he knew who that person was in the photograph. It was Cal, Cal maybe twenty years ago. He looked over, considering a call to Cal, but if he turned away he might miss what was going on. He wanted to wring the scrawny neck of the woman next to him, who kept talking, but he held his peace and glared at the television set.

And there she was. She was different. No doubt about it, older, thinner, stronger-looking. Pretty but not soft pretty like that one time. It was a kind of pretty he liked. He had passed women with that look on the street. Cal would say he'd like to wipe that look away by shoving it where it would make her cry for mercy, but this woman was different. He had seen her maybe a hundred times in dreams, looking out of that car window, her mouth open, her eyes magic and burning into his eyes, his brain. And then he would wake up and imagine what he would like to do to her.

On the TV, she was sitting on a brown sofa with a man and a little girl. No, it wasn't a man. It was a kid and he was wearing glasses. The little girl was like a smaller version of the woman.

He never did quite hear what they were saying clearly, but he did piece some of it together. They were looking for him and Cal. They knew their names, knew they were the ones who had killed that guy in Chicago, at least that bitch with the kids was saying it. The honey blonde ended by saying something about the police still having witnesses and the interviewer wondering how witnesses could remember faces of the killers for so long, but the woman on the couch with the kids said that they were faces *she* would never forget, that she had tried but failed to forget completely. Then the woman said the police weren't interested in finding Marty and Cal. They had given up. She was interested. She was after them.

Then the red-mouthed interviewer named Jo Ann something said this was the first of a series on unsolved Chicago murders and asked that anyone who knew Cal or Martin should call their local police. Marty could feel his fingers vibrating. He looked around the bar at the faces to see if anyone was staring at him, but no one was. No one had pieced that story, those pictures, to him and Cal. But that wasn't what worried him. Someone was after them now, and they might some time be picked up for running a red light or getting in a fight, and a cop might put it together. If only they had taken a few more seconds eight years back, that bitch wouldn't be alive to go on TV and show their pictures.

He got off the stool, elbowed his way around a table, where

two black guys ready for an argument looked up at him and changed their minds fast. He got to Cal, who was saying, "No point in taking it from anybody. World's full of them. Even around here you got fags."

"You got a point there honey," the old blond whore said. She said it almost all the time to anything Cal had an opinion on. He'd usually answer, "Fuckin' right."

"Cal," Marty said, standing over him. "We got some talking to do."

Cal looked up, annoyed, at the familiar bulk of his cousin, who blocked out the brown tavern light.

"Later," hissed Cal. "Lady and I are talking goddamn philosophy. World picture."

Cal was wearing a white T-shirt and his old jeans with boots. He was still surprisingly well muscled in spite of his drinking. It came from lifting machines and the fact that his mother's family had all been built like that, lean and mean. Marty, on the other hand, had been an exception, the one big man in the clan.

"Got to be now, Cal," Marty said softly. Marty's hand gripped his cousin's shoulder and pulled the smaller man toward him. "We've got to go home and talk," Marty whispered.

"All right," Cal hissed.

The bar was on Farrell and there weren't a hell of a lot of people out on a Wednesday afternoon in this heat. Marty didn't say anything till they got to the van. The pickup truck was long gone and they had been driving the orange van for almost four years now. When they got in and Marty pulled into traffic, Cal said, "What the hell's going on?"

At the corner, they caught a red light, and a young Mexican woman pushing a baby in a stroller moved in front of them. They both watched her. Marty thought he could see a little trickle of sweat going down her arm. He liked that. When things got tough, and he had to think for both of them, he could see little things, a drop of sweat, something moving, even some ant or bug crawling on the sidewalk.

"We got to go out to Chicago," Marty said, turning on Third and driving into the sun.

"Chicago, shit," said Cal, leaning back and folding his arms. "What the hell for?"

"She's looking for us," Marty explained. "That whore in the car is bringing it up on TV, saying we killed that smartass in the parking lot way back in Chicago."

"We didn't . . ." Cal began angrily, and then paused. "I remember. Who the hell cares about that? That was self-defense."

That was all Cal had ever said about the incident, self-defense, all he could remember, but Marty had remembered much more. He tightened his grip on the steering wheel. It wasn't fair. Cal could forget, walk away. Hell, Cal could wring a baby's neck and eat the kid for lunch and forget about it in two days, but sometimes things were different for Marty. Pictures stuck in his head, faces, those little drops of sweat, the ants crawling on the sidewalk. He suddenly thought of himself, saw himself lying in his bed, asleep, and a long wormlike bug crawling in his ear.

"She got our names," Marty said. "Our pictures. People who saw us. She saw us."

When they got back to their house, he let Cal wander over to the television and turn it on. There was some game show and a woman in glasses and big tits jumping up and down. Marty went for the book. There wasn't that much in the one-bedroom house. It was lots smaller than their house back near Chester, but it was clean from corner to corner. At night Marty even scrubbed the cracks in the tile in the bathroom. He found the book with the peeling brown leather cover in the closet and took it down. The newspaper articles were there, just as he knew they would be.

The articles were yellow and brittle, the corners frayed. He reread them, handling them carefully, and looked at the underlined names, the old man and woman, that couple of kids, the guy who owned the hot dog place, who had taken the knife to them, and the girl who had worked the counter. Their names were all there. And there was the name of the woman, Maureen Dietz. The last article had said she was in a hospital, but that was almost eight years ago. The woman on the TV wasn't broken down. She wasn't quite the woman of his nightmares, but she was that woman at the same time and something more. She had a kind of craziness in her, the kind that says I'm going to do what I got in mind and no one but the devil himself is going to have a chink's chance at stopping me.

Marty did the packing while Cal sat in the chair and watched shows, complaining. By the time the packing was finished an hour later, Cal had sobered up some.

"We're going in the morning," Marty said, coming in after he had put the three suitcases in the back of the van.

"Going where, Martin?" Cal said, playing with a screwdriver and circuit he had picked up from the table. Beyond him a soap opera was on, and a woman was talking angrily to a thin boy.

"We're going to Chicago to stop that woman from bearing witness against us," Marty explained patiently. "We got a debt to settle with her."

"I got this circuit to finish. It'll take me two, three days."

"You'll finish it when we get back," said Marty. Cal shrugged, put the circuit down, and pushed up out of the chair. "Get some sleep," sighed Marty. "I want to be on the way when the sun's up."

"You shouldn't have done it?" Miles asked incredulously. "Are you kidding? You had to do it. We've got to do anything to catch those two . . . two . . ."

"They may be dead," said Mike, looking at his watch.

"Not hardly," answered Miles. "They're out there. I'd like to see them caught, tortured."

"Then you'll have to get them convicted of something in Argentina or Albania," said Maureen. "The best you'll get if they're caught is a lot of years in Joliet."

"That's not right," said Miles, getting up to turn off the television set. "We've got a death penalty in this state."

"According to Helen Katz, this isn't the kind of crime that will get them the electric chair," said Maureen, gesturing for Miles to join her on the couch. She needed him close. The pressure in her chest was there, but he took her gesture as a sign that she wanted to comfort him, and he wasn't having any.

"They beat a man to death in a parking lot, a man who didn't do anything to them, and they tried to kill you, and they go to jail and that's all?" Miles asked, looking at both his mother and Mike.

"Why don't we catch them first and then worry about what happens to them," said Maureen. "One step at a time."

She looked at Mike, who smiled supportively back at her. She wanted to return the smile, but she couldn't help feeling resentment. Helen Katz, Mike, Miles had all helped convince her to do this thing, to set up the television interview, to bring back the past, but the decision had been hers. There was no denying the fear, the memory of that night. It came back in the sudden, imagined smell of ketchup, the sensation in her shoulder, the flicker image of a face and hand through the jagged car window. There was also no denying her anger. Miles was right. It wasn't fair that those two animals should be out there uncaged. She did have some regrets that Miles had seen the whole Barelli file, that she hadn't had the sense to hide it, but he had seen it, had read it, and now knew the details of his father's murder that she had kept from him for eight years.

Miles took the opportunity to once again tell Mike the story of David's murder. It had bothered Maureen for the last five years that Miles liked to talk about his father's murder. It was a constant what-if motif. What if they had eaten inside Bittie's instead of waited in the car? What if Maureen had tried to help? What if Lou and the black man had come out a few seconds earlier? What if his father had not been the next in line but . . .

Maureen blamed part of it on herself. The two men had followed her. It was her they had wanted. David had simply gotten in the way. Her own wish to keep the past in the past had encouraged Miles to take the past on himself, to talk about, push, dig out the clippings, ask his grandmother. It was one reason she had agreed to do the television interview, to face it once more for Miles in the hope that there might be an end to it.

"I'm going to my room," Miles finally announced, looking first at Maureen and then at Mike for a possible argument.

"Whatever," said Maureen.

"Go for it," added Mike, and Miles bounded out, heading for his video games or David Letterman.

When he was gone, Maureen fixed her eyes on Mike. "You were a big help," she said with equal parts of sarcasm and challenge.

He shifted to get a better view of her and said, "I didn't know you were looking for help. I thought I was supposed to stand back and be the neutral, benevolent observer. Getting soft in your old declining years, huh, queen of the Amazons?"

Mike was wearing a black short-sleeved turtleneck shirt, which was not only sadly out of date but a poor choice for the hot weather. The air conditioner was off, but the windows were open and a movement of air kept the room reasonably comfortable. Somewhere above them they could hear Miles's window air conditioner turn on, an act of minor rebellion.

"You think I was right, don't you, Coach?" Maureen said, curling her leg under her. The movement reminded her of something in the past. She remembered those weeks in the hospital when that nurse kept telling her not to sit with her feet curled up on the furniture.

"Beats me, Maureen," Mike said. "I'd like to know, now that the cameras are gone, the kids are tucked in under their *Star Wars* blankets, and we are alone, just why did you really do it?"

"You mean," she said, putting the cold glass down on the table, "beyond my responsibility, a belief in justice, a desire to protect potential victims?"

"Beyond that," said Mike, reaching over for her drink. She beat him to it and moved the glass. She didn't like people sharing food or glasses, but she knew a lifetime of doing it was hard for Mike to forget.

"Just," she went on, "the need to face the past and put it behind me."

"That's a good one," he said, getting up with a grunt and reaching over to pour himself another glass of iced tea. "Okay. You just faced the past. Now what about the future? I don't have half a century more. It's nice playing courtship games, Maureen, but I'm a little old to keep this up much longer. I'm talking about marriage, vows, together for keeps, and if you don't think it's hard for me to talk like this you're making a big mistake. I'm the one who had the bum marriage. . . ."

"And I had a marriage that ended in hell. The rotten egg can break anytime, Coach," she countered.

He took a big drink of his tea and walked over to turn off the television set. The picture had been moving, but the sound was off. The click and dying hum filled the time of a heartbeat.

Maureen looked at him for a long time with neither of them speaking. He stood there bouncing on his heels just the way she had seen him do on the sidelines during a football game.

"You are some homespun philosopher," he said finally. "Maybe we can get you a radio show of your own. The Garrison Killer of the suburbs."

"Everyday bread-and-butter stuff," she said, grinning. Maureen got up, stretched, and took a step toward him.

"You're almost young enough to be one of my daughters," he said, raising his eyebrows.

"If you were twelve when you had me." She grinned, putting her arms around his neck. "You're good, but I don't think you're that good."

"You mean I am snug and comfortable or you find me comforting like a teddy bear or a nice pillow? I had a comfortable pillow when I was a kid, big giant thing with baseball cartoons on it."

Maureen kissed him on the cheek and laughed a small, too serious laugh, and said, "That's the same pillow that's still on your bed."

"A replacement," he said, putting his arms around her. "Got it two years ago. Janet said it messed up the decor. Had to wait till she ran away to trot it out and suck my thumb."

"You want to make love?" she whispered.

"Does Nixon want to forget Watergate?" he answered. "What about Miles?"

"Miles," she said, "will have to get his own girl."

"I'd introduce him to my younger daughter, but I like Miles too much," Mike whispered back. "She'd devour him."

"Miles knows we do it," she said, enjoying the solid heaviness of his body as her arms encircled him. "Not only does he not mind, he thinks it's good for me. Before you came around I had a reputation in this house for being a prime contender for the next Christian Crusade to abolish good times. I worked at it too hard for the kids' sake. Miles likes you."

"He likes going to football games," Mike countered.

"Are we going to keep talking or are you going to come upstairs with me?" she said, stepping back. "Miles has never, not since the age of seven at least, come to my room at night. I'll lock the door. Michael, use it or lose it."

Maureen had always been the leader in their sex and tonight was no different. When she had made the suggestion, she felt no great feeling of lust or love, simply a need. And she realized that she planned to use Mike the way she used her exercise, to forget herself and the past, to lose the idea of time. When she said it to herself, it felt better. Why shouldn't she? There was no harm in it. Damn, she thought, guilt is coming back. Maybe the huge, warm bear of a body would blanket her from it for an hour or two.

They were on the second-floor landing, with Mike doing his best to be quiet so Miles wouldn't hear and Maureen going out of her way to make a little normal noise. She grinned at him and unbuttoned the top button of her white blouse as she pointed at her bedroom door in a mock gesture of command. He had taken a step past her outstretched arm when the phone rang. "Miles will get it," she said.

Mike stopped and waited, and Maureen let her shoulders drop, knowing they would not enter till they were sure the call was not for her.

The ringing stopped, and they could hear Miles's voice, beyond his closed door at the top of the stairs, over the sound of his television. Miles's room was the only one on the third level. It was a converted attic, which could be very warm in the summer without air-conditioning and cold in the winter even with heat, but it gave him privacy. They stood waiting on the landing, unable to make out his words. Just as they decided that the call was indeed for Miles, his door came open.

They looked up and could see him in dark silhouette, his arms on the doorjambs, looking down. "It's for you, Mom, a *Sun-Times* reporter. I told him it was too late, but he wants to talk to you about the interview. He says it was used on the network."

"I'll take it," she said. "Hell of a way to get famous."

"You want me to make us an omelette, Mike?" Miles called down.

Maureen could see that it wasn't what Mike had in mind for the rest of the evening, but he said, "Sure."

Maureen gave him a squeeze of his hairy hand and went into her bedroom to take the call. Behind her, as she moved toward the small table near her bed where the phone was, she could hear another door open and Nancy's voice, sounding a little frightened, saying, "What's wrong? What's wrong?"

She hesitated, turned to go back out to the girl, but was stopped by Mike's voice. "Omelette party, Princess Daisy. Why don't you come down and join us? Chocolate ice cream and mushroom omelettes."

"That's gross," giggled Nancy.

Maureen picked up the phone and put her hand to her chest, hoping that it would help to control the throbbing that demanded attention.

Mike left a little after one in the morning, never having gotten back to Maureen's bedroom. His grade point had shot up somewhere near the maximum with both Nancy and Miles. By the time Maureen had finished her phone call and gone down to the kitchen, the two kids and Mike had been solemnly and appreciatively at work consuming an eight-egg omelette.

"That sucker can eat," Nancy had said, doing her Mr. T imitation and nodding at Mike, who'd shrugged sheepishly.

Even if the call had not rubbed away the edges of sexual feeling, the sight of the three of them in the kitchen had. Mike's teddy bear frame had seemed to fill the room, reminding her of his desire for a full-time role in her life. She'd imagined him filling her life as he filled the room. The image had been both comforting and somehow chilling.

"What did the reporter want?" Miles had said between bites of what looked to Maureen like a far-too-runny yellow glop.

"Just wanted to get some more details after seeing the television show," she had replied. "He thinks we'll get more calls tomorrow."

When they had finished a quart of generic cola and the kids were back in bed, Mike had raised his eyebrows in a ludicrous Groucho imitation and pointed upstairs. Maureen had given him a small smile and touched his arm, shaking her head no.

Mike had put his arm around her, a single great arm, and had given her a hug as they moved to the front door. It was, she'd thought, the kind of consoling hug she had once seen him give a quarterback who had just thrown an interception. Instead of resenting it, she had put her own arm around him and hugged back, which she had not seen the quarterback do.

He'd kissed her, smelling of salami and onions, and she'd said, "It feels good to have you around."

"Feels good to be around," he had answered. "You want me to stay the night? I'll sleep downstairs."

"No, thanks," Maureen had said. "I'm a big girl. Besides, what happens tomorrow night and the night after?"

"That's my question," Mike had said. There'd been nothing more to say and Mike had left with a promise to call the following night.

Maureen spent another hour looking through the thick file Helen Katz had given her. She had gone through it several times quickly, looking for something startling, important, but it was mostly lists of places, phone calls, checklists of dead ends. The few photographs of the Vanbeeber cousins held no special impact for her. In fact, she was finding it hard to believe that the two men in the photographs taken from the file were the same two she had seen murder David. She would never forget the face of the big one who had looked into the car window, but she wasn't sure the man in the photograph and the killer in the parking lot were the same. Helen had said that eight years and a major breakdown can cause some fantasy and distortion. Maureen knew that. She knew the feeling of seeing a fantasy. The sight of a large

— 74 —

and a small man together had cut through her hundreds of times, sending her in a determined run to get in front of them, to see their faces.

Maureen considered calling Nancy in to sleep with her and fought it off. When she had been in the hospital, right after David's murder, she had found that the only way to deal with the vulnerability of those she loved was to concentrate on getting better, stronger. It had started from fear, but it was evident in her obsessive determination. She would take care of her mind and body. She would be strong, ready, concentrating on taking care of Miles and Nancy and taking satisfaction in the moment. Being happy, she decided, was overrated. Being at peace was the real trick, and she found a way to achieve it through her work.

The street was quiet, but with the window open as she lay in bed Maureen could hear cars three blocks away on Dodge Avenue. Though the dawn light streaming in got her up early each morning in the summer, Maureen preferred that to the darkness with the shades drawn. Now the streetlight created fluttering shadow images on the ceiling of the leaves from the tree in the front yard. The tree shadows danced to the sound of distant automobiles, a modern dance. Maureen let her body relax and gave her full attention to the shadow pattern on the ceiling. Her thoughts moved to the fringe of fear, and she gently called them back to focus on the pattern, not interpreting it, not putting what she saw into words, not seeing Rorschach shapes. The line between watching and sleeping was so thin, so without boundaries, that she was over it without knowing it had happened.

Maureen didn't know where she was, but she knew there was something familiar about the place. She was sitting in a car or truck. Miles was on one side and Nancy on the other. They were all strapped into seat belts and couldn't move. She first looked at Miles, who shimmered, vibrated from being a little boy to being a teenager. Then she looked at Nancy, who changed from a baby to a little girl.

She tried to close her eyes because the changing of the children made her dizzy, filled her with nausea, but her eyes wouldn't close. They stayed open and she felt her hands moving, moving without commands from her. She looked down and in each hand was a plastic container, a yellow one in her right, a red one in her left. She watched as both hands began to squeeze and liquid flowed, gushed from the containers, flying around the car, covering herself, the children.

She forced herself to look up. Something drew her eyes away from her hands. There was a sound out the window to her left and she found herself staring through the glass at him, the big man. His face was pressed to the window, his nose distorted, his purple baseball hat at a mad angle. Miles and Nancy were covered in red and yellow, and screaming. She could hear them, sense them, but she couldn't look away from the big man, who stared at her as if he wanted to get in. She wanted to scream too, but no scream came out, and the man's face was gone, as if he had backed into a cloud outside the car window. She tried to let go of the two tubes in her hands but couldn't. She strained, turning as far as she could past Miles, who was now a little boy again. Caught in her seat belt, she could barely see over the bottom of the window, but she could see. In a black circle on the ground lay David, and over him stood the big man. David was bloody, a massive clot of blood, and the big man was about to hit him; but David shimmered, vibrated, and changed into someone else, another man and then a woman and finally into the big man himself. And the big man stood there looking down at himself, his arms drawn back to bring down on his duplicate the full weight of the bar he held in his hands.

As he brought the bar down, he looked once more toward Maureen with a look of helplessness and hatred that made her scream, scream so loud that she woke herself up as she had done from the same dream dozens of times before. But even when she was awake and she held back the next scream, the piercing sound quivered through her and then she realized the phone was ringing.

She took two quick, deep breaths, glanced at the illuminated clock on the table, which told her it was three-ten in the morning, and grabbed for the phone in the hope of cutting it off before it woke the children.

"Hello," she panted.

"You shoulda let it alone," came the man's voice. "You should have let it die, bitch."

"Who is this?" she asked, but she knew who it was.

"We're coming, you slut. You wanted us and you're going to get us. And when you see us you won't have anything more to say to anyone, not ever."

There was a click on the phone. Maureen closed her eyes. Maybe it was a dream inside of a dream. She knew it wasn't, but maybe, just maybe. And then she smelled something or imagined she smelled something like a dead animal, or her own fear, or a rotten egg.

Helen Katz stood tall, straight, and gently tanned in front of Maureen's house at seven the next morning. She had just dropped her huge denim bag under the oak on the front lawn. She was wearing a pair of loose-fitting white shorts and an oversize blue T-shirt, making it evident that there was more to her bust than Maureen's. She wore a white sweatband to keep her hair back. Maureen greeted her with a wave, pausing in her warm-up exercises. Maureen was wearing ultra-lightweight running pants and a white T-shirt. Her hair was held back in a ponytail with a thick red rubber band.

A few minutes after the call had come, Maureen had called the Evanston police. The woman who'd answered the phone had turned her over to a sergeant whose name she hadn't caught. Maureen had told him about the call and he had been sympathetic and calm, maddeningly calm rather than reassuringly calm.

"He said he was going to kill me," she had explained. "That they were going to kill me."

"Yes, ma'am," the sergeant had said. "But like you said, you were on television. Your phone is listed. Any freak could have picked up the book or dialed information and just called to give you a scare."

"That's sick," she had said.

"It can get a lot sicker, ma'am," he'd said. "I don't want to scare you more than you are, but don't you think if it was this guy and he wanted to get you he'd just come and not reach out and just say hi?"

"It was his voice," she'd said, knowing her teeth were clenched.

"You're sure of that?" he'd asked, still calmly. "Just a second. I've got an emergency on the other line."

"I'm an emerg—" she'd begun but the line went dead. She was considering hanging up when he had come back on the line.

"Sorry," he'd said. "Look, I'll send a car over right away. We can even have a man stay at your house till morning," he'd said.

"And then?" she'd asked, looking toward the window for the first signs of dawn, which was hours away.

"And then they go," he had said. "We can't assign someone to you full time, ma'am, not on the basis of what sounds like it might be a psycho call. I can send a man over for you now and leave a report for a detective to come see you tomorrow."

"Forget it, just forget it, Sergeant," she had said angrily.

"If it makes you feel better, ma'am, I don't think I will forget it," he'd said, "but there's only so much I can do on something like this."

She had hung up with a sharp "Thank you" and then got out of bed and searched through her purse for the number Helen Katz had given her.

"The truth," Helen Katz said now, standing in front of her. "You didn't think I'd be here on time."

"I didn't think you'd be here on time," Maureen said, smiling weakly. "I'm just finishing my warm-ups and then we can get started when you're finished warming up."

"I don't warm up," said Helen, leaning back against the big oak on the front lawn. "I get warm enough running. A jock I knew a few years ago didn't believe in warm-ups for running, playing basketball, or sex. He was pretty good at two of those so I figured I'd try it."

"Well," said Maureen, looking up from a sit-up.

"Well?" countered Helen innocently.

"Which two was he good at?"

"Basketball wasn't his game," Helen sighed. "Couldn't go to his left and his jump shot was shit."

Maureen got up and began doing her trunk twists, starting gently to right and increasing as she moved, stretching and breathing. A battered van pulled down the street and both of them looked at it. It was a one-way street and the van was moving slowly, much too slowly. Maureen turned her eyes to Helen and watched her. The policewoman bent down to pick up her denim bag. The van pulled even with the house and Helen reached into the bag.

Inside the vehicle, a man, well back in the shadows, paused, looked at the two of them for an instant, and then reached for something at his side.

"Don't pull out the gun," Maureen said softly. Helen hesitated. "If you shoot the *Sun-Times* delivery man, I'll have to walk an extra block each morning to get the paper."

The man threw the paper underhand out the window. It turned three or four times, like the bone thrown by the ape at the beginning of *2001*. At least that was how it looked to

Maureen, who waved at the man. He waved back. They met like this several times a week when their schedules overlapped.

Helen put her bag down and turned to Maureen, who was well warmed up and stood with hands on hips, looking amused. "If you don't want to lose my company, don't go showing off by running forty or fifty miles this morning, and keep the speed down to well below Evelyn Ashford," the policewoman said.

"I run from here to the park, about three blocks, and then two or three times around the park before sprinting back here. That's a little over three miles. I do it in a little under half an hour."

Helen shrugged, adjusted her sweatband, checked the strings on her running shoes, which Maureen could tell had seen some use, and said, "Sounds all right if you aren't conning me."

"You'll make it a lot easier if you don't run down the street carrying a pistol," Maureen added. "This neighborhood isn't perfect, but it might cause some talk."

Helen picked up her bag, walked over to her Datsun, unlocked it, dropped her bag in, locked the door, and displayed her car keys, which she dropped into a pocket in her shorts. Maureen picked up the newspaper, tempted to see if the reporter who called the night before had gotten his story in. She resisted and threw the folded paper up on the porch.

"Let the games begin," Helen said, and Maureen took off down the street. They moved slowly at first, not talking, listening to each other breathe, their feet hitting the street. A car passed, heading in their direction, and moved far to the right to avoid them.

Neither of them was breathing heavily when they hit Main Street and ran in place while some of the early morning to-work traffic sped by. Across the street, Maureen took off to the right to begin the broad circle around the block. She alternated day to day. One day she went right to left, the next she went left to right. This early in the morning they were unlikely to meet anyone. On weekends, there would be soccer players—Mexicans, Japanese—who had a league in the park. Sometimes too there would be a lone black boy shooting baskets at the court next to the playground, a would-be Dr. J or Michael Jordan. The women padded past the basketball courts. Miles came out to play a few afternoons a week and held his own in the games. Maureen had come to watch a few times, but he had made it clear that her presence embarrassed him.

"It is hard enough being a small, white kid with glasses trying to make it in an all-black pickup game," he had explained, alternating between insistence and apology, "without my mother looking on." It had seemed reasonable to her and she had stopped coming.

"Watch for dog shit on the turn near the ball field," Maureen said to Helen at her side as they rounded the far corner of the park.

"Okay," panted Helen.

They ran on and Helen kept pace, side by side. Maureen figured that the other woman was about six years younger than she was, maybe thirty-one, thirty-two.

They went down the straightway of the street paralleling the far side of the park and past the four tennis courts, which often had players even at seven in the morning. This morning the temperature was already well into the upper seventies, and no one was on the courts. Maureen and Nancy, at Nancy's request, came here about once a week to search for tennis balls lost in the tall grass or lodged in the shrubs. Nancy had amassed a reasonably large collection, sixteen balls of various colors and conditions. It was the only real interest Nancy had in the park. She preferred her yard and Paulette's wading pool.

There was a reasonable amount of early morning traffic on Dodge as they went down the sidewalk around the park bordering the street. From the corner of her eye, Maureen saw a battered, rusting car slow down and a dark youngish man lean out toward them. "Say babies, you like a little ride on this?" he called. The joke tickled another young man in the car, who choked with laughter.

Maureen's usual response to this when it happened—about once a week—was to ignore it and keep running. The first time it had happened she had felt the finger of fear on her spine, but she had kept running, lost herself in the run. It had been only a car pool of men on the way to work trying to impress each other. None but the truly feebleminded would think they could pick up a woman jogging in the park with such an offer. Helen, however, slowed down, turned toward the car, which was a few feet away, and gave them the finger. "Go play with yourself, putz," she said.

The choker in the car went into convulsions, and the guy leaning out the window yelled, "Bitch, cunt!"

"Add two more words to your limited vocabulary and we'll see what we can do about getting you into remedial kindergarten," Helen shot back.

Maureen was definitely having trouble losing herself in the run this morning.

"She's too fast for you, Paco," the guy in the back seat shouted between laughs.

"More ways than one," Helen said. "Just pedal your trike to work and think of how much you impressed us." The car sped away with a macho squeal of tires, cutting off a station wagon, which had to hit its brakes to avoid collision.

Maureen increased her pace and Helen stayed with her. They caught a green light and dashed across Main, past an abandoned gas station where Maureen began to sprint as she always did for the final three blocks. She didn't look back for Helen, but sped away, and for the first time during the run she did lose herself.

Turning the corner on her street she felt Helen not far behind but didn't look, didn't acknowledge the end until she slowed down in front of her house. Maureen eased into a slow jog as she went up the narrow driveway and around the back. She slowed to a walk as she made her first circle around the house, pausing to pick up the newspaper, and found Helen at her side.

"You always go that fast?" Helen said.

Maureen looked at the woman, who was drenched in sweat. "I don't know," Maureen admitted, feeling the heat now that the run was over. "I just do it."

"I kept up with you to impress you," Helen said. "But I'm not sure it was worth it. Let's do it a little slower tomorrow, okay?" They were walking slowly around the house now.

"You're coming back?"

"You thought you'd lose me this easily?"

Helen stopped at her car for her denim bag and followed Maureen into the house. Maureen had locked the door this morning. Normally she just left it open. The key was in the little pocket of her pants. She fished it out and went in, holding the door open for Helen, who had fished a big blue towel from her bag and draped it around her neck.

In the living room Nancy, still in an enormous yellow night-gown—a present from Grandma Darla—was holding her pillow on her lap and watching "The Flintstones" on Channel 32. She looked up at her mother and Helen, nodded in response to their "hi," and turned back to the television. The routine was for Maureen to shower and have her breakfast with Nancy, who usually made herself something Maureen disapproved of but accepted with the knowledge that tastes change. In this case, Nancy had poured herself a big bowl of PacMan cereal, which included little marshmallow Pac men.

"Want some PacMan cereal?" Maureen asked Helen.

"You're kidding?" the policewoman replied.

"Mom," whined Nancy without taking her eyes from "The Flintstones," "don't make fun of me. You promised."

"I promised, Daisy," Maureen said.

Maureen showered upstairs and Helen downstairs in the small stall in the workout room. Maureen made toast and orange juice and they sat in the kitchen, within hearing distance of the end of "The Flintstones." Maureen found the story on page three, read it quickly, and passed it to the policewoman.

"We had six calls last night and this morning," Helen Katz said, sitting on the wooden kitchen chair, taking a respectable bite out of her piece of buttered toast and looking at the article. "All from people who had seen or thought they had seen . . . the Vanbeebers. Four were from the Chicago area. One call came in from Virginia. One from Phoenix. One from St. Louis. We don't think any of them were the Vanbeebers, but it's good to know people were listening."

"Good to know," Maureen agreed, making it clear that she did not share Helen's enthusiasm for the situation. "You think they might come here, don't you? You think that it was one of them on the phone this morning?"

"Truth?" said Helen, after washing down a bit of toast with a gulp of orange juice. "No. Truth is I think it was a nut who watches too much TV, but I'm not sure. If it goes the way things usually do, we'll get a few more reports. The newspapers will carry a story or two, maybe not."

"But your boss took the call seriously enough to send you here," Maureen continued.

"Nope," Helen said, playing with a few dark crumbs on her plate. "This visit was on my own time. It'll take more than a phone call to get any official protection for you."

"I see," said Maureen. "They've got to actually maim or kill me or one of my kids before the manpower can be spared."

"Something like that," agreed Helen, "but woman power is another thing."

Maureen finished her toast and reached for a second. She allowed herself a large orange juice and two pieces of buttered toast in the morning. She normally ate no lunch and had a dinner of anything she wanted, and she usually wanted what the kids wanted: hot dogs, pizza, ribs, burgers. Her only evening concession to good health was a nightly salad of fresh vegetables.

"So," Helen went on, "get yourself an unlisted phone and stay near the kids as much as you can. Maureen, it probably was a nut on the phone."

"That sounds reasonable in the daylight but I'm not so sure about when the sun goes down."

From the living room Fred Flintstone shouted, "Yabadabadoo."

"I hate that," Helen said. "Sorry."

"I hate it too," admitted Maureen. "May she outgrow it soon. She took up television when she stopped sucking her thumb. I've got to drive Nancy to summer camp at the community center."

"And I've got to get to work," added Helen, getting up. "You sure you don't mind my running with you in the morning? If you'd rather be alone . . ."

They were both standing now and Maureen was clearing the table and putting the juice away. "I'll take all the company I can get," she said. Normally, she hated having anyone run with her, even Miles, who stayed with her for the first two miles and then shot out and away for the final mile as if she had been jogging it instead of running. Miles always made it seem like a race instead of a run. Helen hadn't thought she had been a distraction. The possibility existed, Maureen thought, that Helen might actually be a friend. Friends tended to become dependent, to assert their needs, and Maureen had not wanted to give herself to that, but something was changing in Maureen. Besides, Helen had made no emotional demands.

"Good," said Helen, picking up her bag. "I'll see you tomorrow or give you a call before then if anything comes up. You'll be all right?"

"Sure. Maybe we can get together tomorrow or the next day for dinner," Maureen tried.

"Sounds fine," the policewoman said. She was wearing her skirt and blouse again. "We'll set it up."

"Without Mike," Maureen added.

"I like Mike," Helen said. They had met two nights before when Helen had come for dinner before the Channel 9 interview. Maureen had sensed a cautious initial response to Mike, as if she were waiting for the male signs that inevitably come. Since Mike was big, burly, and a football coach, Helen had looked particularly wary, but Mike had proved himself comfortable and respectful, with more questions about Helen's job as a cop than Miles or Nancy had.

Miles, she knew, was sleeping and would probably stay in bed till noon. He stayed up till at least three in the morning in the summer. Sometimes a friend joined him and once in a while, when she had no school the next day, he even let Nancy into his room to watch television or play a game of Risk or chess till midnight.

Nancy had dressed herself by the time Maureen came into the living room. Nancy had six favorite dresses, which she alternated. One of them was a year old and too small, a pink dress she now wore. Her closet was also full of skirts and blouses, but Nancy wouldn't wear them, sneakers, or jeans.

"You look terrific," Maureen said, advancing with the hair brush.

"I brushed my hair, Mom," Nancy said, glancing at the Popeye cartoon that had just replaced "The Flintstones."

"Humor me," Maureen said, kissing her daughter and standing up to brush.

"Have you got a hard day?" Nancy asked, looking from the television to her mother with sudden, surprising, and genuine concern.

"I hope not, Daisy," she said, reaching over to brush the girl's bangs.

"You think they'll get them?" Nancy whispered. Bluto laughed behind them, filling up the room.

"The ones who killed your father?" Maureen whispered back, taking the girl's now-serious face in her hands. Nancy nodded. She had no memory of her father outside of a few stories imperfectly remembered by Miles, and some photographs. "They'll get them," Maureen said firmly and with great sincerity, which she most certainly did not feel. "You want to go swimming tonight at the Y?"

"I'd rather rent a tape of *Grease I* or *II*." Nancy smiled back with a baby face that had proved its power over her mother.

Maureen smiled also. "No *Grease*, Daisy Duck, but the swimming offer holds. Maybe Miles will join us. Think about it."

She dropped Nancy off at the community center at nine and tried to get out of the door quickly, but the camp director, Barbara, stopped her and asked if she had a minute.

"I'm running late," Maureen said. "But sure."

Barbara was neat, slightly heavy at fifty, with short, straight gray hair. Maureen liked her efficiency and the fact that the children obviously respected her. They moved into her small cluttered office and Barbara closed the door. They didn't sit.

"I saw you on the news last night," she said. Maureen tensed, ready for the kind of morbid questions she had feared might come. "This must be very hard on Nancy," she said. "Maybe we should talk, meet with Millie Weiss. You know Millie? She does some social counseling."

Maureen's tension eased. "Do you really . . ." she began.

"I think so," Barbara said. "I've seen similar situations. A girl like Nancy will keep it in. She admires you a great deal. She'll try to face it the way you do, but she's just a little girl."

"I can make it any afternoon around three just before I pick up Nancy, if that will be all right," she said.

"Fine," Barbara said, and smiled. "I'll set something up with Millie and let you know. Is there anything we can do for you?"

"Two thousand dollars, a new car, a trip to Europe," Maureen said. "Just joking. A bad joke. You're right. Things are a bit tense, and I appreciate your thinking about Nancy."

The rest of the morning went badly. She had a class at her center, which she made on time, though she had the feeling that the car brakes were starting to go, which would mean the loss of the car for a day and a steep bill. It was a '78 Olds Omega, which she had bought, used, from an Episcopalian minister who retired with his wife to Vermont. The car was fine, but had its reasonable share of problems and a love of gasoline. Someone had also parked in her reserved space next to the building. She had called Miles to wake him and assure herself that he was all right. He had been irritable.

The exercise class itself was only a minor disaster. It was clear from the looks on the faces of the people before her in the room that they had either seen her on television the night before, read something in the newspaper this morning, or had been told what had happened.

Maureen faced it head on, told the class she was fine and that she simply wanted to go on with the class. It didn't work. There were twenty-three bodies moving for the next hour, but there were an equal number of minds not attuned to the moving bodies. Maureen had to admit that even she was having trouble giving herself up to the workout.

To compensate she made the routine even more rigorous and turned up the volume on her cassette player as Handel's *Water Music* came on, but she wound up losing a few more women who were not in shape for the forty push-ups that alternated with knee bends.

The problem with sessions like this was that instead of revitalizing her they took something away, made her feel a little tired. They did just the opposite of what they were supposed to do.

She found herself thinking about, beside the brakes, the young man at Barnaby's—Simcox—who had stopped awkwardly at their table. He had been a kind of omen, the first reopening of the wound, a sign that David's murder would force itself back to her consciousness. She also remembered that she had not been particularly cordial to him. "Let go of the guilt," she said aloud. And then to herself, "Let it go."

The rest of her classes went about the same way, and she had little to say to Miles and Nancy in the evening. She hoped Nancy wouldn't ask to go swimming and was relieved when she didn't. Miles made a few stabs at jokes, teased his sister, and then went to his room. Maureen went to bed early, but before she did she double-checked the doors and windows to be sure they were locked, and she left the kitchen light on. When she got to her room, she pulled out the Barelli file and found the two sheets she was looking for.

# 4

The orange van was caught in a hell of a traffic jam on the expressway heading out of St. Louis. There was no exit in sight, and the trucks and cars were barely moving. Marty wiped his brow with the gray handkerchief in his shirt pocket and glanced out of the window at the factory far back in the grassy field, spitting fire and smoke into the sky. He hadn't slept more than an hour. He'd thought calling her would make it better, hose him down a little, but hearing her had just made him madder. He had sat up watching the window for the first sun. Now they were on the way and the car radio was playing loud country and western music Cal had found. It was Dolly Parton or Barbara Mandrell or one of those sexy ones almost crying about losing a guy to her best friend. It was loud and squawky and Marty didn't like it at all.

"How about turning that down," he said, looking in the rearview mirror for an opening to wedge into and give himself the impression that he was making progress.

"I like it," Cal shouted from behind him in the van.

"I'm turning it down," Marty said, and he reached over and turned it down.

"How the shit am I supposed to hear it back here if you turn it down like that?" Cal shouted.

"Well stop all the time playing with yourself back there and come up here and sit near the radio," Marty answered. He was feeling irritable and getting to the point where he didn't mind who knew it.

"I ain't playing with myself," Cal shouted back. "Don't need to play with myself the way you do, Martin. I got no trouble picking up broads, and I got no regrets if I have to pay for 'em here and there."

"Cal," Martin said gently. "You shut up. I'm in no mood. No mood at all. You mind what I'm saying?"

Cal shuffled in the van and coughed before he spoke. He was still sounding tough and spiteful, but Cal had read something in Marty's tone that made him a little cautious. Marty knew that there wasn't anything in or on God's green earth or in the devil's dark that could stop Cal when he lost control. When the anger took him, there was no holding on to Cal, and short of sitting on him, there was nothing to do but back away and save some face. "I don't give a shit what you say, cousin. You hear me? Turn the damn radio down if you got a mind to. How about we stop somewhere and get us something to drink? I'm frying alive back here."

A trucker gave Marty a blast of his horn as Marty eased the van in front of him, almost causing a crash. Marty ignored the driver and began looking for another hole in the traffic. "When we get to Springfield," Marty said, "we'll get something to eat and drink. We've got things to do, Calvin. Let's keep our minds on it. You hear me?"

"I'm not deaf," Cal grumbled behind him. "Shit, shut the damn radio off. I can't hear it now."

Marty reached over and turned the radio volume up again, higher than it had been before when he had complained and

—— 91 ——

lowered it. He saw a break in the traffic and stepped on the gas to take advantage of it.

"Sometimes," Cal cried from the darkness, "I think you are crazier than I am, and that's a fact."

"That's a fact," Marty agreed.

Barbara or Dolly or Crystal or whoever it was wailed a song and felt sorry for herself, and Marty looked straight ahead, forcing himself to be calm. It might take hours to get where they were going, but he would get there. They had come a long way, and he had to tell himself that there was no hurry. She was waiting there for him, waiting for him to come and end the nightmare.

By noon they had made it to Springfield. They pulled off the expressway because the van was overheating badly in the ninety-degree heat. The neighborhood was black and so was the guy at the gas station, but Marty didn't give a shit what color he was as long as he gave him water for the radiator and gas for the tank.

"Radiator's overheated pretty bad," the black guy told Marty, who had stepped out of the van. Cal was silent in the rear of the van. Marty had left the radio on, and Marty Robbins was singing into the warm air about a honky-tonk man.

The black man was wearing a mechanic's suit. He was maybe forty, maybe less. His head was bald and he had a cautious look on his face.

"I know the radiator's overheating," said Marty. "You think I just stopped here to chew the fat with you? Open it up and get some water in there."

"Too hot to open," the man said. "You'll have to sit while it cools down a little."

Marty looked at the man and knew that someone was going to back down here. "What's all this about?" Cal shouted, sticking his head out of the window. "Get done what has to be done and let's get out of here."

"Man says the radiator's too hot to open," Marty called back over his shoulder. It was the start of a routine familiar to the cousins, a routine they had been working on most of their lives. Behind him Marty could hear the van door open and Cal get out. The black guy touched his sweaty bald head and glanced over at the station for help. Cal was at Marty's side now, shrugging off the cramps in his legs. His hair was wild, and he needed a shave. His gray T-shirt was sweaty, clinging to his chest, and he was grinning a mean-ass grin.

"Man's job is to service vehicles," Cal said. "That's what the Shell ads say, isn't it, Marty?"

"It's what the Shell ads say," Marty agreed, enjoying this.

"It's too damned hot to touch," insisted the black man, who too casually put his hand down to his pocket, from which a gray greasy wrench protruded. "Even if I opened the cap, it would stream over. You'd still have to wait. Now you don't want to wait, just drive on down the street to Texaco."

Cal put his hands in the back pockets of his jeans and took a step closer to the man, whose hand was now on the wrench.

"We don't want no fuckin' Texaco station," Cal said. "We want Shell. We love Shell. And you are going to open that radiator or I'm gonna take that wrench you got in your hand and poke it through your eye and out your ear."

"You shit," said the man, pulling the wrench out and stepping back. He was scared, real scared. Marty laughed and shook his head. "Ben," the black man shouted. "Ben, Arch, come out here, shake your ass."

"You better have six of you in there," Cal said.

Marty stepped forward fast as the black man pulled out the wrench and held it high. He moved in front of Cal and was ready to reach out and grab the black man.

"Back off," came a voice, a deep voice. Marty and the black man with the wrench were looking into each other's eyes, and Marty knew that the man was pissing or shitting in his pants.

"Back off," the voice repeated, and Marty looked toward it. He saw two men, really a young skinny boy and a man who must have been seventy at least. They were both black and no match for Cal and Marty. At least they wouldn't have been if it hadn't been for the big pistol in the old man's hand.

Marty raised his hands up and took a step back from the bald man. It was a comic exaggeration, showing that Marty wasn't going to do anything.

"Let's take their ass," Cal hissed.

"We didn't mean anything by it, old-timer," Marty said, putting out a big hand to keep Cal from getting killed. A pair of black kids had picked up on the action and stopped to watch. They were about ten or twelve. One of them dribbled a battered leather basketball on the sidewalk as Marty guided Cal back to the van. "Just hold your wad in," Marty said, opening the van door, "and we'll be on our way."

"Just take your white-trash ass out of here," said the old man. He stepped forward, waving his gun, and the bald man near them, encouraged by the support added, "You got fifteen seconds or this place is going to be covered with cops."

"Who you shitting, man?" Marty laughed, easing Cal inside the van. He had to shout now to be heard over Marty Robbins. "Cops don't come running to a call in this neighborhood. If it weren't for the old shit with the gun, we would have had you swallowin' wrench. You sleep on that and remember next time to be nice to customers."

Marty closed the van door and started the engine. The old man with the gun and the boy behind him stayed where they were, a good fifteen feet away. The black bald man kicked the side of the van as it pulled away, and Marty swerved, knocking over a trash can filled with empty oil-change cans that went flying, clattering and rolling. For good luck he aimed at the two kids watching. They froze, and he missed the nearest one by no more than four or five inches. The basketball flew out of the kid's hands and under the van, exploding like a bomb.

Cal was doubled up with laughter and Marty was grinning. "You see that? You see that?" Cal screamed. "Hot mad damn. That was worth it, though I'd truly like to have stomped that boy once or twice."

"Let's find another station," Marty said, feeling better. He had nothing against blacks. In fact, Cal had a sweet tooth for black whores, and that was a fact. Hell, a man is a man. Color had nothing to do with it. He knew black guys who would stand with you when trouble came and white guys who were supposed to be buddies who turned ass and left a trail of shit when the woods started to burn. No, Marty thought. The real business was up ahead somewhere, just waiting for them, just waiting in the August heat.

Maureen's decision was actually made at some point during the night, in the half-light between sleep and wakefulness, at the moment between two dreams. When she felt the sunlight touch her in the morning, she sat up, resolved, got out of bed, and walked to her desk to pull out the Barelli file. She flipped through the pages till she came to the ones that had drawn her the night before.

Before she could read them through, the phone rang. A glance at the clock near the bed told her it was slightly after seven. The phone company had agreed to change her number immediately and she had had time to give the new number to only one person after the special services operator called to tell her the change had been made.

By seven-thirty she had had four calls, all about the Vanbeebers and David's murder. So much for unlisted numbers, she thought. One call was from a newspaper in Belleville, Illinois, not far from where the Vanbeebers had lived and where Maureen had decided in the last few hours to visit. No, visit wasn't the right word. Maybe the word was pilgrimage, or investigation. If that phone call had really been from one of them, there was no sense in sitting there and waiting. Except for Helen Katz, the police didn't seem interested in either reopening the case or protecting her and the children. She would have to do something, try something. She had only one class set up for the day, and a call to her studio canceled that. No more than a dozen people were enrolled for it and they were all regulars. There was some guilt involved in making the call, but it wasn't strong enough to stop her.

Nancy trundled down to the kitchen when the phone rang a second time. Maureen was drinking a small glass of cold water prior to going out to run. Nancy's straight hair was clinging to her face, and she looked as if she were still asleep. "My air conditioner didn't work," she said, sitting sullenly.

"It wasn't hot last night," Maureen answered, reaching over to straighten her daughter's hair and touch her cheek.

"My window was locked," Nancy countered, pulling up the fringe of her pink nightgown to wipe her moist hair from her face. "Why did you lock my window?"

"I'll have Miles check the air conditioner," Maureen said, putting her glass in the dishwasher. "Can I get you some breakfast?"

The girl puffed out her cheeks, let the air out with a massive sigh, and said, "I'll get myself some Donkey Kong cereal and juice and watch 'Underdog.' You can go run."

As Nancy pushed herself away from the wooden table, Maureen said, "Nancy, I've got to go out of town today. I'll be back tomorrow afternoon. I just called Mike and he's going to stay here with you and Miles, okay?"

"Why can't I go with you?" Nancy said, throwing open the refrigerator. Maureen could see only the bottom of her gown and her small bare feet behind the open door.

"It's far, boring, and you can probably talk Mike into taking you out for dinner and a movie."

The refrigerator door closed and revealed Nancy holding a bottle of orange juice in two hands. "I don't like the same movies he likes."

"He'll be accommodating," Maureen said.

"What's that mean?"

"He'll be very anxious to make you happy," Maureen explained. "I'm going to tell Miles and then run. Stay in the house till I get back. Right after that I'm taking off as soon as Mike comes. I'll bring you a present."

"A new Barbie?"

"Not a new Barbie."

Maureen had already packed. The small brown imitation leather overnight bag was at the front door. Mike had tried to find out where she was going, but she had decided that secrecy in this case would be easier than remembering a lie.

"We'll talk about it when I get back," she said. "I'm getting calls from newspapers, television, nuts of all kinds. I just want to get away for a day by myself and there's something I have to do. Trust me, Coach."

"Consider yourself trusted," he said. "I'll take care of Miles and Daisy. But we've got a lot to talk about when you get back."

Maureen knocked at Miles's door. She could hear the rush of his air conditioner inside and a shifting in his bed. She could see by looking at the bottom of the door that no light was coming through the thin opening, that Miles had as usual pulled his shade and his drapes and come as close to total darkness as was possible outside of an experimental lab. "Huh, yeah," he groaned.

"Miles, it's Mom, I've got to go away for the day after I run. Mike is coming over in a little while. Help him with the princess."

"Going?" Miles said blearily and half-asleep. "Going where?"

"Business, just came up, I'll be back as early as I can tomorrow. If the phone rings before Mike gets here, let it ring. I've been getting calls all morning about our television appearance." To confirm her statement, the phone rang again. "See what I mean?" she said.

"I hear it," Miles mumbled. "I haven't got my glasses on."

"Go back to sleep," she said, putting her head to his door and smiling. "I'll see you tomorrow."

The call was from *The National Enquirer*. She said she had no comment and hung up.

She warmed up, ran, and urged her body to absorb her thoughts about what she had decided to do. She fought to make the trip vanish for the duration of the run, but fighting the thought didn't work. It never did. She thought of colors and her breath, and by the one-mile mark, passing the tennis courts, she was at ease.

When she got home, however, the thoughts returned, and she let them. There was nothing dangerous in what she was doing. The Vanbeebers had left where she was going years ago. It wasn't likely to be a very fruitful move in terms of learning anything, but she had to do it.

She showered quickly, changed into a lightweight green skirt and matching blouse, and headed for the living room. Miles was still upstairs. Nancy was parked in front of the television now, watching "Popeye."

"I think I'll be happy when school starts again," she said, looking at her mother, who reached over to hug and kiss her good-bye.

"Don't answer the phone. Mike will be here in a few minutes. Wear something light today."

"My bathing suit?" Nancy said, looking back at the television.

"Your blue cotton dress will be fine."

She went out, hurried to the Omega, opened the door, and threw her bag on the passenger seat. Then she sat and waited. For an instant she considered changing her mind, but she knew she would not. Somehow, this trip had to be made. It had to be made for David, for herself. In a sense, she was touching their territory as they had touched and violated hers. Maybe it would confirm to her that she was right, that these were the men. Another thought scratched from within her. The trip would also confirm the reality, the reality of David's death that she had found so elusive. It had been her goal to bury the past, but, at some level, she knew that it had also been her burden. Barelli had, for whatever reasons, carried her burden for eight years while she struggled to block it out. She would have to reclaim some part of it, if not in reality, at least symbolically. She wasn't sure that anyone else could understand what she was doing. She was sure that she didn't care.

After ten minutes of sitting in the Omega with the windows open and the sound of neighborhood birds in the nearby trees, she was aware that Mike's station wagon was turning down the street. She started her engine and pulled away when he was half a block behind. She had waited to be sure Nancy and Miles wouldn't be alone, but she didn't want to talk to him. He deserved more at this point, but she wasn't ready to give it.

When she cleared the city, she took I-57 straight south and listened to news on WBBM till she started to lose the station just before Champaign-Urbana. She stopped for a light lunch, slightly dazed by the flat land and apparently endless dry stalks of corn that blanketed the state outside of Chicago.

She stopped again at Effingham for a drink of orange juice and gas and the twenty minutes needed to reorient herself, to wake up from the hypnotizing hot trip of hazy highway and bored humming tires. It struck her at one point that this was probably the way they had come after they had killed David. She was going over their tracks, coming after them. She shuddered, leaning forward to free her sweating back from the seat. It gave her a little relief.

It was late in the afternoon when she turned off I-57 near Marion and headed west past Carbondale. The land changed. Hills appeared and the road began a welcoming rise and fall. She almost got lost finding 149, but asked directions, and then found herself on State Highway 3, which took her right into Chester just before four in the afternoon.

She had a few ideas of how to find the Vanbeeber house. She had the location in Barelli's file in her bag, but someone might be living there. She could ask directions. She considered going to the police, but that would certainly have resulted in a strong suggestion that she turn around and go home. Instead, she found the office of the weekly newspaper, where a pleasant, thin, sixtyish woman behind a high mahogany desk told her that the Vanbeebers' property was handled by Burnham Realty. She knew, said the woman, because she handled the listings for property in the paper.

"You a reporter from St. Louis?" asked the woman, who looked wily and formidable.

"No," said Maureen with a smile. "I'm from Chicago."

"*Tribune?*" the woman tried.

"No," Maureen said, walking back to the door of the newspaper office.

"I don't think you'll find a lot of people who want to talk about the Vanbeebers," the woman said, putting her hands on the counter and waiting for her words to stop Maureen. Maureen stopped.

"Why not?"

"Not too many people in town were friendly with the family," the woman explained. "And they didn't spend a lot of time in town. Their place was out on Sixteen-A and they didn't come to town a lot. Besides, no one wants to talk for fear Martin and

Calvin might take it into their minds to come back through here someday. Their departure was welcome from here to Red Bud, and their return will not be greeted as the Second Coming."

"Thanks," said Maureen.

"Luck to you," said the woman, still examining her with unblinking blue eyes.

Burnham Realty was easy to find. She got there just before five. It was a newish brown-brick building set back off of the main street of the town. It was surrounded by well-trimmed grass and had a white stone parking lot big enough for about six cars and a white colonial sign announcing that Burnham Realty had been in business since 1886. What it didn't seem to have was someone inside. Maureen tried the door and then knocked. There was no response and it was dark inside. She tried to peer through the window but could see nothing. If it weren't for the new blue Buick parked in the lot, she would have given up and tried to find the place herself.

Then something stirred inside, and she thought she could see a door opening beyond the dark room and a figure moving forward. The door opened in front of her, and she found herself facing a lean man her own height. He was about forty and, in spite of the heat of the day, wearing a lightweight suit with a tie. His hair was recently cut and just turning gray. He gave her an efficient business-curious smile.

"Yes," he said. "We're really closed for the day."

"I'm sorry," Maureen answered. "I'm only in town for the day and there is some property I'd like to see."

The man looked at her without speaking, pursed his lips, and shrugged. "Come on in," he said pleasantly.

Maureen went into the office, into the dim light coming through the shaded windows. The man flipped on the lights and held out his hand, which she shook. His grip was firm and confident. "I'm Van Burnham," he said. "Now which piece of property might you be interested in?" He offered her a seat in an old, well-polished wooden armchair and sat behind the desk nearby.

"The Vanbeeber house," she said, watching for his reaction.

He didn't appear to be surprised, but leaned back, rubbed the space just below his lips with his little finger, and thought for a moment. "No one's lived there for four or five years," he said. "The owner left without leaving instructions. Truth is I handle it and keep an eye on it because the owner is a relative."

Maureen looked at him with new interest. "You . . ." she began.

"Calvin Vanbeeber is a third cousin, something like that," he explained, looking back at her as if trying to see what she was really after. "Calvin's father was a Burnham on his mother's side. That's how he got the name, Burnham Vanbeeber. I'm said to favor him a bit. Calvin's mother, Norma, a fine-looking woman, was a Calvin. Family tradition, carry on the maternal name. Could get you into trouble naming your kid, if you marry a woman named Kiebenbauer—which, as a matter of fact, is precisely what I did."

Maureen smiled politely as Van Burnham looked at her. "I take it you would like to look at the place?" he asked, getting up out of his chair.

"I'd like to, if it's possible," Maureen said, also getting up.

"It's possible," Burnham said. "I'll find the keys and run you out. Wife's at a friend's and I'm staying in town for dinner and a meeting so I've got a bit of time."

"I really appreciate this, Mr. Burnham," Maureen said.

He found the keys he was looking for in a wooden rack behind a small counter, went to the door, and held it open for her. She went into the late afternoon sun and followed him to the Buick. The car smelled, and she didn't object when he turned on the air conditioner.

"Why the Vanbeeber place?" he asked, looking back over his shoulder as he backed out of the small gravel lot.

"I just like the location," she said. "And a friend who lives nearby thought it might be a good place to bring my kids. My son's thinking of going to Southern Illinois in Carbondale and I have a business. . . ."

"Uh . . . huh," he said. "We turn over at the Willow Road and go out, not far from the Mississippi. On a bad day you can smell the river from the Vanbeeber porch."

They were silent for the rest of the trip. Maureen wasn't sure of the turns, but they found themselves on a relatively traffic-free road in ten minutes and turned into the driveway. There were no other houses nearby. In the distance, down the road, she thought she saw a white mailbox with a little red flag.

"Here we are," said Burnham, turning off the air conditioner and engine and stepping out. Maureen got out after him and stood on the stone driveway. It looked, felt, familiar and unfamiliar at the same time. It seemed right that the house should be a small, two-story frame building, that the driveway should lead to a flat-roofed garage with peeling red wooden doors, that grass and weeds should be growing through the stones beneath her feet, that a soft hum should rustle through the weeds beyond.

"I have Al Slingo's boy come out here every other week in the summer and cut the grass," said Van Burnham, walking toward the front porch. "But for what I'm paying I can't expect it to look like the governor's mansion up in Springfield."

Maureen followed him to the porch. The steps were wood, painted gray, and peeling. "Exterior needs a painting," he said, putting the key in the door. "Interior might give you a bit of a surprise."

He opened the door and stepped back so she could go in ahead of him. The interior of the house was indeed unexpected. The small wooden-floored alcove Maureen stepped into was well lit from the windows in the living room. In fact, every room on the first and second floor was well windowed and let in the sun.

But that wasn't the surprise. She had expected to step into the smell of animals, the sense of the two things that had killed David. As she followed Van Burnham through the house, she found no visible sign of dark horror. Each room, though dusty, was clean. The furniture was old but well taken care of. Had she not known, she would have guessed that the house had been home to a fussy old spinster.

"These are the bedrooms," Burnham said, pushing open a door on the second floor. "This one was Marty and Calvin's. Don't ask me why they slept in the same room when there was another bedroom."

Maureen looked around the brightly lit room. There were two beds, two dressers. The beds were covered with army blankets. The dressers were unblemished, or seemed to be, until Maureen walked over to the one near the window and saw that there were a dozen or more burn marks etched in the wood. The room looked institutional, like a hospital, a prison, or any army barracks.

"Left it just the way it was when they went," Van Burnham said, looking around. "I should put up a few dollars and have the place cleaned. Madge Kennedy in town will come out for ten or fifteen on an off day. Marty and Calvin left suddenly about four or five years back. They had a little trouble with a fella who owns a tavern out on One-Fifty."

He stepped back onto a small second-floor landing when Maureen had finished looking at the room. She followed him and stopped to examine the photograph of an old man on the wall. The photograph seemed to be from another century.

"That's Calvin and Marty's grandfather, James Martin," Burnham said, clapping his hands together to get rid of some of the dust he had touched. "It has been suggested that he was less than a savory member of the family."

He looked around for something else to show her and shook his head. "The loft," he said. "I almost forgot. There's a loft, an attic that can be used for sleeping. I think Marty and Cal slept there when they were kids. There's a ladder behind the door in that closet." He stepped over, opened the door to darkness, and coughed when a whiff of dust hit him.

"I think we can skip that," Maureen said. It didn't feel the way she had expected it to. Instead of a ghost being set to rest, this one was coming to life. It seemed, felt, as if they were there, nearby, standing, watching. She could almost smell them in this house that stood waiting for their return, but she wasn't going to let the house or this man know.

"I've seen enough," she said.

"Suit yourself," Burnham said, leading the way to the steps. "Have you got enough now to make your decision?" He was three steps down the narrow stairway when he stopped as if suddenly remembering something and turned to face her. The hall was dark except for a single, thin stained-glass window on the stairway, an old blue-and-gold designed window that turned Burnham's face into a ghastly mask. "Dietz," he said. "Your name is Dietz." He laughed to himself and shook his head. "It's funny. I knew who you were when you walked into the office, but I couldn't remember your name. You know how that is? I've been going through the alphabet and it just came to me."

Maureen took a step backwards up the landing where the bedrooms were. Burnham, holding the wooden rail, took a step after her. He was the cousin of the two men who had killed David. He had watched their house, protected their property. "I . . ." she began.

"I know," he said as she backed away. "You were just curious. Didn't you think we have television and newspapers down here? Jesus God, when you mentioned that policeman on TV—what was his name, Barelli—I remembered talking to him. I brought him out here, and we went through the house, just the way you and I just did." Burnham took another step toward her, and she considered jumping into the bedroom to her right and trying to barricade the door. "Martin and Calvin are my cousins," he said seriously, looking into her eyes. Maureen reached over to feel for the door and couldn't find it. She had decided to turn and push through the door when he said, "And, Lord help me, I wish they were both dead."

Maureen looked at the man, whose head was turned away from her. He was leaning on the railing looking over at the photograph of Cal and Marty's grandfather. "Mrs. Dietz," he said, still not looking at her, his voice a soft whisper, "I brought you out here because you seemed to need it, to touch it, to feel that it's real. My family has known that the Vanbeebers were real for three generations. I'm what you would call an old-fashioned God-fearing man. I wasn't always. There was a little of that family spirit in me as a kid. You remember maybe twenty years back the mysterious craters around here? Everyone thought they were made by space visitors. Cal, Marty, and I dug those. Did other things not so light too. Things I'm not proud of, but they were spirited things that didn't hurt anyone. Then I went off to school, and Marty and Cal stayed here and their spirit turned wild. I lived in St. Louis for seven years, met my wife, never thought I'd be coming back here, but blood calls." He stood up and sighed and looked around the landing. "And here I am. I hope I never see those two again. If I do see them, I'll turn them in to the state police or, if I have to, I'll shoot them myself. I haven't shot a rifle since my father forced me to go hunting when I was a kid, but I'd do it if need be."

Maureen moved to his side and said, "I'm sorry, Mr. Burnham."

He turned to face her and shrugged. "I saw the look in your eyes a few minutes back," he said. "You were ready to turn and run from me. I was one of them to you. Don't bother denying it. And don't look at me with all that sympathy. The truth is I don't spend more than a few minutes a week or a month thinking about my demonic kin. It takes a visit from Marty or Cal or an outsider like you or that policeman to bring it all up. It's something you learn to live with. Damn, I think about it a lot more than my neighbors do. You know what I'm saying?"

"I know what you're saying," she said.

"Good," he sighed, and started down the steps slowly with Maureen behind. "You have any more questions about Cal and Marty I'll be happy to tell you. I can give you life histories in some detail if that will make it any better for you." In the front hallway he stopped and turned to her. "For what it's worth," he said, "I'm truly sorry for what they did to you."

"It wasn't your responsibility," she said, giving him a supportive smile, wanting to get out of the house. The sense that those two were above her, upstairs, watching, angry at her intrusion, ready to rush down the stairs, prodded her into near-panic, but she stood consoling this apparently decent man.

"Each man is the responsibility of his brother," Burnham said. "There is a certain literalness to that, which makes it impossible for me to avoid all sense of responsibility."

He opened the door, and they stepped out onto the little gray wooden porch. The sun was lower in the sky behind the house, but it was still bright. She breathed deeply only when he closed the door. They paused on the porch, and Van Burnham looked around, down the road, across the highway into the trees, and down at the ground. He played with the keys in his hands and didn't move, as if he had something else to say. Maureen waited.

"Would you like to join me for dinner?" he said finally. "Nothing special, but there is a good restaurant at the Holiday Inn."

"No thanks," she said, knowing that there had been no sexual innuendo in the offer but not wanting to spend any more time within the aura of the man's undeserved guilt. "I really have to start back."

"Want to take a look in the barn before we go?" he said, stepping over to the car.

"I think I've seen enough," she said, getting into the Buick.

"I think you have too," he said and got into the driver's seat, closing the door behind him.

They got back to Chester in about fifteen minutes. Burnham drove slowly, as if trying to come up with the right words, but the words never came. He pulled into the driveway of Burnham Realty, parked, turned off the engine, and kept both hands on the steering wheel as he finally spoke, looking out the window in front of him. "If they die before I do," he said quietly, "I'll tear the house down, bulldoze it, sell the land dirt cheap to Jason Norman to add to his farm, and turn the money over to some charity. What's your favorite charity, Mrs. Dietz?"

"I don't know," she said, never having been asked the question before. "C.A.R.E. or cancer research, I suppose."

"That's what it will be then," he said, and turned to her with a small grin. She put out her hand and he shook it.

"Thanks, Mr. Burnham," she said, getting out of the car.

"While it would be a bit foolish to say that it has been a pleasure," he said, getting out and closing the door, "I can say that I feel better having met you. Take care of yourself and your family."

"I will," she said, moving quickly to her Omega. She had left the windows open, so the seat wasn't terribly hot. As she drove away she saw Burnham standing next to his car, the keys to the Vanbeeber house in his hand, his eyes watching her.

She drove for four hours and found a Ramada Inn near Vandalia. In the coffee shop she had a tuna salad sandwich and an iced tea before going to her room. She took a hot bath to wash away the memory of the house and Burnham, and then she went to bed to the drone of the air conditioner.

She didn't know how long she had been sleeping when she woke up feeling someone was in the room with her. She reached, fumbled for the light switch, and turned it on. There was no one there. The air conditioner droned on and she sat up, trying to catch her breath. It was four in the morning but she didn't want to go back to sleep in this room, in any room but her own. She threw her things together and left before the sun came up.

It wasn't until she was twenty miles south of Chicago that she remembered promising Nancy a present. She pulled into a tourist gas station, filled the tank, checked the oil, and bought an overpriced five pounds of pistachio nuts for Miles and an equally overpriced plastic turtle that could be attached to a garden hose and that sprinkled water. It was hit or miss whether Nancy would like it. Mike deserved something too, but she couldn't think of a thing. Hell, she thought, I feel like I've just come back from a nightmare, and I'm bringing presents.

For the rest of the twenty miles home she felt weary, and then as she turned into familiar streets within a few miles of home, it felt a bit better. She had journeyed into the nightmare, chosen the route, taken the ride, and returned. She had faced the past and come out of it.

The next afternoon, when Maureen got home after her class and a meeting with Billy Stultz, she seriously considered turning on the air conditioner in the living room. All it would have taken was a small complaint from Nancy, but her daughter wasn't in the mood for complaining. Nancy grabbed her plastic turtle, threw it in the wicker clothes hamper in the bathroom, and put on her one-piece bathing suit with the faded yellow flower.

"I'm going under the turtle sprinkler," she said, bouncing.

"You mean, 'Mom, may I go under the turtle sprinkler?'" Maureen answered. "And I answer, 'Yes, if Miles sets it up.'"

Miles agreed, and followed his sister through the back door and into the yard.

"Well," asked Maureen, turning to Mike, who stood with his arms folded.

"You don't plan to tell me where you were yesterday, do you?" he asked.

"No," she said. "Not now, but I really thank you." She moved to kiss him, and he accepted it with reservation.

"I've got to go back," he said with barely disguised irritation. "I'll talk to you later." And he went without looking back.

She considered calling out to him but instead moved to the kitchen, where she could see part of the Johnstons' yard. With the windows open, she could hear the squealing of little girls. She found the *Sun-Times* and opened it again. If Mike didn't call her, she would call him later, try to make it up. She had used him and he deserved more then the "I'm not talking thanks a lot" she had given him. In the morning she had been to her one class and feared something of the reactions of others, first the people in her class and later Billy Stultz. The people she met treated her as if she were taboo. That was the word that had struck her, and she vaguely remembered reading something by Sigmund Freud about taboo. David's books had all been sent to his brother in Vermont, but that one had been hers from college. In any case, the people she had met today projected a fearful sympathy, looking at her as if she had been touched by a dreaded disease they didn't want to catch.

There had been a bit less of it in Billy, who had a series of his own hobby horses to ride through each day. Billy had gotten into production of videotapes when his specialized employment agency had failed after doing well for a decade. Companies no longer wanted to pay premium finder's fees for scientists.

"So," he had said, nervously flicking on the remote-controlled television and turning it off again. Billy lived alone. Maureen didn't know if he kept the place clean himself, had someone come in, or if the exclusive Sheridan Road apartment building provided such things.

"I saw the paper this morning," he said, searching for

something and finding it, a golf ball. "Are you all right? I mean, are you okay?"

"I'm okay, Billy," Maureen had told him with a smile. "Look, I've got to pick up Nancy. If you've got the contract . . ."

Billy had the contract ready on the dining-room table in the corner of his large living room, which had been tastefully decorated in the late 1950s. The table was empty except for the three-page contract and a white ballpoint pen. She signed all three copies without reading them.

"We've got a good up-front on this one," he said, rolling the golf ball over the back of his hand nervously. "These health club people who saw the first tape like the voice-over you did, just the right touch of something different, makes exercising sound like the work of God. Good stuff."

"When are we going to do it, tape it?" Maureen asked.

Billy shrugged, played with the ball a little more, picked up the television remote control, put it down again, and made Maureen want to escape.

"Well, I thought with everything going on," he said tentatively. "The television, newspaper stuff. Maybe we should hold off till you're feeling—"

"I'm feeling fine, Billy," she said. "Remember you asked me and I said I was feeling okay. It was what I meant. You can use the money. I can use the money. What are you worried about?"

Billy stopped fidgeting, looked at her seriously, and said, "You want a drink, diet drink, Sprite or something?"

"Billy," she repeated.

"The paper this morning hit pretty hard on the business about your being . . . having that emotional and physical breakdown after the accident. And the police don't seem to be taking it all seriously. That lieutenant they quoted made you sound like some . . . some poor booby who needs to be humored. Didn't you read it?"

"I read it," she said. "And I've been reading people's faces, like yours. Where's your old enterprise, Billy? We can turn this into a selling point. On the voice-over, I'll talk about how exercise pulled me back from depression and pain. No details, but that's true. I talk about that in my classes; I can do it on a tape."

Billy started to shake his head no, reconsidered, and began to see the possibilities. "You mean these health club people might want to pick up on the idea that exercising is as good for you as going to a shrink, maybe better?" he asked, but the question was addressed to his muse rather than to Maureen.

"I wouldn't go that far," Maureen said. "Not publicly. Now I've really got to go, Billy. When do you want to tape and, more important, when do we get some money? I have worn-out brakes and a kid starting college next year."

"Next week too soon?" Billy asked, walking over to pick up the contract and blow on the signature, though it had been written in ballpoint pen. "I'll see if I can get studio time."

"See if you can get me some choices so I can work around my classes," she said, reaching for the door.

"Will do," said Billy. "I'll push the club people on the money. Maybe they'll want an exclusive on the tapes. Maybe even want you to represent them, travel, who knows? You know what I mean. They really like the first tape."

"We can talk about it when and if it's more real," she said. "I've got to run, Billy."

"Did you bring your car, or are you going to run home?" he said, picking up his remote control TV channel changer. It was his single recurrent joke with her. Billy lived near Montrose in Chicago, right along the shore of Lake Michigan, across from the Outer Drive. It was about ten miles to Maureen's house. She had once been dropped off at his apartment by Miles and run home, but she had found the traffic too distracting.

When she didn't answer, he turned to his television to watch the Cubs, saying, "Take care, Wonder Woman."

Now back home, she sat down at the kitchen table again, listening through the open window to the giggling and shouts of Nancy and Paulette. She hadn't bothered to check on Miles. At this hour he was almost certainly playing ball in the park or, if he had any money left for the week, at a video arcade with a friend.

She turned to the article on page three again. There were the photographs of the two men who had murdered David. They looked even less like the memory of them in the newspaper. The headline read: WOMAN'S EIGHT-YEAR NIGHTMARE GOES ON.

So, she thought, even the headline is inaccurate. A major point of the meaning of her existence had been her conquering of the nightmare, or at least her control of it. This article was implying that she had spent the last eight years in terror. No wonder her class had looked at her like that. No wonder the two sessions she had done today had failed. They were seeing this woman, who promised them meditative release and calmness, as a walking nervous wreck.

The article itself was only a little better. What she had hoped for was more on the two men. There was some but not too much, a reference to their murky reputation in the southern Illinois town they came from, a suggestion of minor mob contact with a bar owner, and a not-very-accurate description of the night of David's murder. She read it as if it were the description of a scene in a movie and not her own experience. She felt that the writer had left something out that was particularly important. He left out the heat, the sense of being trapped in the car, her inability to see David when he was down, the . . . shit. She closed the paper and touched her chest. Some mild meditative exercise downstairs was, she decided, what she needed. A half hour, no more. Then she would spend an hour thinking about the new videotape, maybe even writing out some of the narration. If she felt better after that, she might call Mike. Mike was always available, always willing to go to a movie, a play, swimming. For a man with his bulk and the amount of hair on his body, Mike was remarkably unembarrassed about walking around in a bathing suit.

"He looks like a fur-covered Dick Butkus who just swallowed a beach ball live," Miles had commented once to Maureen. It was an accurate description.

Maureen was about to push herself up from the table when the phone rang. She reached back and picked it up from the counter. "Hello," she said.

"Mrs. Dietz," came a voice she recognized. "I've been trying to reach you all day."

"I've been working," Maureen said. "Though it has been a bit tough after your story."

"You didn't like the story?" said the reporter.

"Mr. Donnelly," she said calmly, "you make me look like a . . . Rochester's wife in *Jane Eyre*. Have you ever read that?"

"I saw the movie when I was a kid," he said. "Orson Welles before he went fat. He could have used one of your classes."

"If people think I'm a weak, twitching marionette, there won't be any classes," she said.

"I don't want to make you angry, Mrs. Dietz," he said. "I'm really trying to help."

"Mr. Donnelly, in a few days you will be done with me and my story and be involved with someone else's life, but I will still be living down the melodrama you wrote this morning."

"I wrote it last night," he said. "I thought the idea was to get publicity out to help catch those two guys. I wanted a story and you wanted publicity, right?"

"Right," Maureen agreed, leaning forward to try to get a glimpse of Nancy through the window. The girls weren't screaming and hadn't been for a few minutes. Maybe they had gone inside for some Kool-Aid or to use the toilet.

"I'd like to do a follow-up for tomorrow," Donnelly said. He sounded young, not much older than Miles.

"I'm listening," she said.

"I've got a good angle," he said with enthusiasm.

"I didn't know reporters used words like 'angle' except in movies made before 1945," Maureen said. A faint splash of water and a girl's voice convinced her that Paulette and Nancy were back in the pool.

"I've even been known to say 'scoop,'" Donnelly countered. "I do it mostly for my father, who gets his ideas of what a reporter does from those same movies. Do you want to hear my angle or are you going to hang up on me?"

"Talk," she said.

"Barelli," Donnelly came back. "The man who wouldn't give up. He spent eight years working on this case on his own, even after he left the police."

"A good angle," she agreed.

"You don't sound too enthusiastic."

"From your point of view, it's a good angle," she said. "From my point of view—"

"It keeps the story alive, reminds people that those two guys are out there. You don't want to forget those two guys are out there."

"I'm not likely to forget," said Maureen, growing a little impatient with Donnelly's enthusiasm and lack of tact.

"I didn't mean you. Shit, I'm a good writer and a third-rate talker. Bear with me."

"You asked me once already," she reminded him. "What do you want from me?"

"On the television interview, you mentioned a file, a file Barelli gave you when he died."

Helen had asked that she not be mentioned in the television interview, and Maureen had not done so. Helen hadn't thought her bosses would think it a good idea to get involved. "You want the file?"

"An hour or two to copy it," he said, not quite pleading,

but close. "I've already talked to Barelli's widow. Can it hurt? It might be the thing we need to get those two."

"Donnelly, do you really think a television show and two stories in your paper are going to catch these guys after eight years?" she said.

"No, but it might. Why did you go on television if you didn't think so?"

"Because," she said, "partly because of the file, what Barelli had put into finding them. I wanted to give him a last chance. There are other reasons, too, but they're mine. I don't want some commuter with a late breakfast to spill coffee on them."

"Can I borrow the file?" Donnelly said.

"You can borrow the file," Maureen said, catching a glimpse of Nancy in the yard. Nancy was laughing and screaming and trying to jump away from a spray of water aimed at her by some unseen person hidden behind the Johnstons' house.

"I'll send a pickup for it right now and get it back to you tomorrow," he said. "Okay?"

"No more Mrs. Rochester, Donnelly?"

"I'll do my best," he said, and she hung up.

The front door opened and Maureen called out, "Miles?"

"Mom?" he answered, coming around the living room and into the kitchen. He was drenched in sweat, dripping. His cutoff blue shirt was soaked almost black.

"Basketball?" she asked.

"Yeah," he said, opening the refrigerator and adroitly catching his glasses as they fell off his nose while he leaned over to pull out a bottle of Pepsi. He closed the refrigerator, gauged his thirst, unscrewed the cap, and began to gulp it down. Maureen watched his Adam's apple bob as he drank.

"You read the paper?" she said.

He removed the bottle from his mouth, perched his glasses back on his nose, and, without looking at her, said, "Yeah."

"And?" she pushed.

"Made us look like jelly doughnuts, something out of Dickens," he said. "See, I'm getting ready for college. Literary parallels and everything."

"Well, what do you think?" she said, getting up.

He finished the cola and held the bottle up to catch the last few drops on his tongue before he answered. "It's worth doing if they catch them, even if it only makes them hide," he said. "You do what you think is best, Mom. I don't want to talk about it." He took a turn-around jump shot, and the empty plastic bottle landed neatly in the garbage pail near the sink.

"I'm going to take a shower and lock myself in my room with the air conditioner," he said, changing the subject. "I saw Princess Daisy outside. What are we doing for dinner?"

"I thought we might call Mike and go out," she said. "How does Wendy's sound?"

"Arby's sounds better," Miles said, leaning against the refrigerator. "You giving up on cooking?"

"No, just using this," she said, tapping the newspaper, "as an excuse, I guess."

"You don't need an excuse," said Miles, examining a scratch on his arm. She didn't bother to ask him about it. Basketball wounds were too common. "You are one tough lady."

"Woman," she corrected.

"Jedi warrior, for all I care," countered Miles. "Hey, that policewoman who was here the other day, Katz. She called you earlier, said it was kind of important. Number's over on the pad near the phone." With that, Miles ran out of the room, and she could hear him going upstairs two or three steps at a time.

Maureen found the number and considered yelling up to Miles to be sure the last number was a three instead of an eight, but he had already started the water in the shower. She bet on the eight and dialed the number, which turned out to be the police.

—— 117 ——

"Sunnyside District, Officer Reinberg," came the man's weary voice.

"I'm calling Sergeant Katz, returning her call. My name is Dietz."

"Hold," he said, and the line went dead. Maureen closed her eyes, listening to Nancy's screams and the running water of Miles's shower. When he was feeling particularly good, Miles sang in the shower, though the songs were no known ones that Maureen recognized. There was no singing coming from upstairs.

"Maureen?" Helen Katz's voice said suddenly.

"Helen," she answered. "What's up?"

"Maybe something, maybe nothing," the policewoman said, very slowly and calmly. Maureen could hear voices behind her, particularly the voice of a man shouting, "Tell them I'll come when I can come. That's when I'll come for chrissake, you dumb fuck."

"You found them?" Maureen said, sitting down.

"No," Helen Katz said with a long pause. "You remember the name Simcox?"

"I remember the name Simcox," Maureen said. "He was the young man in the hot dog shop, Bittie's, that night." She was about to mention that she had seen Simcox in Barnaby's a week ago, but it didn't seem particularly relevant, and she wanted Helen to go on with what she had to say.

"Simcox is dead," she said.

"Dead?"

"He was found in the alley behind his apartment this morning," Helen said. "He left for work about seven-thirty. Garbage collectors found him. I wouldn't have made this connection if . . ."

"If . . ." Maureen prompted.

"It could be coincidence," Helen said. "This is a violent city, and we haven't had time to check his friends, enemies. He was killed in a kind of fringey neighborhood just outside Lincoln Park and—"

"Helen, will you please just say it," Maureen interrupted firmly.

"He was beaten to death," she said. "No weapon found yet. Could be a wrench . . ."

"Or a baseball bat," Maureen added, feeling the throbbing in her chest again.

"Could be," Helen Katz sighed. "I'm on my way to see the wife."

"No," Maureen said. "I want to come."

"No way, Maureen," Helen said firmly. Behind Helen, the man who was coming when he was coming shouted an obscenity.

"He may be dead because I talked to the six o'clock news and a newspaper," Maureen said. "And I talked to them because you pushed me into it."

"Now wait a minute," Helen said sharply.

"I'm not blaming you; I made the decision. But it was you who handed me the past in that file. . . . You've got some responsibility. I'm not asking you to take it all, just share it with me and let me come." Except for the shouting man on the other end of the phone, there was silence for about five seconds. "Helen?" said Maureen.

"I'm here. I'll talk to my partner. Maybe you could help talk to the widow, something. I don't know. I'll call you back in a few minutes. Maureen, this could be, probably is, a coincidence. Somebody might even have used the story as an excuse to get Simcox for something."

"They're back," Maureen said. "We brought them back."

Before Helen Katz could reply, Maureen hung up the phone. She sat at the table, resisting the urge, the screaming urge, to pull Nancy into the house, call Miles out of the shower, and huddle somewhere with her arms around them. The idea made her chest ache, made her suck in a deep breath. She put her hands on her breasts and felt them heaving. She touched her nipples through her shirt and wondered why they were suddenly hard.

"No," she said aloud and then repeated the no silently as she stood up and forced herself to move out of the kitchen to the stairs. She went down the stairs slowly to the basement and moved across the room and past the mat to the full-length mirror. Maureen Dietz stood before the mirror, forcing herself to look and telling herself—willing—that it would not happen again, that she would not let it happen again.

She took a deep breath, looked at herself again and stretched her arms out in isometric tension. Never again, she told the mirror Maureen silently. Never again. She moved her body slowly to the beat of her heart and tried to let herself flow into the movement.

The phone and doorbell rang almost at the same instant. Maureen shouted "Just a minute" in the general direction of the front door, hoping that her voice would carry through the open window in the living room, and then she picked up the phone in the kitchen.

"Maureen," Helen Katz's voice came through firmly, making it clear already what the answer would be.

"I can't go," Maureen said. the doorbell rang again. Maureen covered the phone speaker and shouted, nearly screamed, "Just . . . a . . . second."

"I asked," Helen said, "but I didn't push. This Simcox isn't my case. There's only the slightest chance that it might be connected to you."

"I'm sure you tried," Maureen said evenly.

"I'll tell you once more, Maureen," Helen Katz said, now clearly trying to keep herself under control. "I asked. Then I dropped it. I don't have a hell of a lot of clout around here. I'm not one of the boys."

"I'm sorry," Maureen said, trying to make it sound as if she meant it, which she did, though she still felt some resentment. Touched with the resentment was something else that she didn't like, relief—she was off the hook. She had tried to face the possibility, talk to the widow, maybe see the body, and she had been told no. She could now turn her anger toward some unidentified male cop and away from herself. The doorbell rang again. "I'm really sorry. Can I call you later or tomorrow about this?"

"I'll call you," Helen said and hung up.

Maureen hung up the phone and ran for the front door and the ringing bell. She opened it and stood face-to-face with a graying, average-size man with the beaten face of a boxer. He was wearing a wrinkled yellow long-sleeve shirt and black slacks and bore a resemblance to the smaller man in the photograph, the man who had killed David. She stepped back to slam the door in his face.

"Miz Dietz?" he said, startled as the door slammed closed. And then through the closed door, he shouted, as if used to humoring people who slammed the door on him, "I come for the stuff for Mr. Donnelly at the *Sun-Times.*"

Maureen reopened the door and said, "Sorry."

"That's okay," the man said with a shrug. "You got the stuff for me?"

She had promised. The news about Simcox had come after the promise, but it had come. Now she didn't want the headlines the next day about Simcox. But Simcox was a human being, a man she had met, who had seemed . . . Damn the day she decided to come back to life eight years ago.

"You all right, lady?" the more-than-middle-aged delivery boy asked, cocking his head to one side.

"I'm all right," she said. He nodded his head and let his eyes take her in from the neck down. She knew the look and she didn't like it. It was one thing for a man to take her in entirely and indicate in small ways that he admired what he saw. She did that frequently enough with men, but the look she was getting from the man in the doorway was a depersonalized strip search. She had been about to invite him in, but instead she said, "Wait there, I'll bring it."

Then she closed the door and went for the file. It was upstairs in the drawer of her desk near her bed where she had left it. She had gone through it carefully and closely and knew just where to find what she wanted. Barelli had prepared a page or two on each of the witnesses to David's murder, each report badly typed on onionskin paper. Those more than two pages in length were stapled in the left-hand corner. Simcox had a single sheet. She removed all five of the reports on the witnesses. Helen had said there was a chance, a good chance, that Simcox's murder and her story were not linked. Maureen didn't want to suggest to Donnelly the possibility of a connection. He probably would, but she wasn't going to help. She didn't remove any of the information on herself, not even the two typed sheets that Barelli had prepared and which she had read over at least ten times.

Something that the old policeman had seen in her face the one time he visited her in the hospital had altered his life. Maureen knew what it was. She had seen the look in a mirror right after David's murder. It had been the face of a Gorgon, a frightened and frightening Medusa, the sight of which exposed the beholder to the stone-chilling depths of terror. Barelli had checked her progress for four years without making contact with her. The report made that clear. Feelings had to be read through the official jargon of Barelli's document, but they were there, and when she had been released from the hospital, he had obviously been nearby, across the street watching when Darla and her brother Ralph had picked her up.

She put the file of reports on her desk and hurried down the stairs with the remaining clippings and reports and a large envelope to put them in. The man was sitting on the stone wall along the concrete steps in front of the house. He was smoking and looking up at the oak tree on the lawn. He turned to her when the door opened and looked up as if he had just bitten into a hot pepper but didn't want to show it.

"Sorry," she said, handing him the envelope. "Please remind Mr. Donnelly that I want all of this back just as soon as he copies it."

"I'll remind him," the man said, taking the envelope and tucking it under his arm. "But I don't think I'll be making another run this way today. I might be tomorrow."

"Just remind Mr. Donnelly, please."

Instead of answering he turned away and waved the envelope in her direction as he hurried to his car parked at the curb. It was a small car, not old, not new, with rust problems. She regretted not inviting the man in and offering him a cold drink.

"Who's that?" Miles said, coming down the stairs as she closed the door.

"Man from the *Sun-Times*," she said. "I gave him the file to copy."

Miles adjusted his glasses, and frowned. His hair was flat and wet from the shower.

"Back in the newspapers," he said.

"I guess," she replied. There was no point in mentioning Simcox to Miles. Among other things, Miles had not been particularly civil when Simcox had stopped by to talk in Barnaby's. The possibility that Miles would feel guilty was a good one. If she was feeling it, Miles was enough like her to feel it too. Besides, Miles might with good reason be a bit frightened by the news.

"I'm going out," he said, walking past her to the door.

"Nice to feel good on a summer afternoon," Maureen said.

Miles held the door open and turned to look at her. "If you

don't worry about some nut grabbing you when you turn the corner," he said. He was looking down, his glasses dangerously close to falling.

"It's hard on you," she said quietly. "Sometimes I'm thinking so much of me that I forget the yous around me."

"Princess Daisy doesn't worry," he said. It was not a bitter statement. Rather it was tinged with envy for her assumed innocence.

"I think she knows more than she shows," Maureen said. "How about we go to Dairy Queen after dinner?"

"With or without Big Mike?" he asked, lifting his head to her.

"Which way do you want it?"

"Hell, he can come," sighed Miles. "The princess likes him."

"And you?"

"How can a guy with my appetite like someone who can outpig him on a pizza?" Miles asked. "The man's a gastronomic menace and a threat to my self-respect." Then Miles let out a very small grin. "Yeah, I like him."

When Miles went out, Maureen walked around to the rear of the house to stand in the yard. Beyond the fence she could see Nancy and Paulette sitting on small lawn chairs near the wading pool. Maureen didn't feel like talking, so she went back in and upstairs to take another look at the reports by a dead man on people whose lives might not be worth very much.

Barelli's list was almost complete. There was a report on Louis Parenti, who would now be in his sixties. According to Barelli's report, as of a year ago, Parenti still owned Bittie's. Maureen had for eight years not only avoided Diversey west of Clark but had tried not to get within a mile or two of the corner. Her heart and chest reacted like a geiger counter when she approached the area. So Parenti was still there. It had astonished her when she first read it in the report. For reasons she had never explored, she had assumed that the murder of David Dietz had changed the lives of everyone involved as it had changed hers. It was a reasonable assumption. She had seen a CBS special on television the month before with Bill Kurtis about a TWA flight in which the crew and passengers had plunged almost six miles and miraculously not crashed. Their lives had all been changed by the kiss of death, but apparently the kiss had not been indelible for Lou Parenti. Was she somehow angry? That was absurd. Why should she be angry that a man had kept his business even though someone had been murdered in his parking lot? Parenti, according to the report, had a wife, a son, a daughter, and two grandchildren. He lived on Nagle Street in Chicago just off Foster, in the heart of the territory of Alderman Roman Pucinski, the silver-haired Polish saviour.

Susan Breen, the girl behind the counter, would be about twenty-eight now, according to Barelli's report. Maureen's impression had been that she was one of a never-ending army of tired, decent, and not-too-bright skinny girls from too-large families who would get married young, lose their husbands to indifference, and spend a hard life taking care of three children. The report was a further blow to Maureen's assessment of both the event of that night and the people who were involved. Susan Breen had been going to Northwestern University's continuing education program when David was killed. She lived at home with her parents. Two years after the murder that sent Maureen to the mental hospital, Susan Breen had received her undergraduate degree and had gone on with financial aid to graduate work at Northwestern in television. Two years after that she had a Master of Fine Arts degree in television production and management and was hired as production assistant at WGN, less than two miles from where she had once served hot dogs and taken insults at Bittie's. The last notation on Susan Breen by Barelli was that she had had some very close relationships with men at the station and that she lived alone in an apartment in Lincoln Park.

The old couple shared a report, but they were no longer an old couple. The woman, whose name was Elsa Brinkmann, had died in 1980 at the age of eighty-six, of a heart attack. It was not likely that the attack was a long-term result of the witnessing of David's murder. Her husband, who was now eighty-eight, was August Brinkmann, a retired pharmacist, who lived alone in a west Rogers Park high-rise condominium on the North Side of the city.

She didn't want to review the Simcox file, but the obligation was there. If the man had died because of her—and that was a possibility she wanted to face—then she had to respect him enough to deal with what he had been. It struck her suddenly that one might well accuse her of not having faced what David had been, but her feelings would not sort themselves out.

Maureen looked at the sheet on Simcox and his wife Allie, put it down, got up from her chair, and walked to the window. Below she could see the neighbor's yard and the two girls now eating what looked like sandwiches that had been trimmed of the crusts. It was the way Nancy particularly liked them, and Maureen wondered if Paulette's family were suddenly catering to her daughter's taste because they were aware of the story, the television show. Of course they were, Maureen knew. She went back to the desk and picked up the report on Simcox.

He had died a few hours ago at the age of thirty. To be precise, he had died two days short of his thirty-first birthday. Barelli's report, clearly dated in the upper right-hand corner as December 5, 1981, showed Roger Simcox's address as 876 Flower Lane, Atlanta, Georgia. The Simcoxes had had two children as of December 5, 1981, and Simcox had been a salesman for a Datsun dealer.

Barelli had been a fanatic; had apparently questioned each one of the witnesses, come back to them, badgered them for details, even followed up the possibility that the killers had known one of them, recognized them, though there was no evidence. Apparently, according to Barelli's own report, August Brinkmann had actually complained to the police about Barelli.

And he never talked to me, Maureen thought, putting the reports neatly in a pile topped by the clippings.

Maureen was jerked out of a drowsy fixation on the pattern of the comforter on her bed. It was a soft, brown comforter, designed, sewn, labored over by Darla, and given to her as a coming-home present after she had left the hospital. It was one of the few things she owned when they had moved into this house. She had had all of her old furniture, clothes—everything—sold for any price they could get. Her brother Ralph, feeling guilty over having been of so little support to her during her hospitalization, had willingly taken on the task and had gotten a good price for the furniture. He had even helped her get this house, through a friend from high school days who was the vice-president at a real estate company. Six months later Darla had moved to Los Angeles to be near her only living brother and sister.

Maureen glanced over at the door, thinking that something was missing from the list of reports, something she had forgotten to remove before giving it to Donnelly. And then she remembered: the report on the black man.

Barelli had no name for the black man, whom Maureen remembered quite vividly, though she was beginning to question the accuracy of her memories. Barelli had tried to track the man down with little success. The man had no name. None of the other witnesses had ever seen him before, and the police had not been concerned, concluding that one more witness would make little difference. They had plenty of witnesses. It was the killers they couldn't find. There wasn't much Donnelly could do with the typed sheet on: MALE, BLACK, AGE: circa 50. Beyond a description of the man's clothes, there was nothing to follow. It might, Maureen thought, turn out to be ironic. The man had disappeared eight years ago, apparently because he didn't want to be involved. As it was turning out, it looked as if he had done the right thing. In a way he had gone into an oblivion, erased himself from the event, which was exactly what Maureen had tried to do after that August night. And now it was all back for her, but not for the black man with the kind face.

The phone was ringing. It rang twice, and she had her hand out when she paused. It might be Mike, she thought. She had asked him to call and now wasn't sure she wanted to talk to him.

"Okay," she said to herself and reached for the phone, into which she said, "Hello."

"Helen," came the voice. "I just got back from talking to the investigator on the case and the woman at the address where Simcox was staying. That woman is *not* his wife, and Roger Simcox did not live there. He lived in Atlanta. He comes here from time to time to trade shows, dealer meetings, and, apparently, any excuse to get back with his old friends and spend a few days with Susan Breen."

"Susan Breen," Maureen repeated.

"Right, the same one. According to Miss Breen, they got to know each other after your husband's death."

"David's death was responsible for them having an eight-year-long affair?" Maureen said, not at all sure of how to take this.

"They didn't get together all that much," Helen said. "More like *Same Time Next Year*. And according to her she wasn't just sitting at home and waiting for him. Anyway, I'll give you the rest fast. I've got to get back to work. Simcox did leave from her apartment for work early this morning. He was going to see some dealer about buying a piece of his business and moving back to Chicago. And that was it. There are a few of Susan's male friends who might be suspects, but Dan White, the investigator on this case, doesn't think that looks too promising. He knows about your husband, read the reports, saw the body of Simcox. We don't think it's the same killer. Simcox was beaten pretty badly, first hit from behind, but the medical examiner says it was probably one person delivering the blows, and they weren't as savage as the ones that killed your husband. In addition, Simcox seems to have been robbed. It happens."

"It's been a long time, Helen," Maureen said, her mouth prickly and dry. "Maybe only one of those men came back. Maybe they don't kill quite the same way anymore."

"Maybe," Helen agreed. "I didn't say we're ruling it out. All I said was that it looks more like coincidence than connection. You'd be surprised at how many times two murders look as if they're connected and prove to be unrelated. Early this year I was on a case where two brothers were killed, Puerto Rican kids in their twenties, three days apart. We got the killers, different ones for different reasons. One was a gang killing. The other was a simple straight-out robbery. We waited a month looking for a connection, and there wasn't one."

"Thanks," said Maureen.

"You're welcome," Helen answered. "I gather I haven't been altogether successful at convincing you."

"Not altogether, but I appreciate the try. I'm sorry I lost control earlier."

Helen Katz laughed. "I've only seen you out of control once, lady, and that was a long time ago. I'll get in touch if anything else turns up."

"You coming over in the morning?" Damn, Maureen told herself, biting on her lower lip. She didn't want it to sound like a plea for friendship or protection.

"Seven sharp," Helen said, "but don't expect a dazzling new running suit. I've got that one pair of running shorts, and the shirt I wore is my favorite."

"We're running, not modeling," Maureen said.

"Tell it to those putzes in the car the other day. If we time it right we might get a few more seconds of intellectual exchange with them. I picked up a few special Spanish idioms from a detective named Gutierez. See you in the morning, and do me a favor?"

"What?"

"Don't have a glass of orange juice ready for me. I drank it that morning to be polite, but it reminded me of bad mornings as a kid in my mother's kitchen."

"Coffee?"

"Fine."

"Iced?"

"Even better," said Helen.

"You've got it."

Maureen hung up first and knew that she had made a decision. She would believe that she didn't think the Simcox murder had anything to do with her. She would believe it until she had no choice, and when and if she was convinced that there was a tie-in, she would have to act, though she had no idea of what that action might be.

"Mom," Miles called after knocking at her door.

"Come in," she answered, sitting down on her bed. Miles came in barefoot, wearing a fresh pair of jeans and a short-sleeved red pullover shirt with brown horizontal stripes. The collar was tucked awkwardly under one side and she got up to pull it out. Somehow, his face looked far too serious for his years. At this moment, she thought, I should be saying to myself that he looks like his father, but he doesn't. She examined his serious face and thought that he didn't look like David, and he didn't look like her. He looked firm, serious, and somewhat alien and vulnerable.

"Mom, are you all right?" he said, stepping away from her.

"Miles," she said. "You've spent too much of your life looking at me like that. I'm not going to crack up again. I'm not going to go away and leave you. I'm going to be fine. You've got to let me be frightened and angry when it's reasonable to be frightened and angry."

"Right," he said, "but are you okay?"

"I am," she said, "okay. In addition, I am getting hungry. And unless you stopped on the way home from the park at McDonald's for a burger or Rick's for a large bag of that chocolate-covered gunk, you must be hungry too. I'll call Big Mike, and you get your sister in here to change her clothes."

Miles backed away in mock panic, his hands out.

"Hold it," he said. "I'll face muggers in the park, challenge Big Mike to a sumo contest or even full-contact karate, but I'm not going out there to face the demon princess and tell her to cut her pool party short. There are some jobs it isn't reasonable to ask a man to do."

As it turned out, Miles did go down for his sister, who complained only minimally, while Maureen called Mike. The coach not only said he would be right over but suggested that they go to Barnaby's.

"No," Maureen said. "Let's go somewhere else. Let's go deep dish, Carmen's."

Mike agreed and she hung up, thinking little by little she might be drawing circles around more places she didn't want to go near, places that had become taboo because of her fear of ghosts. When the circles grew too large or too numerous, there might not be any more space for Maureen to move in. She might develop a new kind of madness, one involving a mental map of the area with imaginary narrow corridors in which she could safely travel.

She glanced at the clock and decided that she had enough time for a concentrated workout in the basement on a cool blue mat. She stretched out, extended her arms as far back as she could reach, and pointed her toes, balancing on the muscles of her buttocks. An image came to her of a dark circle, a perfect dark circle. She imagined herself stepping into the dark circle, which shrank as her foot touched it. It shrank and shrank until it was gone. Then she imagined herself leaning over and finding the near pinpoint of darkness clinging to her big toe. She reached down in her imagination, balanced the small black spot on her finger and her body, and for a moment she felt the peacefulness of nothing at all.

Her moment ended with the appearance of Nancy at the door. "Mom," she whined, hands on hips, her blue one-piece bathing suit demonstrating clearly that she had a long way to go before she looked like Olivia Newton-John. Nancy tossed her long hair as she stepped in, clopping with her oversized clogs. "Mom."

"I gather there is a problem," Maureen said, pulled out of her meditation.

"Cynthia and I already ate," the girl said. "Can't I just stay here at the pool?"

"Cynthia?"

"Paulette's name is Cynthia," Nancy explained. "She told me this afternoon. She's Cynthia now."

"The last time she said her real name was Darlene," said Maureen, sitting up on the floor and folding her arms around her knees, trying not to show how amused she was.

"Garlene, not Darlene," Nancy corrected. "And that wasn't her real name. Cynthia is her real name."

"I think if we ask her mother we will find that her real name is Paulette Johnston," Maureen said gently. "Paulette has an active and fickle imagination."

"I believe her," Nancy repeated, "and can I stay, Mom, please? Her aunt doesn't care. Please, just this one time, and I'll never ask for another thing in the world, not ever."

"I believe you," Maureen said, getting up, "but I want you near me tonight. We're celebrating."

"What?"

"We're celebrating your successful completion of a whole day without skinning your knees," Maureen said solemnly.

"Mom, that's not funny," the girl cried.

"I'm sorry, Daisy, I know, but you've got to come. You can skip dinner and have dessert. You can even wear your clogs. For added inducement I'll give you fifteen hundred dollars."

"Mom, you're making fun," Nancy whined. "But you mean it about the clogs and dessert?"

"I mean it," said Maureen. "You can even invite Paul— Cynthia if you want to."

Nancy thought about it, shifted her weight to her other foot, considered the offer with various extreme changes of expression, and said, "No, if she sees me too much, she might not invite me to her pool when the new baby comes. She might get tired of me. Besides you're sort of right. She's starting to tell stories again."

Maureen had wandered over to her closet, and Nancy clopped over to the bed and sat down. "Like what, Daisy?"

"Mom you promised not to call me that. It's bad enough Miles does. You promised."

"Sorry," Maureen said, holding up her hand in a peace gesture without turning around. She picked out a lightweight, sleeveless red-and-white dress, which she knew Mike particularly liked. "What kind of stories is Cynthia telling now, Nancy?" she said, removing the dress and checking it for marks or dirt.

"The men in the van," Nancy said, bouncing on the bed. "Can I bring my Malibu Barbie and Ken?"

"What men in what van?" Maureen asked, turning to her bouncing daughter.

"She said that there were two men in an orange van going round the block this afternoon. She said one man looked like a combination of the Incredible Hulk and a walrus, and the other looked like Mr. Harkart at school, the one we call Vitamin Harkart."

Maureen forced herself to put the dress down gently on the bed and turn to her daughter. "And these men just drove around the block and drove away?"

"Cynthia said they looked like creeps."

"Did Cynthia say something else about the van, about the men?" Maureen asked, putting her hand on her daughter's leg to signal her to stop bouncing.

"Something Electric." Nancy shrugged. "That's what it said on the van. I think Cynthia made it up."

"And I," sighed Maureen, "think it was some repairmen. Now go get dressed. We're meeting Mike."

"Again?"

"Come on Nancy Marie, you like Mike. You just want to get in a last grouch or two."

They had deep-dish sausage-and-onion pizza at Carmen's. Mike and Miles spent a lot of time talking about someone named Gault's decision to try for the Olympics instead of playing for the Bears. Miles, who was more interested in improving the Bears than in the ambitions of a man he didn't know, argued that Gault was wrong. Maureen thought that Miles was just going through the motions, repeating an argument he had made before, that his mind was someplace else, and she thought she knew where his mind might be.

Mike had consumed most of the large pizza and clearly could have eaten more, though he politely declined and suggested that since tomorrow was Saturday, why didn't they go to a movie. Surprisingly, Miles was indifferent, though willing. It was Nancy who swung the vote to the movie, and it was Nancy who decided they would see *Trading Places,* though Mike had held out surprisingly long for *Fanny and Alexander.*

The show was crowded. People were talking and everyone laughed at Eddie Murphy, whom Maureen had a hell of a time understanding. After the show, Nancy announced that she liked the joke about farting in the Jacuzzi. Miles agreed and Maureen, who had not heard the joke, said that it was funny. Mike, who had laughed nearly out of control for most of the movie, announced that he had found it only mildly funny.

"I laugh easily," he said apologetically as they got into the car. Mike always assumed that he would drive his own car and Miles or Maureen would drive theirs. So he did the driving.

Nancy voted to stop for a Dairy Queen, but Miles and Maureen were negative and they went home instead. Nancy announced that she had had a good time and went to bed with no argument within minutes after they got back. She even gave Mike a kiss on the cheek.

"Thanks," Miles announced after his sister was gone. "I'm going upstairs."

When they were alone Mike turned to her and said, "Why the lights? You left almost every light on. Are you that scared?" He took her hand. He was wearing a yellow shirt with a little blue panther sewn on the pocket.

Maureen fingered the panther and whispered, "I guess I'm that scared." Then she told him about Simcox, and Mike popped air from his cheeks and said, "You're right, you should be scared. At the risk of going out of that door rejected, I'm going to ask you if you want to go upstairs and get in bed with a slightly overweight, overage, and very overeager football coach with a bad knee."

"How could a woman in her right mind resist such an invitation?" she said with a smile, stepping up to kiss him. He tasted like popcorn salt and felt like a vibrating, gentle animal. She liked the feeling.

"Let's give it a try," she said softly.

"I have every hope of success," Mike said, putting a massive hand around her head and kissing the top of her nose.

Through two closed doors, they heard the occasional laughter of some talk show coming from Miles's room while they made love. When they had first come together, Maureen had feared having him on top of her. David had been of medium height and build, and the few others had been the same or less. Mike had been a radically different encounter, and she had found, to her surprise, that his bulk was remarkably light. He was graceful, hairy, and no bigger sexually than anyone she had coupled with in the past. He was each time, as he was tonight, comfortable, accommodating, and—when things were right—exciting. Mike could let himself go, and she could appreciate it, and encourage him, even if she herself couldn't let go.

"What do you like better, sex or exercise?" he asked her in the darkness after she had rolled away. Both of them were slippery with sweat.

"Exercise," she answered before she had a chance to think that the answer might hurt him.

"Why?" he asked in the darkness, clearly curious but not hurt.

"Exercise lasts longer," Maureen said, lying back and feeling very sleepy. "And you?"

Mike rolled over and sat up with a laugh. "Sex," he said. "I get plenty of exercise, but not much sex. You can live without exercise but not without sex."

"I can live without sex but not without exercise," she countered, "but I'd rather have both."

"We should tape this conversation," Mike said, chuckling.

About fifteen minutes later they made love again, slower and more aware of each other. They rarely did it twice in one night. Maureen never wanted to, but this time she did, starting as a kind of reward to Mike for being available and reliable. By being indifferent instead of intense, she lost herself in the act, actually felt herself let go with an animal feeling she had never let surface before. It was Mike who broke his mouth from hers and moved away.

"That was as good as a ten-kilometer run," she said with a smile he couldn't see.

"I'll consider my life fulfilled when I'm rated on a par with fifty push-ups. Can one man aspire to such a rating?"

Maureen clung to him for an hour, her head resting on his

hairy, moist left arm. Neither of them spoke and she thought that he had fallen asleep. "Mike?" she said without moving.

"Time to go," he sighed, recognizing her tone. He got up and reached for his pants. Against the streetlight and the shadow of dancing leaves, he looked like a cutout of a giant panda. Dressed, he turned to the bed, found her, kissed her gently, and said, "I thought I was too far over the hill to find someone like you."

"Over the hill," she said, taking his hand. "You're standing on the peak."

"Maureen," he said almost as an afterthought, though she could tell that he had been preparing for this, weighing his words. "When this is over, this thing you're going through, you've got to make up your mind about us. I'm having a lot of trouble playing the happy teddy bear. I don't want to lose you, but it's time to get serious."

When he was gone, Maureen got up, went to the bathroom, put on her cutoff pajamas, and returned to bed, leaving her door partly open. Miles had turned down his television, but she could still hear an occasional voice, a movie shot, a distant electronic shout.

Somewhere deep inside her the image of Roger Simcox surfaced, but she painted a white box over it and watched it float away as she fell asleep, exhausted.

Maureen was up at six-thirty. She found an envelope under the front door containing the Barelli file and a one-word note from Donnelly: "Thanks." She had her orange juice and changed into her running clothes. She watched through the window, tempted to have a second glass of orange juice but knowing it wasn't a good idea before she ran, especially on a humid day. When the van came down the street she moved to the door and reached the sidewalk in time to pick up the newspaper before it came to a stop on the driveway. She waved at the delivery man and removed the string from the paper.

There was nothing on the first three pages. On the fourth was the feature about Barelli. There was a photograph of the dead detective, looking like a clean-cut version of the washed-out man she had met in the hospital in the summer of her madness. The names of the witnesses weren't mentioned, but hers was. Donnelly had not made the connection to Simcox, not yet.

The story on Barelli had suggested more than a hint of madness on the part of the detective. While Maureen couldn't disagree, she would have preferred that his dignity be protected, especially since his widow, according to the article, was living on the fragile image of a husband who had not only been dismissed for alcoholism but had taken his own life.

She almost missed the Simcox story. It wasn't in the front of the paper at all but on the obituary page, a small article announcing that a former Chicagoan who was visiting the city had been murdered in what police believed was a robbery, one of an epidemic of attacks in the Lincoln Park area.

"I saw the story," came a voice behind her, and Maureen dropped the paper.

"Shit," she cried.

"Sorry," said Helen Katz, kneeling to help pick up the newspaper. "But I didn't exactly sneak up on you. I walked up large as a very slightly overweight cop."

Maureen picked up the newspaper. "How is it going, the investigation?"

Helen Katz was wearing the same thing she had the morning they had last run. She had obviously rinsed it out and would do so until she tired of those morning runs or grew serious about them and bought more running clothes.

"How's it going," Helen repeated, pushing dark hair from her eyes and looking up at the sun. "I had the pleasant job of calling Simcox's widow in Atlanta. My boss, Lieutenant Kiley, thinks things like that need a woman's touch. She's coming in today to make funeral arrangements. As far as she's concerned, she thinks it was a robbery, which is what I think it was."

"And if it wasn't," said Maureen, starting her warm-up exercises. "She was a witness too. Those two might be after her."

"Put it together, Maureen," Helen said wearily, arms folded, looking down at her. "First, no one knows she's coming. When they decide on where the funeral will be, if it's going to be in Chicago, we'll be there. If the Vanbeebers show up, we'll have them."

"Then Susan Breen," Maureen went on, twisting her neck in a circle first in one direction, then another.

"She saw the article on you in the paper the other day," Helen said, stopping to pluck out a blade of grass, which she placed in the corner of her mouth. "She doesn't think there's a connection, but we told her to be careful just in case."

"You've got someone watching her?" Maureen said, her hands behind her neck, her legs spread as she began to touch her elbows to her knees.

"You know what it would cost to put a twenty-four-hour guard on her?" Helen Katz said with a cynical smile. "If—and that 'if' is a big one—we had a definite threat against her or hard evidence to show that someone was out to kill her, there is still only a slight chance that the department would assign anyone to her. Even if they did, it would only be for a few days. Then they'd tell her to pack up and move out and leave no forwarding address."

Maureen stood up and brought her knees alternately up to her chest. "Is that what you're planning to tell me if it turns out that they have come back?" she said.

"Would you go?" Helen asked.

"Who knows?" Maureen said, stopping and looking at the other woman. "Right now I think that the answer is no, but it's not real for me. I'm not sure I want to think about it being real to me. I keep thinking about Nancy and Miles. You know something, policewoman? Sometimes I'm a little sorry I agreed to that television interview and that story. I had some good reasons, but I also wanted to impress you, show you I was as cool and responsible as you are. I was at least in part a victim of feminist thinking."

"And that's bad?"

"It can be dangerous," Maureen said, letting herself smile slightly.

"You're telling me?" Helen said, pointing to herself. "I've been a cop for nine years. If I told you half the stupid things I've done to prove that I wasn't afraid to do them, you would realize that impressing me is not a reasonable thing for a human being to do."

"Let's run," said Maureen.

"Fine with me," agreed Helen Katz. "What's your afternoon like? I'm off. How'd you like to invite me over?"

"So you could keep an eye on me," Maureen said, putting her tongue in her cheek. "I thought the police department wasn't interested."

"My own time again," Helen said. "Hey, I'm just making a social contact. Don't turn me down just because I'm a cop. What can I say, I'm not an elephant, I'm a human being. Or what was it Bette Davis said to Joan Crawford at the end of *Whatever Happened to Baby Jane?*"

"'You mean,'" Maureen said in an awful imitation of Bette Davis, "'all this time we could have been friends?'"

"Just as I thought," Helen said, throwing away the piece of grass she had been chewing on. "We even like the same movies."

"Let's make it around six," Maureen said, starting off in a jog. "For dinner. I've got something to do this afternoon."

Helen nodded, saving her breath, and took off. Maureen had made up her mind when she read the article that she would pay a visit to Susan Breen. She had left the paper on the lawn next to the house with a stone holding it down in case a highly unlikely breeze lost its way in the August heat.

Miles's plan for the afternoon, was, essentially, "I don't know. Turn on the air conditioner in my room, call Mark. I guess I'll go to a movie later if Mark wants to. You want me to take Daisy?"

Maureen considered it and told him that he could go when she came back from some business if he wanted to use the car. Nancy would spend the afternoon with Paulette/Cynthia Johnston and her aunt, who had invited her.

Maureen found that Susan Breen's telephone number was unlisted, so she called WGN to leave a message and found herself connected to Susan Breen. "I didn't expect to find you at work on Saturday," Maureen said. She was in the basement exercise room with the door closed.

"We're on the air twenty-four hours a day," the woman answered in distinct businesslike English. "Whom am I talking to?"

"I'm sorry," Maureen said. "My name is Maureen Dietz. I doubt if you'd remember . . ."

"I remember you," the woman said, keeping her businesslike tone, though her voice dropped just a touch. "And if I hadn't, the police reminded me yesterday. What can I do for you? I'm sorry I can't talk too long. I'm working on a show for tonight."

"Roger Simcox," Maureen said. The pause at the end of the line was long, but Maureen was sure the woman had not hung up.

"Yes," she finally said.

"And about you," Maureen went on. "It really might be important."

"I . . ."

"I can meet you wherever you say," Maureen pushed on.

"All right," Susan Breen gave in. "I'm having dinner with some people on staff. If you want to come to the station this afternoon, about three, I'll take a break. I'll leave your name with the guard at the desk, and we can get a cup of coffee in the cafeteria. Will that be all right?"

"Fine," said Maureen. "I'll see you then." When she hung up, Maureen wasn't looking forward to the encounter, but she was sure it was a meeting she had to have. And then another realization struck her. The television studio just off Western was well within the dark circle of Bittie's Red Hots, the circle she had been determined to avoid, but there was no avoiding it now unless she called Susan Breen back and made an excuse. Since Maureen knew that she had already taken a step into the dark circle in her memory, a literal step into the taboo territory seemed a reasonable though not comfortable suggestion.

She exercised lightly and tried to read a book in the bathtub, a novel titled *Peregrine,* about a woman held captive by a madman who wants her to think she is a falcon. Maureen found it compelling and sick but finished it. When she got out of the tub and changed into a white skirt and white cotton blouse, it had begun to rain. The sky was black and the thunder was deep and rumbling after the cracks of lightning.

"You really have to go out in this?" Miles asked from the kitchen as she passed. He was, from the smell, making himself an omelette of leftovers, one of his favorite foods. In the living room the television was on, and two remarkably well built and sweaty young black men were fighting it out from Atlantic City. Miles kept ducking his head through the archway in the kitchen to watch a few punches.

"I've got to go," Maureen said. "I'll be back in about two hours. If Nancy comes back, keep her inside and don't let anyone in. If there's any . . ." She paused, looking over at Miles. Spatula in hand, he was examining her critically over the tops of his glasses. "You know all that," she said.

"I know all that," Miles said. "Those guys aren't coming here. If it will make you feel better, I'll call Mike and ask him to come over and watch the Canadian football game."

"What," asked Maureen, moving to the door as thunder clapped outside, "makes you think Mike will be available?"

"Mom, Mike is always available. If his daughters aren't in town on Saturday, he's at home watching sports or reading. There is no one more predictable in the world than your friend and mine, Mike Rothman. Are Jews generally particularly reliable in your experience?"

"No more than any other group," Maureen answered as casually as possible, wondering what the point was of this sudden and for-the-first-time bringing up of Mike's ethnicity.

"If you and Mike got married," he said, returning to his omelette, which, from the smell, threatened to burn, "would you turn Jewish?"

"I'm not planning to marry Big Mike," she said. "Don't worry about it."

"I'm not worried," he said too quickly. "But if you did, would you expect Nancy to be Jewish and what about—"

"I have no plans to marry Mike or anyone else," she said, checking her watch as the announcer on television shouted, indicating that someone was engaging in particularly effective mayhem. "And if I did marry, I can give you an oath that I won't have any children. Miles, I am almost thirty-nine years old."

"Raquel Welch was over forty when—" He stopped, having revealed more than he wanted to about his knowledge of sexually related gossip.

"There's nothing to talk about, Kareem, but I'll elaborate on my position later if you want. Now I've got to go. Take care and be sure to clean up that pan."

When she stepped into the humid afternoon, the rain was splattering down noisily, but it wasn't making things much cooler. It would have been better to wait, but there could be no waiting if she was to get to the studio by three. Maureen dashed across the lawn and sidewalk, hoping that she had left the front door of the Omega open. She had and got in without too much of a soaking.

The drive was slow, dark, and muggy. She turned the air conditioner on since the downpour through the open window would have drenched her, but the traffic proved surprisingly heavy on Western Avenue, so she turned the air conditioner off after a few miles, fearing that the car might—as it was known to do—overheat. Maureen had purposely avoided taking the expressway, which would have brought her past Bittie's when she got off at Diversey.

When she made the turn onto Diversey into what was surely the black circle, her chest gave her one throbbing warning as she whispered, "Oh, Lord," but kept going till she found the small street with the arrow pointing the way to the television station parking lot. She slowed down as she turned and drove down a street lined with small factories, all closed on a Saturday afternoon, giving her the impression that she was suddenly alone in the heart of a crowded city. Her lights were on, had been on all the time, and they guided the way through the gray pelting rain and into the station's parking lot.

The building itself was glass fronted and well lit. She could see the lobby, the guard through the revolving door, and the adjacent small cafeteria. She had been to the station twice before, both times for television interviews on her theories of exercise. One show had been directed at women. The other had been a late-night panel on exercise, mental health, and nutrition. The interviewer, a woman, had been intense and interested while the cameras were on, eager and supportive of health and nutrition for women. As soon as they cut to a commercial, the woman had reached for a cigarette and clung to it, smoking to the last possible second and asking quickly if any of the three guests wanted to remain after the show to go for a drink to continue the conversation.

Maureen parked as close to the front door as she could. As she leapt out of the Omega and dashed for the front door, she saw a van pull into the parking lot. She kept running and pushed through the revolving door into the blast of air-conditioning, which chilled the rain against her body. Inside, she turned to look out of the window at the van, which was searching for a parking space. She couldn't tell what color the van was or how many people were in it. The rain had blanketed it in darkness. The van parked and turned off its lights. She watched to see who was getting out, angry with herself for having clutched the fantasy of Paulette/Cynthia.

"Can I help you, ma'am?" a voice came behind her.

"Just a second," she said, without turning to the voice. "I have an appointment. I just want to catch my breath."

No one got out for a minute. Maureen was on the verge of suggesting to the guard at the desk that he go out and investigate, that she might have been followed, that there might be killers in that van, two killers who had followed her into the dark circle of the past. And then the door to the van opened and someone jumped down, a woman, who came running across the lot, her jeans tight and wet, her breasts bouncing against the soaked tan man's shirt tied across her stomach to reveal her navel. The woman brushed back her long wet hair and came through the revolving door, panting.

"Shit," she said, looking around, then throwing her hair back. Up close, Maureen could see that the yellow hair was dyed. Brown streaks showed through. As the woman shook herself off, Maureen could also see that she was appreciably older than she had thought and that the exposed stomach wasn't tight.

"Can I help you, ma'am?" the guard repeated, this time to

the newcomer. The guard was a young black man in uniform. His cap was on straight and his mustache well trimmed.

"I'm looking for Clyde Dunnagan," she said. "Clyde Kelly Dunnagan. He's supposed to meet me. He's my cousin."

She moved to the desk, panting heavily, her shirt plastered against her breasts, which the guard managed to ignore. He went through a printed book in front of him and said, "That's Dunnagan with D, right?"

"Right," she said, giving Maureen a quick disinterested glance and then looking back at him.

"Sorry," he said. "I've got no Dunnagan listed. What department is he in?"

"I don't know," the woman said, shrugging with irritation. "He's a janitor or something."

"Sorry," the guard said, looking up. "There's no WGN employee by that name."

"WGN?" she said in a near-squeak. "I thought this was WLS. That motherfucker at the gas station . . ."

The guard came out from behind the desk, glanced apologetically at Maureen, and moved toward the woman, gently saying, "I'm sorry, ma'am, but you've got the wrong station. I'll be glad to tell you how to get where you want to go if you'll just hold your voice down, control your language, and step outside."

"Forget it," said the woman, her voice still high. "Just fucking forget it." She stormed out. The door was still revolving as she dashed back toward her van. Maureen watched the woman dash across the lot and open the door of the van. In the flash of time it took her to get in and close the door, Maureen thought she saw a hulking figure in the driver's seat.

"Sorry about that," the guard said behind Maureen. "Now, whom did you have an appointment with?"

"Susan Breen," she said, glancing over her shoulder at the van. The lights came on in the vehicle and it moved gently back into the dark rain.

"Are you Mrs. Dietz?" he said.

"I am."

"I'll tell Miss Breen you are here."

A newscaster Maureen recognized pulled up in a cab, dashed into the building, and passed her, waving his hand at the guard, who smiled. Through the same door the newscaster had darted, a woman stepped into the lobby, walked up to her, and put out her right hand and said, "Hello, Mrs. Dietz, I'm sorry to make you wait."

Time makes changes, but Maureen wasn't prepared for this one. She had expected a variation on the skinny counter girl at Bittie's, but this was more than a variation, it was a major transformation. Susan Breen was a well-endowed woman who outdid the ideal of Rubens, the kind of woman Mike described with admiration as *zaftig,* one of the few Yiddish words she had ever heard him use. Her face was clear, serious, and definitely pretty. She had oversized fashion glasses, and her hair was brown, straight, and shoulder length. She wore a blue skirt and a light blue blouse with a very colorful red, yellow, and white scarf as a belt. She looked, in fact, like the ideal young woman executive.

"You look different," Susan Breen said, her eyes on Maureen's face.

"That's what I was thinking about you," Maureen countered with a small smile.

"I mean you look different from the way I saw you last, about a year ago when you did Ellen Mane's show," Susan said.

"I don't remember seeing you. . . ."

"I didn't talk to you," Susan said. "I heard you were on and I came to watch the taping in the booth. I didn't think you'd want a reminder of the past. And now, here you are reminding me of the past. Shall we go into the cafeteria?"

The young woman led the way on clapping high heels. She walked erect, her back straight and confident. Inside the almost empty cafeteria she suggested that they have coffee and made it clear that she was paying. Normally Maureen would have turned down the coffee for a juice or ice water, but she wanted to get past the social awkwardness and down to the reason for her visit. Susan went for the coffee while Maureen sat at one of the white Formica tables and watched a man in full clown makeup smoking a pipe and conducting what looked like a friendly argument with a gray-haired thin man, who refused to look up from his cup of what looked like hot water.

"I've got about fifteen minutes," Susan said, returning with two coffees and sitting across from Maureen. Maureen had her back to the window. A snap of lightning and a crack shook the window.

"I'm not sure how to put this," Maureen said, picking up the coffee in both hands. Susan watched without drinking and said nothing. "First, I'm sorry about what happened to Roger Simcox."

"I'm sorry too," Susan said, picking up her cup to take a sip. "He was a good person who didn't deserve . . . But you know about that. Your husband . . . I'm sorry."

"Don't be," Maureen said. The coffee was hot and had too much cream, which was just the way she liked it.

"Well," Susan said, adjusting her large glasses as if she were going to make an important statement. "Maybe it will be easier for you if I make some things clear. I didn't love Roger Simcox. He came to Chicago once or twice a year to see his parents, old friends, and me. Sometimes we got together. Sometimes I made an excuse and avoided him. Roger had started to talk about moving back to Chicago, and this trip I was going to tell him it would be better if we didn't see each other anymore. I was going to tell him I was getting married to someone at the station."

"And are you?" Maureen asked.

"No," Susan said with a sigh that made it clear that there might indeed be someone at the station she would like to verify the lie with. "When I met Roger Simcox he was a slightly older, slightly better educated, good-looking guy with a wife who, he said, was along for the ride, betting on his making it big. I don't know if that was true. I've only met her a few times, most of those when he brought her into Bittie's years ago. I thought she seemed nice."

"And?" Maureen prompted.

Across the room, the clown with the pipe demanded of the man with him that he at least pretend that he was paying attention.

"And," Susan went on, "I thought I was lucky to have him wanting a skinny kid who worked behind a hot dog counter. I'm from this neighborhood. My parents still live about six blocks from here and two blocks from Bittie's. I used to go past here on the bus and think I'd never work in a place like this, but I am, and on the way Roger Simcox stood still, dropped out of Chicago State University before he got his degree, and started selling cars. If this was a network soap, I'd say I passed him. After a while he didn't seem quite so bright, so good-looking, and didn't seem to have much future ahead of him. I still liked him, but he had never indicated that he wanted to leave his wife, and after a while I was glad of it. I know I could have married him as recently as four years ago, and I would have regretted it."

"I'm sorry," Maureen said.

"That doesn't mean I didn't cry for him," Susan Breen said, looking up with near-defiance.

"It didn't sound that way to me. Listen Susan, I'm trying to be sure that there's no chance, no chance at all, that Roger was killed because of me, because of my going on television, talking to the newspapers, bringing everything up again."

Susan shook her head and drank her coffee and then looked up again. "Why would those killers come after Roger?" she asked. "There were lots of witnesses, you especially. Lou certainly."

"And you," Maureen said softly.

"And me," Susan agreed. "You're not suggesting that these maniacs have come back and plan to kill every witness."

"It doesn't make sense," Maureen agreed, "but you can see that—"

"How did they find Roger?" Susan asked reasonably. "How did they come to Chicago and find Roger, who was staying with me? How . . ." And then the fear that had struck Maureen appeared in the eyes of this self-possessed young woman. "You mean . . ." she began.

And Maureen finished. "They could find you. They could get your name from the old stories. They could even send someone to Bittie's to ask how you were doing, where you might be. It could have been you they were looking for and Roger they found coming out of your apartment."

Susan laughed nervously and bit her lower lip, her eyes misting. "That's crazy," she said. "You mean Roger died because he was staying with me? You mean they wanted to kill me and found him instead?"

"They might not even have recognized you," Maureen said. "I certainly didn't, but Roger hadn't changed very much. They could have seen him coming out of your apartment while they were waiting for you and decided to get him instead."

Susan banged her cup down on the table. The teaspoon bounced and she said, "Stop it."

The man with the clown turned around to see what was happening, but the clown went on talking.

"I'm sorry," Maureen said, getting up. "You're right. I'm almost certainly imagining a lot that couldn't be. The police don't think much of the possibility and to tell the truth, I don't think it's a particularly strong likelihood. I shouldn't have come here, and I shouldn't have done this. I am sorry." Maureen stood up, thanked Susan for the coffee, promised not to bother her again, and turned to go.

"Wait," Susan said, and Maureen turned to her. She was

standing now, and there was a slight easing of the role she had worked so hard to live out. Maureen thought she saw behind the glasses, makeup, and grooming something of the frightened, scrawny teenager at Bittie's. "There is something, something we can talk about, something about those two men. It doesn't mean much. I didn't remember it till a few years ago, and then it seemed silly. I didn't even consider going to the police with it. I've got to get back now. I'm late. Would it be possible for you to come by my place tonight, about ten?"

"I don't . . ." Maureen began.

"Fair is fair," Susan said, regaining her composure a bit and trying to smile. "You just tried to scare the hell out of me. The least you could do is have another cup of coffee and listen to what I have to say."

"I'll be there," Maureen said. "Is it all right if I bring a friend?"

"The more the merrier," Susan said, running her manicured hand down the front of her skirt to remove a nonexistent crease. "We'll sit around telling ghost stories. I think I'd rather not be alone tonight."

With that, Susan Breen turned and moved quickly down the small row of tables, glanced up at the wall clock, which showed it was three-twenty, and pushed through the double doors into the lobby. A few more people had come into the cafeteria. A trio of men wearing overalls had gathered in a corner. They looked old and tired. The clown and the gray-haired man were still there on a second or third cup of coffee and hot water. Maureen turned to look into the afternoon darkness. It was still raining, but the sky was clearing a bit, and it looked as if it would soon stop. As she crossed the lobby a few seconds later, she glanced out the window after saying "thank you" to the guard behind the counter.

There was, as she was sure there would be, no van parked in the lot. There was, however, her Olds Omega, its lights clearly on. She pushed through the revolving door and dashed across the lot, kicking up water from a puddle at the curbing.

"How about a break?" she said, putting her key into the ignition and speaking to the car, fate, and any gods or goddesses that might care or be interested. She turned the key, heard the sick grinding of an abused battery, and then the catching of the engine. It turned over and she sat feeding it gas gently and being thankful for small engines.

# 5

"Now do you two mind telling me what the fuck that was all about?" the woman said, readjusting her wet shirt. Her name was Myrna. She was married to a cab driver named Sol, and she spent most of her spare time—which was, as far as Marty could see, as ample as her ass—in a trio of bars on Howard Street east of Clark.

They were in the van driving west on Diversey, and neither of the men on either side of her answered. "There it is," the smaller man said suddenly, pointing a finger past her at a hot dog stand.

"I see it," the big one answered without looking.

"You're not gonna tell me, are you?" Myrna said, shifting her weight.

They had picked her up the night before. Marty, Cal, and Myrna had been the last customers at Irvine's Bar, lingering until two in the morning. She'd been drunk and Cal had been plastered out of his head, moaning about not being able to find a goddamn television store.

Myrna had accepted a drink from the two of them, though she might have turned them down had it been a few hours earlier and she a little less stewed. She was pretty good at picking out the crazies, the brawlers, the talkers. Marty was sure of that. He had seen the type from Carbondale to Calabassas. When the bartender had told them it was time to close up, Cal had gotten that look in his eye that could have meant trouble. It was Myrna who had said that she would take them to a place she knew where they could have a good time any time of the day or night.

She had led them to a place called the Gold Tack, one of the crummiest bars Marty had ever seen, and in his travels with Cal he had seen places that a pus-covered rat wouldn't go in. He'd hated the place, but Cal had wanted to stay. There'd been a few guys at the bar who looked like trouble, but Marty had made it clear that he was far from drunk, and they'd turned their eyes away.

After trading dumb shit talk with the woman for an hour and fumbling for her tits, Cal had passed out. Marty had dropped a ten-dollar bill and picked up his cousin. He had been surprised when Myrna followed him out.

"Where are you going?" she'd said in the hot night air.

A cruising cop car had been coming down Clark Street, so Marty had hustled toward the van, opening it and pushing the limp body of his cousin into the back.

"Hey," Myrna had said, running after him, "you dumping me out here in this neighborhood at this time of night? You know what could happen to me here?"

Whatever it was, Marty had been sure it had already happened to her more than once, but with the cops cruising closer, he wasn't about to start something.

"Can I come with you or what?" she'd said loudly.

"Suit yourself," Marty had said, and she'd jumped in, closing the passenger door behind her.

She had fallen asleep about ten minutes later while Marty was looking for old places he and Cal had worked or played when they came to Chicago. They couldn't go back to their room, not with Myrna, who'd sat snoring like a dying racoon with her mouth open. So he had driven and finally parked on a side street in a neighborhood where no one was likely to bother them. It had been about five, and Marty had leaned back in his seat, looked over at the available woman, shook his head, and said aloud, "Used-up shit," and then he'd fallen asleep.

Marty had been the first to wake up, around noon. He'd pushed the woman in the ribs to stop her from snoring and called back to Cal to wake up.

"I didn't get home," she had said, beginning to realize where she was. "Hell, Sol is a good guy to stay away from when you don't get home for a night."

"I'll stay away from him," Marty had said. Behind them, Cal had begun to cough. The cough had turned bad, and Marty had called back, "Cal, hey, you all right?"

"I'm all fuckin' right," he'd called back irritably. "What's she still doing with us?"

"Thanks a lot," Myrna had said angrily, looking back at him and trying to pull herself together. "You can just take me back where you picked me up, and that'll be jake with me."

The rain had started by then, and as they drove, Cal had awakened a little, stuck his head into the front of the van, examined Myrna, whom he clearly didn't remember very well, and suggested to her that there was no damned hurry.

"All we got to do is pick up a television set and a fan," he'd said. "When my head clears, you can climb on back here with me."

"And what are we gonna do back there?" Myrna had said playfully.

Marty had wanted to reach over, open the door, and kick her into the street. "We got things to do, Calvin," Marty had said warningly.

"Like what?" Cal had said, breathing putrid air on his cousin's neck.

"Like follow that woman," Marty had said. "We're doing some detective work," he'd thrown at Myrna. "Following a woman who's cheating on her husband."

"I hate that, cheating," Myrna had said indignantly. "If Sol ever cheated on me, I'd put a bomb in his cab."

"Shit," Cal had said wearily, ignoring her and rubbing his hair back. "We can do that tomorrow."

"We'll do it today," Marty had said. "We'll do it now."

"Myrna can stay with us," Cal had insisted, and Marty had shaken his head. Cal's dumbness was going to get them caught, and that was a fact, but it had been a toss-up, having Cal grumbling all day, maybe thinking and starting to ask questions again about what they were doing, or letting the woman stay to keep him busy. Marty had decided to let her stay.

After they had stopped for sinkers at a doughnut place, they had driven to Evanston and waited until Maureen headed out into the rain. Marty had been parked almost a full block away, and he'd been sure she hadn't seen him follow her.

Myrna had climbed into the back when they'd hit Western, and from the sound of the moaning, groaning, and comments, Marty'd been sure Cal wasn't getting it up. He'd also been sure by this time that Myrna was reasonably sober and beginning to appreciate how dangerous Cal could be. Whatever he had been doing back there in the dark as the rain punched against the van's roof, she'd been telling him it was just fine and dandy.

Marty had been careful following Maureen and had almost lost her a couple of times, but never quite. He had pulled into the television station lot after she had parked and driven straight to a spot, but something had been wrong. When he'd parked and turned off the lights, he'd been able to see Maureen standing inside the lighted lobby, looking out at the van. She hadn't seen them, couldn't have. Maybe she was just being careful because of the shit she had started. Whatever the reason, she'd been standing there looking straight across the parking lot at him and the parked van no one was getting out of.

"Hey you, Myrna," he'd called back. "Get your ass up here fast, real fast."

She had muttered something real low and not so nice, thinking he couldn't hear, but Cal had shouted, "You heard him, move."

When her head came out of the back, Marty had said, "I want you to go across through the door over there, say you're looking for someone, say anything you want to say, and then come back and get in the van."

"You're out of your damn mind," she'd screeched.

Marty had put his right hand around her neck and squeezed. "That woman we're following is in there. I think she spotted us. Now you just climb over me and do it. You follow?"

"Yeah," Myrna had whined, trying to push his hand away, but he wasn't having any. He'd squeezed harder. "Wait. It's raining out there."

"There's worse things than getting a little wet, Snow White. You hear where I'm coming from?"

From behind, Cal had laughed and Myrna knew she had no choice.

Later, when she'd gotten back in the van and they had driven away, she had tried to get in the back, away from Marty, but Cal had grown tired of her and pushed her back in the seat.

Now she was about to protest. Marty could feel it, so he turned to look at her as he drove. There was no hate in his eyes, but he could see on her face that she was reading him real good. She turned forward and shut her mouth. When she reached over to turn on the radio, Marty slapped her hand away. Twenty minutes later he pulled over to the corner of Clark and Foster and said, "Out."

She got out, looking back toward Cal, who said nothing. Marty reached over to close the passenger door.

"Who are we?" he asked her. The rain had stopped, and she stood in the gutter fiddling with her shirt.

"I don't know," she said, trying to find the answer that would please him and get her away.

Marty could see her fear, and it was just what he wanted. "We aren't anybody," he said with a pleased grin. "We don't exist. We just plain ain't. You never met us."

She shuddered and shook her head in agreement. "I never met you guys," she said, and Marty could see that she wanted it so much to be true that with a few drinks she might well convince herself.

Helen arrived just before six and made several pointed comments about the heat, which led to an admission from Maureen that it was pretty damned hot. They closed the windows and turned on the air conditioners.

"You know one reason I don't like turning on the air conditioners?" she asked Helen, who was making the salad while she worked on the chicken. Miles was upstairs, door closed as usual, and Nancy was watching a rerun of a rerun of "The Brady Bunch" or "The Partridge Family."

"Sure," Helen said, slicing radishes into the huge bowl in front of her on the kitchen table. "You want to tough it out, not be dependent on a machine that might break down. More of the self-reliance, self-discipline. Don't count on anything or anybody that might let you down. Show you can take the hard way. Prove yourself."

"Pretty good," Maureen admitted, pulling the last piece of baked chicken from the aluminum foil–covered platter she had just taken from the oven. "But I've got another one I just thought of. I didn't want it to look like I was sealing us in, closing the windows, trying to protect us from whatever is out there."

"So you keep your windows open in the summer?" Helen asked. "Remind me not to accept any invitations from you after December. No, make that November."

"It's all right to keep them closed in the winter. It's . . . you think I'm a little nuts, don't you?"

"No." Helen shrugged, pouring salad dressing—oil and vinegar—on the massive concoction in the wooden bowl. "Some time I'll tell you about nuts I have met. It'll cheer you up. Trouble with you is that you don't know you're like other people. You're scared of the lunatic world, and you cover for it by acting brave. You think everyone is divided into the brave and the scared when in fact almost everyone is like you. You just had an experience that pushed the limits too far. And that's about the extent of the analysis you are going to get from me. I think we're ready. You want to call the kids?"

"Before I call them," Maureen said, putting four cups around the table near the plates, "I want to ask you a favor."

Quickly, she told Helen Katz about her visit to Susan Breen, that Susan had some information, and that she wanted Maureen to come to her apartment tonight.

"I'll go with you," Helen said, shaking her head to show that there were people who would never learn but were worth humoring, "but she's not going to have any big news. This isn't 'Barnaby Jones.' What she has to tell you is out-of-date. What she wants is some late-night company. You scared her. I scared her. Whoever killed Simcox scared her. After all, she'd been playing with the guy under the sheets for a long time. You don't just walk away from that when he gets his last rites."

"She didn't look scared," Maureen said. The air-conditioning was working reasonably well now.

"Tell me something now, exercise lady. You don't look

scared. You look just as tough as you hope you do. Now, enough of who's scared, you scared? I'm hungry. Call the A-team."

Nancy reluctantly gave up the Bradys, and Miles came flying down the stairs. Over the years he had managed to fall several times, once breaking an arm, but it didn't stop him from trying to set some new record for carpeted-stair descent.

"I'm in the wrong house," he said, "or it's the Twilight Zone. My house isn't air-conditioned. You are a trio of aliens posing as my mother, a policewoman, and the humanoid from the deep who has been telling us her name is Nancy Dietz for the last nine years." He sat at his regular place at the kitchen table, poured himself a full glass of cola, and reached for the chicken.

"You aren't funny, Miles," Nancy said. "Tell him he's not funny, Mom."

"You're not funny, Miles," Maureen said, straight-faced, reaching for the salad.

"You're not funny, Miles," Helen added, handing him her glass. He took it and filled it with cola.

"The car, Mom," he said, starting on the first of three chicken legs he had piled on his plate. "I'm getting it tonight, right? "Remember, Mark and I are going to a movie."

"I forgot," Maureen said, sucking air between her teeth. "Helen?"

"I'll drive. Buddy Hackett can take your car."

"You want me to take Daisy?" he asked, his mouth full.

"Don't talk with your mouth full of food," Nancy said. "And I don't want to see a scary movie. Besides, I told you, I'm staying at Paulette's tonight. We're setting up a tent."

"You arc not sleeping in her yard," Maureen put in quickly.

"Mother," Nancy said, looking to the sky for help in explaining things to her remarkably dense mother. "We're putting the tent up in her bedroom."

"Why didn't I think of that?" Miles said, raising his eyebrows in a terrible imitation of Groucho Marx.

"Sounds fine with me," Maureen said. "Remember—get to sleep no later than eleven."

"Paulette can stay up till midnight on not school days," Nancy whined.

"And," countered Maureen, "I'm sure there's a kid in Singapore, an eight-year-old girl, who goes to bed every morning at three."

"And a five-year-old girl in Bristol, England, who never sleeps," added Miles, adjusting his glasses.

"Don't make fun of me," Nancy insisted. Maureen noted that her daughter had not yet taken a bite of either chicken or salad.

"Is it like this at every meal?" Helen asked.

"The good ones," Maureen answered, reaching for additional salad.

When they finished dinner, which included frozen Dilly Bars from Dairy Queen, Miles agreed to clean up, take Nancy over to the neighbors with her *Star Wars* sleeping bag, and turn off the air conditioners. He zipped through the chores and was gone before Helen and Maureen left.

Then Helen said that she had to stop at home to leave a message for her husband. "I thought I'd be home when he got in," she explained. "We see each other about ten minutes every other day. I'll tape it on the television or the beer in the refrigerator so he can't miss it."

The drive to Helen's in Rogers Park took about ten minutes, which made them only a few minutes later than Maureen had promised to arrive at Susan Breen's apartment. Helen suggested that Maureen wait in the car.

"Two reasons," she explained. "My husband, Mojo Porkbelly, alias Howard Bruckner, might be there and we might, to put it nicely, exchange some caustic words. He would surely, sober or not, go out of his way to make a sexist remark to—or about—you."

"You ever think about a divorce?" Maureen said.

"A lot, especially recently," Helen said with a look of near-pain. "You want to hear the second reason?"

"I might as well," Maureen said. "But the first one was good enough."

"Thanks. Reason two is the place is a perpetual mess. He never cleans and I have not lifted a broom in weeks, hoping that the state of chaos would drive him away, but he thrives on it. Your place is, if I can presume on our brief friendship, disgustingly clean."

"I'm obsessive, remember," Maureen said.

"I almost forgot," Helen said, getting out of the car. "I'll try to make it fast."

Fast turned out to be nearly ten minutes. Maureen had gotten out of the car. She was halfway up the walk to the small townhouse in the middle of a row of identical houses when Helen came running out, her denim bag slung over her shoulder.

"Let's go," she said, taking Maureen's arm and turning her around. "Sorry about this, but Mojo was home and wanted a little verbal warm-up before he hit the streets or the sheets. I don't know whether he was coming or going, and I don't think he does either." Without waiting for comment, Helen got in the car and started the engine.

"Maybe I should just catch a cab," Maureen said, standing outside and leaning over to talk through the open window.

"Get in fast or Porkbelly will be out and drag you into his cave," Helen said between clenched teeth, looking forward. Maureen got in and Helen pulled away from the curb, burning rubber. "I told him that this was a particularly important date to add to the anniversary of our romance," Helen went on, driving, Maureen thought, more than a little recklessly. "This is the day I've had it. I told him to move out by tomorrow. I even told him where to find the garbage bags to pack his things. He suggested in return that I leave, and I said that I'd be happy to do so and

I'd even call the garbage collectors to come by and clean the place out tomorrow. It went back and forth like that. Real Noel Coward stuff. If they ever do a movie about me and the Creature, we'll be played by Jeremy Irons and Kate Nelligan."

"I'm sorry," Maureen whispered.

"Thanks," Helen said, biting her upper lip. "If I weren't a cop, I'd probably cry. Cops don't cry when they're sober. They teach you that in cop school the first day." She reached over and turned on the radio to discover that the night, the next day, and the day after would be hot. A woman's voice took over, singing passionately, and Helen flicked off the radio, muttering, "I don't listen to singers who say, 'Hey, baby.'"

"How about spending tomorrow with us?" Maureen said. "Mike and the kids and I are going to have a picnic, possibly in the living room with the air conditioning on."

Helen faced straight ahead. "Thanks, but I'm on shift tomorrow afternoon. Cops work on Sunday."

They said no more even when they got to Susan Breen's apartment on Goethe Street. It was a street lined with two- and three-story stone townhouses with renovated fronts, and a few small, very new apartment buildings. Parking on the street was a miracle in this neighborhood, night or day. Helen pulled in front of a fire hydrant and dropped the sun visor, which had a police card on it.

Night was just coming, settling in, and the afternoon rain— puddles of which still remained on the sidewalks—made it one of the most clothes-clinging nights of the summer. A dying many-legged insect quivered on the windshield in front of Maureen. She got out, trying to ignore it. Susan Breen lived in one of the apartment buildings. Her name was in the lobby. Maureen pushed the button but heard nothing.

"Probably not home yet," Maureen said.

"Bell might not work," said Helen, her face set, holding back her own thoughts and anger. "Let's go up and knock."

Helen rang another bell, and a man's voice came back. "Yes?"

"Police," Helen shouted, "open up."

The glass-fronted inner door buzzed and Helen opened it, slinging her denim bag over her shoulder. She led the way to the small elevator. The hall floor was darkly carpeted, and from above the smell of something sweet and meaty filled the corridor. The elevator was there and open. They stepped in and Helen pressed three.

"Maybe we should tell that man something, the one who opened the door?"

"We should tell him not to open the door when someone says 'police,'" Helen answered, facing front. "Saying you're a cop doesn't make you a cop. He should have got his shorts on and trotted down to check us out. Buildings like this are supposed to be secure, but any thief with an I.Q. slightly higher than a moron can get in and out."

"You learn that in cop school too?" Maureen said as the elevator stopped at three and slid open with a tinkle of a bell.

"On-the-job training," Helen said and strode to 3A, which was easy to find since there were only four doors on the floor. The door to 3A was slightly open.

"She's either here or she left her door open all day," Helen said.

"She's not the type to leave it open. Maybe she's throwing out the garbage?"

Helen pressed the white button next to the slightly open door. They heard the chime clearly, followed by a sound inside the apartment but no answer.

Helen reached into her bag, found a small pistol, and pulled it out of the leather holster. Maureen couldn't take it seriously, not that little gun, not Helen's seriousness. They were going to scare the hell out of Susan Breen, who was probably soaking in her bathtub or taking a shower.

"Wait . . ." Maureen whispered, reaching out to touch Helen's arm.

Helen pushed her back with her free hand and stepped into the apartment. "Susan?" she called. Maureen stepped in beside her. "Miss Breen?"

It didn't take a cop to see something was wrong. The apartment was small, looked as if it had been furnished within the past week with expensive furniture, or furniture that at least looked expensive. White was the principal theme. White carpet, white sofa, and matching lounge. Even white director's chairs around the living room table. On the wall was a painting of a Latino woman in a shawl. It looked like an original. The whole room could have been photographed and put into a magazine for working women except for the lamp that lay on its side on the floor and the trail of red that speckled the carpet and the sofa.

"Holy . . ." Helen whispered. "Susan, are you here?" Then to Maureen: "Get out of here, find a phone, call nine-one-one and tell them an officer needs their help here."

Helen had taken a step toward the partly open door across the room to their left. The red trail led to it. Maureen couldn't help thinking that this woman, somberly dressed with a bag over her arm and a pistol leveled in two hands, looked like a clichéd ad for a television series.

"Move," Helen hissed over her shoulder as she went forward to the bedroom door. Maureen was backing away, her hands behind her, feeling for the wall, when Helen took a final step in front of the closed bedroom door, and the door flew open.

"No," Maureen said, having no idea whether she had said it aloud or to herself. Helen backed away quickly, and the bloody figure lunged out at her. Maureen expected to hear a gunshot, but there was none, just the soft sound of the figure falling to the carpet.

"Susan," Maureen groaned, stepping forward.

"Get back," Helen called, aiming the gun at the bedroom door. "Get out."

But Maureen couldn't go. She wanted to move, to run, but she couldn't leave. She took a step forward as Helen kicked open the door Susan had stumbled through and stepped in, gun held level in both hands. The door bounced back, almost hitting her. Maureen took a few quick steps forward and waited a beat of a heart, trying to take in the motionless, bloody figure on the floor.

Helen came back out of the room quickly, took a step past the fallen figure, and stepped into the kitchen. She opened a door that led to a closet and closed it. "Gone," she said. "Close the door. Get on the phone. We must have just missed whoever did this. Get to the phone."

Maureen moved to the kitchen, where a blue phone hung on the white wall. She looked back over her shoulder at Helen, who had put her pistol away and was turning over the figure on the floor.

"How . . . is she?" Maureen said, trying to dial 911 and watch what was going on.

Susan Breen was a vision from a horror film. Her face was bloody and unrecognizable. Her nose was pushed to one side, her dark hair was caked with blood. There was an oozing, a pulsing, on her forehead. She was wearing the same skirt and blouse she had on when Maureen had seen her at the television station. Both were soaked in blood.

"Police," someone said on the phone.

She gave Helen's message and added that someone had been attacked. When she finished she found the phone hook on the second try and turned quickly. She didn't want to turn her back on Susan. Maureen had the sudden, horrible fantasy that if she turned her back, the blood-drenched woman would leap from the floor in a last accusing spasm and attack her.

"She's alive," Helen said, leaning over her. "Susan, do you hear me?"

There was no answer, nothing, but now Maureen could hear a horrible labored sound coming from the figure on the bloodied white carpet. The sound was the woman's attempt to breathe.

"Nose is shattered and who the hell knows what else," Helen said without looking up. "I'll do mouth-to-mouth. You prop up her legs for shock and then help me stop the bleeding."

Maureen pulled a pillow from the white chair. She got on her knees and lifted Susan's legs to push the pillow under them. Then she looked up. Helen's face was just coming up from the battered mask of the young woman. Now Helen's face was covered in blood, the visage of a crazed vampire pulling away from a feast.

"You going to be sick?" Helen said, glancing at Maureen. A bead of blood clung to the policewoman's lower lip. "If you're going to be sick or go nuts on me, get out. I need help, not another case of shock." She didn't wait for an answer but bent back to give more mouth-to-mouth aid.

Maureen moved to get around Helen and into the bedroom. There was more blood, but she didn't stop. She found the bathroom, which was unbloodied, grabbed a green towel with a swan embroidered on it, and ran back to try to stop the bleeding.

The first sign of help was the sound of the paramedic truck coming down the street. Neither Helen nor Maureen had said a word for the five or six minutes it had taken. Helen had worked on her resuscitation, and Maureen had pressed gently on the open wounds. The side of Susan's head where the skull had been crushed felt crunchy and brittle.

"Open the door," Helen said, sitting up and putting her hand on her back. Maureen got up and hurried over to open the door as the elevator bell rang. None of the other three doors on the landing was open. Two paramedics in blue, one looking like a kid, the other like a baseball player with a thick mustache, rushed in past her. One was carrying a big dark satchel. The other cradled some kind of machine. The older one with the mustache took in the scene and moved over to look at Helen's face. "I'm all right," Helen said irritably. "This is her blood on me."

The man nodded, and both he and his partner knelt next to Susan. Helen stood up and looked at Maureen. The paramedics were talking softly, quickly, as Maureen moved to the kitchen, found a drawer of dish towels, and returned to the living room. She handed a towel to Helen, who didn't take it. She just stood with her back to the wall watching the paramedics. Her hair had come down and dangled in her eyes. Maureen reached over and began to wipe blood from the woman's face. Helen seemed to come awake, looked up briefly, took the towel, and said, "Thanks."

"How bad?" Maureen asked the younger paramedic when the other one ran out of the door.

"Pretty bad," he said. He was holding a tubed mask over Susan's face. Maureen wanted to get a wet towel and clean that face, find the confident pretty woman under the blood, but she didn't move. "She's alive. What happened?"

"We don't know," Helen said softly, breathing deeply, hyperventilating slightly.

I do, Maureen thought, but said nothing. I know. She moved to Helen's side and put her left arm around the policewoman's shoulder. Helen didn't seem to notice. The move was, Maureen knew, as much to comfort her friend, who had taken control but now needed help, as to feel some contact herself. She was rather surprised to feel that she was sure she hadn't broken, hadn't fallen apart, and could breathe. There lay a woman, battered perhaps by the same men who had killed David. She had looked down at the horribly crushed face as she had not looked at David, and she had survived.

When the paramedics had Susan on the portable stretcher the mustached man had brought up quickly, they wheeled her into the hall, and the sound of voices came up behind them, male voices. Helen pulled away from Maureen, took one deep breath, blew it out hard, and rubbed her eyes just before two men came into the room.

"Who . . ." the older man, who was about sixty and had a cop gut, began. Then he stopped. "Katz, is that you?"

"No," Helen shot back, "I'm T. J. Hooker."

The transformation was amazing. Helen stood, cool, talking to the man. She looked over at Maureen, and Maureen knew the look said, "I'm playing it out, just the way you do. Don't tell them the empress had her new clothes on a few minutes ago."

While Helen and Maureen told their story in the kitchen to the old cop, the other man, not much younger but a lot thinner than his partner, began going over the apartment. In a few minutes, more cops came.

"Who's been in the bathroom?" someone called out.

"I was," Maureen answered, interrupted by another voice behind her saying, "Neighbors say they heard, saw, and know nothing. Henderson is downstairs checking the others."

It went on like that for about an hour before the old cop suggested that Helen take Maureen home and get back to him in the morning. Wearily the two women left the apartment and took the elevator down. They said nothing until they got into Helen's car, and then Maureen stated, "It was them. They're back and I brought them. I did that to that girl."

"She's a woman," Helen said, leaning back, now that she was away from the men, and closing her eyes. "If you want to start thinking that way, I did it. I brought you the file, suggested you go on television. I wanted so damn much to have a stupid sentimental tribute to Barelli—who, if the truth be known, was just like my husband and most cops, not too nice, a little selfish and shit . . . Barelli didn't even want to work with me. I was assigned to him as punishment. He got the first woman partner because he was a lush. Before we blame ourselves, there are other possibilities here besides your killers from the past. We're letting our egos seem pretty damned important here." With that she opened her eyes, started the car, and pulled out between the blue-and-white police cars, which partly blocked the street.

"Like?" Maureen said, rubbing her forehead.

"Susan Breen and Roger Simcox were adulterous sack-mates," Helen said with a bit more brutality than Maureen would have liked. "They were connected more with each other than with you. What about his wife having followed him here and doing this? Or what about some jealous boyfriend of Susan's? And that's just off the top of my head."

"Okay," Maureen said. "Okay. We'll wait and see what she has to say."

"If she makes it," Helen said, turning left on Broadway. "If she makes it."


The doorbell was definitely ringing, and no one was answering it. Maureen groggily sat up in bed, shook her head, and forced her eyes open. She stood up, wondering what time it was, and headed for the door. Since she was wearing her normal and favorite sleeping clothes, an oversize YMCA T-shirt and a pair of underpants, she paused at her dresser to pull out some tennis shorts. The doorbell continued to ring as she went down the stairs and crossed the living room.

Miles, who'd had his door closed the night before when Maureen and Helen came in, had probably stayed up most of the night after the movie. Nancy was still sleeping next door, and Helen was surely just as weary from yesterday as Maureen was. Helen had borrowed one of the Y shirts and had slept in Nancy's room.

"I'm on the way," Maureen called out, reaching for the front door and opening it to reveal Mike in a white cotton short-sleeved shirt and a pair of white shorts, and carrying a package under one arm and the Sunday paper under the other. "Mike," she said.

"You mean there's someone else you know who I could be confused with? I'll have to think about that. Picnic day, remember? I wore my shorts so I can amuse the neighbors by running through the sprinkler with Nancy and giggling. As agreed, I also brought my special-recipe potato salad, too much mayonnaise and too many onions, the way Miles likes it."

"I . . ." Maureen stammered, pushing her hair back.

"Look," Mike said, stepping forward to examine her, "you want to just close the door, pretend I didn't ring the bell, and go back to sleep? I told you yesterday I'm getting a little tired of my act. I get these overnight recharges of energy, but you're going to have to provide some applause from time to time."

"Come in," she said, standing back to let him pass. "I'm sorry. What time is it?"

"Almost ten-thirty, Maureen," he said, putting the newspaper down and turning to her. "You've usually run a marathon and lifted the equivalent of the Rocky Mountains by this time. What's wrong? You look—"

"I feel," she said. "Let's go in the kitchen and I'll try to tell you about it. Put the potato salad in the refrigerator."

Over orange juice, Maureen told him what had happened. Mike was a good listener, kept his eyes on her, made a sound from time to time, and said nothing. Maureen finished her telling of the events of the night before, and Mike asked his first question. "How's Susan Breen? We should call the hospital."

"No need," said Helen, stepping into the kitchen. She had on a clean blouse, which she had carried in her denim bag, and wore the same skirt she'd had on yesterday. Maureen could see no signs of blood on it. "I just got off the phone. Good morning, Mike."

"Good morning," Mike answered as Helen reached for the orange juice, changed her mind, and went to the sink to fill the teapot with water and put it on the stove.

"Susan Breen is still alive, comatose, may or may not come out of it," Helen said.

"And the police are looking for those two, the Vanbeebers?" Maureen asked.

"No more than before," Helen said. "You gave Susan Breen a pretty good scare when you saw her yesterday, right?"

"I guess so," Maureen answered.

"And Simcox had been killed the day before, less than a block from her building, after leaving her apartment."

"Yes," Maureen said.

"Whoever killed her came up the elevator and was let in by Susan Breen," Helen said.

"She's not dead yet," Mike said. "Remember."

"Sorry," Helen said, quietly putting her head in her hands. "Whoever tried to kill her. You think she would let one or both of the Vanbeebers in, or some stranger?"

"Now wait a second," Maureen countered. "You told me how easy it is to get into those apartment buildings. They could have made up all kinds of stories when they got to her door. Remember the Boston Strangler? He convinced frightened women to open their doors."

"Maureen, let's face it," Helen went on, looking up at her. "There hasn't been a sign of the Vanbeebers in this area."

"Two out of the eight people who witnessed the murder of my husband have been killed within three days after I went on television to talk about it. You have to admit that's some coincidence."

"Nine witnesses," Helen corrected. "Miles was there, remember, and Nancy, but she was a baby."

Maureen felt dizzy. "Miles was just——"

"Okay," Mike said, "what's the point of this?"

Helen poured some hot water on her instant coffee and sat down. "I don't think it's the Vanbeebers either," she explained, "but I'm not sure so I'll put in as much time as possible checking them out. We did find out what she wanted to tell you. She wrote a note, probably planned to make it a kind of official statement to you to take after she talked to you. About four years ago, Susan Breen thought she saw the Vanbeeber cousins at a bar on Broadway called Kosigian's. Someone is going to check the place out today, but it's not much of a lead, a bar where a pair of guys who looked like two killers were once seen more than four years ago. But it's being checked."

Helen drank her coffee in silence for a minute or two while Mike retrieved the thick Sunday paper, brought it to the kitchen table, and began going through it. "Here it is," he said, pointing a thick finger at an article on page three.

Maureen looked over his shoulder at the side-by-side photographs of Susan Breen and Roger Simcox. Susan Breen looked very much as she had looked at the station the afternoon before, a slight smile, owlish glasses, pretty, confident face. Simcox looked as if he had a secret. The headline indicated LINCOLN PARK LOVERS BEATEN IN SEPARATE ATTACKS, ONE DEAD, OTHER CRITICAL. Mike and Maureen read the story together. There was no linking of the murder and attack with her, no mention of her part or Helen's. It was stated, very carefully, that police were talking to Simcox's widow, who had arrived in Chicago the night before, and several friends of Susan Breen.

"Simcox's wife was one of the witnesses, and she's back in Chicago," Maureen said. "And I suppose if someone bashes her head in, the police will find some elaborate theory to keep it all revolving around adultery and revenge."

"We don't intend to let anything happen to Mrs. Simcox," Helen said.

"I didn't think you intended to," Maureen said, folding her hands in her lap, "but that doesn't mean you'll stop it."

"Have I worn out my welcome here?" Helen said, looking up from her coffee.

"Hey—" Mike began, but Maureen interrupted with, "I'm

sorry, Helen. You have the bad luck to be sitting across the table when I need someone to take it out on. If you weren't here, I'd be giving it to Mike, and if Mike weren't here, I'd probably be taking it out on Miles, who, by the way, should be up by now."

Helen went for more coffee and held up the pot, offering some to Maureen and Mike. Mike nodded his head yes and got up for a cup. He took one from the cupboard near the refrigerator, a faded brown ceramic mug that didn't match the other cups in the house. Helen poured some coffee for him.

"Miles is up," Helen said. "I ran into him in the bathroom. I think I embarrassed him."

"No clothes?" Maureen asked.

"He was wearing a pair of Jockey shorts and his glasses."

"Are we picnicking or are we not picnicking?" Mike asked, hiding the mug in his large fist. "I made about two hundred pounds of potato salad. If we don't have a picnic, it'll take me at least three days to eat it all."

"We picnic," Maureen said. "After I run, do my morning workout, and shower. Helen?"

"I'm coming. I've got my running shoes in the trunk of my car."

When they went out the door, Mike was sitting in the living room with the newspaper and the mug of coffee. "Take your time," he said, without looking up from the sports page.

"You see that mug Mike was drinking from?" Maureen said, starting her stretching. It was later in the day than she liked to run, and the sun was already hot, easily in the upper eighties.

"My favorite color of shit brown," Helen said. "Did Nancy make it in school?"

"Nope," said Maureen, "I made it almost eight years ago in the mental hospital. It's ugly as hell, but I keep it around to remind me of what I don't want to be. Thanks for last night. You handled that—and me—like a pro."

"I am a pro," said Helen. "I've got a badge and a gun to

prove it. I'll tell you the truth. I don't know how I would have done it if you hadn't been there with me. I think I needed an audience to stop me from total panic."

Maureen stood on one leg and bent the other one up under her with her hand on her ankle. She repeated it with the other leg. Stretch and breathe. "You would have done the same thing," Maureen said. "Okay. Fast, Helen, let's do some running."

"Lead the way, former fat lady," Helen said, flexing her shoulders and following as Maureen ran past her.

The run was hot and less than tranquil. It was close to eleven when they hit the park, and it was filled with children's softball or soccer games and their watching families. On the far side of the park, they had to make a choice of running through a family of Mexicans lying comfortably on the grass or going on the street. Maureen led the way to the street, past the baseball diamond and tennis courts, down the sidewalk and around. By the time they finished the second turn around the park, they were both heavy with perspiration.

"How about another mile?" Maureen called over her shoulder.

"No thanks," Helen panted. "You go on. I'll go back to the house."

"Sure?" Maureen asked, slowing down slightly.

"As sure as I am that I'm moving out on Mojo today," Helen said, veering off down the street after a break in the traffic on Main. Maureen didn't look back, but instead of going around the park again, she kept going straight down Main, with only a mild delay on Chicago Avenue. She ran to the park just south of Main Street, to the rocks on the Lake Michigan shoreline, and started back again, avoiding a group of picnickers having a volleyball game.

When she got back home, Miles, Mike, Helen, and Nancy were all seated on the front steps, clearly ready for a picnic. The old, battered yellow blanket was piled high with boxes, balls, and Mike's paper bag, in which resided the potato salad.

"Where did you go?" Helen asked.

"I just ran a little more, maybe a mile or so," Maureen answered, giving Miles and Nancy a big smile. Miles looked particularly serious, and Maureen continued on around the house to cool down. She knew exactly how far she had run—she had measured the distance to the lake and back on the car odometer. In fact, she had measured the distance to seven different sites in both Evanston and Chicago. She had, she knew, just run a little over seven miles. When she came around the house the second time, Nancy was reaching into one of the paper bags.

"Miles," she said. "You all right?"

"We told him," Mike said. "All right?"

Maureen stopped, hands on hips, still breathing heavily. Maybe she should have been bothered, said something about its being her responsibility, but in truth she was relieved; and since she felt good and exhausted after her run, she simply nodded and looked at Miles.

"I'm okay," Miles said. He was wearing an old, favorite shirt, one that was a size too small. Normally, Maureen would have ordered him in to change into something else, but she said nothing.

"What's going on?" Nancy demanded. She was clutching her picnic necessities, which included a battery-operated dog that yelped, a Barbie and Ken, a Popeye coloring book, a pail and shovel, and six crayons held together with a red rubber band.

"Miles doesn't feel too well today," Maureen said, looking at Helen.

"Right," Miles agreed. "The movie last night made me sick. I'll be all right, Daisy."

Maureen showered quickly and changed into an extra-large football jersey that Mike had given her. The jersey was red and white with a big number 7, which Mike explained meant she was a quarterback. They piled into Mike's Buick and headed silently for the beach.

The picnic went well, with Mike holding up most of the conversation on an impressive variety of subjects ranging from the chances for the Chicago Blitz to win the USFL championship next year to classical music. He preferred Bach to Mozart. He also casually mentioned a possible job offer at a junior college in San Diego, not far from where his daughters lived. Maureen knew he had waited to get it properly hidden in casual conversation, just as she knew she would hear more about it later. Helen took off just after noon to get back to her shift, but she promised to be in touch when there was news, or just to be in touch soon.

Nancy had found another little girl who had brought some toys, and they played together through the afternoon while Miles and Mike threw around a football and managed to get a pair of kids interested in joining them for a game of touch.

Maureen had fought off the urge to join them, to try to lose herself in exercise and effort. She forced herself to sit calmly watching, to let what had happened—what she had seen in Susan Breen's apartment—come past her consciousness and drift by. Her chest throbbed when the images came. She concentrated on the white circle in her mind, and it passed. She knew it would be back, but for now she could breathe.

She decided that since the police were still not taking her situation terribly seriously, she would have to do something more. However, sitting there in the park near the beach and watching her children play as she smelled hot dogs broiling, it was difficult to believe in the reality of her fears.

They went back to the house around five, and talked about sunburn. Mike excused himself after they had finished leftovers for dinner.

"Good potato salad," Miles said, and Mike leaned over to kiss Maureen good-bye. She walked him to the door.

"My daughter is in town and wants to see me. Probably wants to hit me for a loan," he sighed. "Which I'll give her. She's married to a good kid, but he's got no push."

"We'll talk later," Maureen said, assuring him and ushering him out the door. The truth was that she didn't want Mike around this evening, didn't want to talk about getting serious and the possibility of San Diego. She wanted to go downstairs, spend an hour on the mat, and then watch junk television with the kids; which was just what she did, though Miles looked distracted for most of the evening, only managing to pull himself out of it every hour or so to show some irritability with his sister.

"You want to talk about it?" Maureen said when Nancy finally went to bed accompanied by two stuffed animals and two Barbies.

"No," Miles answered. "It's just what Mike told me about. You know. What happened. I don't want to talk about it. I think I'll make a shake. Want one?"

"No," she replied. "How about coming with me tomorrow? I've got three sessions."

"Don't worry about me," he answered. "I don't plan to be around here much, and if you like I'll stay away till you come back with Daisy."

She liked. On Monday morning Nancy got up early and as usual turned on the television set to watch cartoons. Maureen tried to speed up her morning run, but a touch of sunburn made it difficult to concentrate. After breakfast she was almost to the door with Nancy, who had put on her much-too-warm dress, when the phone rang. It was Billy.

"I caught you," he said. "I didn't know how early I could call and I was afraid I'd miss you. Remember those kids from Northwestern who did the first tape?"

"I remember," she said.

"Well they can do it again on Thursday. Think you can be ready by then?"

"I suppose," Maureen said. "I have an idea. How about doing the taping outside in the park?"

"Maybe," Billy answered. "Save us studio costs and maybe lights. All voice-over anyway, or almost. I'll call the kid who's directing. What's her name?"

"Jane Chong or Fong," Maureen said. "Look, Billy, I've got to run. Call me back tonight if you set it up. My class Thursday afternoon meets at the Y. We can shoot just before the sun goes down, if that's all right."

"I'll check," said Billy, and hung up.

Nancy gave signs of not wanting to go to camp, which was unusual for her and which led Maureen to the conclusion that her daughter had picked up something of what had been going on.

"You all right, Nancy?" she asked, giving the girl a hug at the front door of the community center.

"I'm fine," she said, "but I thought we could have a day together, just you and me. No Miles. No Helen. No Mike."

"We used to call that a Nancy-Mommie day when you were little," Maureen said, looking down at her daughter.

"We can still call it that," Nancy said, playing with the hair on her Barbie doll. "I'm not that big."

"Okay. I owe you one Nancy and Mommie day."

"When?"

"When?" Maureen repeated as another mother and child moved past them and through the door.

"That was Jules," Nancy said. "He eats his boogers. Gross. You know what I read they feed baby condors? Minced-up mice in soup and vulture vomit. That's more gross than Jules. Well, when?"

"Saturday," Maureen said, trying to remember if she had something scheduled for Saturday. "I think Saturday will be fine. I'll have to check and tell Miles, but let's say Saturday."

"Saturday," Nancy repeated soberly. She hugged her mother and went through the door without looking back.

The rest of the day went well. Maureen had two classes at her studio, and in both she managed to get into the energy of the routine. Apparently, the memories of the people taking the classes did not reach beyond two days. Maureen was surprised at how well she could move from the experience and images of yesterday's horror. As she hurried to pick up Nancy at the community center late in the afternoon, she told herself that Helen was most likely right, that there was more probability that the attack on Susan Breen and the murder of Roger Simcox were not related to her, but she simply couldn't accept that. She had to act, not sit and wait in case they were wrong. If the killers were out there, she had released them. She couldn't bide her time till they came, or killed others on their way to her.

So that evening, Maureen lied to Mike and Miles. She didn't have to lie to Nancy, who paid little attention to her excuses. She told them she had to talk to someone about a new course for a health club in a South Side neighborhood. She gave them details, names, problems—far more than they were interested in or needed—but guilt made her elaborate and apologize.

"It's fine," Mike said. "Miles wants to see the game and I promised Nancy she could meet Jerry Carmello, who, I have sworn, bears an uncanny resemblance to John Travolta."

"I don't want to meet him," Nancy said quickly. "You just talk to him and I'll watch."

"No," Miles kidded, "we'll tell him you want a big hug."

"Miles," Nancy cried. "Mom, tell him not to do that."

"You really think he's going to do that?" Maureen said, stepping back after brushing her daughter's hair. "Come on. He's just teasing you and you always go for it. Just be—"

"Cool," Nancy shouted angrily, glaring at her brother, who grinned.

"Very cool, princess," he said.

Mike was going to take them to a football game. It was supposed to be a pair of neighborhood teams in a new summer league. In fact, it was a bunch of better high school players who had gotten together for a head start on the season. The coaches could come and watch, say hello, but Illinois state high school rules said they couldn't really coach the kids. It was a little more flexible for Mike, who coached at a Catholic school and not a public school, but even there the question of ethics was a bit fuzzy, and Mike didn't want to step over the line. Summer football leagues were something new. The United States Football League and the Canadian Football League had made it acceptable to play in full uniform in ninety-degree heat without people saying you were out of your mind.

"I'll have them home by ten," he told Maureen as Nancy scampered to his car, clutching her Malibu Barbie. "Then I'll stay till you get back." He squeezed her hand.

"Thanks, Mike," she said.

"Don't be so quick to thank me. Nancy might fall for Jerry Carmello, and then you'd be stuck with one of the dumbest potential All-Americans it has been my confused fortune to coach."

Maureen talked to Helen as soon as she was alone, and Helen informed her that she had packed up and moved out on her husband. Considering the condition of the house, he wouldn't notice her departure or the missing items for days, possibly years. Helen also said that Susan Breen had still not regained consciousness and might never do so.

"Simcox's wife, Allie?"

"She's in town," Helen said, sounding very tired. "Between us she seems a damned unlikely murder suspect, but you never know. She's staying with relatives. We're not going to tell the press how to find her, but they might, and we'll be at the funeral just in case your shadows show up."

"Thanks," Maureen said.

"Thanks? We're doing it for her, not for you."

"What about the other witnesses?"

"Give us some credit, Maureen. Mr. Brinkmann is in his eighties and has a history of heart problems. We can't just ring his bell and say, 'Don't worry, but two killers may be around looking for you.' We want to protect citizens, not give them coronaries."

"But—"

"We'll keep an eye on him," Helen said.

"His address and phone number are in the telephone book," Maureen pushed.

"We talked about this before," Helen said, trying to control her irritation. "Look, I've had a hell of a day—make that *two* days. I promise I won't show up at your studio and take over your class. How about you not trying to tell me how to catch criminals and protect the public."

"I'm sorry, Helen, but—"

"Do me a favor. Close your door and windows. Turn on the air conditioner. Use Mike for a pillow and spend the evening watching horror movies on cable. I'll see you in the morning for our Bataan Death Run."

"You want to spend the night here?" Maureen asked, checking the clock. It was almost seven, and she wanted to get along. She didn't know how she would handle it if Helen said yes. Maureen had the feeling that the policewoman would see through her lie, catch something small, the way she answered a question.

"No, thanks," Helen sighed. "I'm on till midnight, and then I'm spending the night with a friend who'll take care of my belongings till I can sue the ass off my soon-to-be-ex-husband."

"I see," said Maureen as easily as possible.

"You think you see," Helen answered. "You think I packed and ran off to some other cop. Well, you're wrong, he's an investigator in the state's attorney's office, unmarried, and doesn't talk with his mouth full."

"What more could you ask?" Maureen said.

Helen laughed. "Don't do anything stupid, Mo," Helen said, much more easily. "I'll get back to you tomorrow."

"Thanks, take care," Maureen said, hanging up. She had never let anyone but David get away with calling her Mo. She hated the nickname, but somehow it was tolerable from Helen. Maybe it was because of what they had been through in Susan Breen's apartment. Maybe she was just ready to accept support. Maureen's father had called her MoMo, which took the masculine sting out of the name. She had vivid memories of her father. She remembered that he was of average height, with a big chest and muscles, which looked to her about like those of Superman in her brother's comic books. He had liked to pick her up when she was a little girl, turn her over, make her giggle, cuddle her. He had come within four percentage points of being seriously considered by the major leagues, but in three years of high-level minor-league baseball, Richard Philip Foran had never batted over .280. He was too smart to stay with a career that looked as if it were going nowhere. So, he had used the training he had obtained as an accountant to get a job. He kept playing baseball for fun and staying in shape. He also kept smoking heavily, which eventually killed him after four heart attacks.

Maureen realized with a small shock that she had a more vivid picture in her mind of her father than she did of David or even of Susan Breen, whom she had seen only two days before. But that image of her father, she realized, was frozen from several photographs in her mother's album and the remembered sensation of being turned upside down by strong hands and giggling, giggling while a voice said, "MoMo makes another giant circle."

Maureen couldn't sort it out and was somewhat annoyed that these memories had moved in. She knew the mind was amazingly tricky, that thoughts were insistent. When she was well into a routine, confident that she had left her thoughts and was floating, merging her mind and body, she'd suddenly realize that thoughts had nudged their way in and were bringing her back to a distorted past or a feared or desired future. If her thoughts were now trying to keep her from facing what she had decided upon, they were going to fail.

She called first and was relieved to hear that Monday night was Lou Parenti's night off from Bittie's. She had told herself that if he was working, she would go to the hot dog stand. That was what she had told herself, though she knew that a journey right to the center of the dark circle might be more than she could bring herself to do. Fortunately, she didn't have to. She had called him at home. She got the number from Barelli's sheet on the man who owned Bittie's, and then she had checked it in the phone book. So, she reasoned, if I can find it easily, they can too. But they know just where to find him almost every day anyway.

"It's my day off," he said over the phone, his voice a little gravelly.

"I won't take long, I promise," Maureen said.

"Come on over, after eight. We're going to my kid Andy's for a barbecue."

"I'll be there at eight," she said.

That was about it. She went out, locked the door behind her, and got into the car, which she had left in the driveway. The sun was just about down and the hint of a breeze came through the open windows of the car. Getting to Lou Parenti's house was easy. She drove to the Edens Expressway, got off at Cicero, took Cicero to Foster, and Foster till she hit Nagle. The ride took her into a neighborhood of small, working-class homes. The homes were mostly brick, variations of each other. They were small but on adequate plots of land, with small front yards and backyards big enough for barbecues, small cement patios, and children's swing sets.

There was plenty of parking on the street, and she pulled up in front of 5433. Before she reached the front door, up three stone steps, the door opened, and he stepped out. He looked the same as he had when she had last seen him, no heavier, no older. He wore saggy shorts, a loose-fitting button-down shirt, and a baseball cap.

"Mrs. Dietz," he said, holding out his hand. "How are you?"

She shook his hand and let him lead her through the door into the cool house. A window air conditioner was humming. As they stepped into the small living room, Lou Parenti took off his baseball cap to wipe his brow, and the years suddenly showed. His once-brown hair was now completely gray.

"You all right?" he said, looking at her.

"Fine," she answered.

"You looked . . . the hair, right? You knew me when I had that mop of brown. It happened fast. My wife likes it, says I look like Jeff Chandler. First of all, I look nothing like Jeff Chandler. I look, if she wants the truth, like Henry Kissinger with a smashed nose. Second of all, who the hell remembers Jeff Chandler? You remember Jeff Chandler?" He pointed to a chair with a flower-patterned slipcover, and she sat down.

"I remember Jeff Chandler," she said. "Cochise."

"I guess," he said. "Can I get you a drink? Coke, beer? Connie even has Diet Pepsi and caffeine-free everything. I get it cheap cause I'm in the business. I think it tastes like cow piss, but Connie likes it. Don't say it. I know what you're thinking. Does this clown go around tasting cow piss to compare it to every-thing-removed cola? The answer is of course he does, but he don't tell it to everyone."

"No drink," Maureen said with a forced smile. It was evi-dent that the man was uncomfortable, overdoing his amiability.

"No drink, right. Mind if I have a beer?"

She didn't mind, and he left the room while she looked

around. There was a television set, a sofa with a slipcover matching the one she was sitting on, a table with some magazines on it, and a lamp. On the wall was a painting of a boy and a girl. The girl was older, about eleven or twelve, and she had her arm around the boy, who was three or four years younger. They were what Darla called "dolled up." The resemblance between both children and Lou Parenti was evident and, Maureen thought, rather touching.

He came bouncing back with a glass of beer in one hand and a can of Miller's in the other. She had the distinct feeling that if she were not there he would be drinking directly from the can but that she was making him feel awkward. He sat on the sofa, took a sip, and said, "Okay, Mrs. Dietz, what can I do for you?"

"Your wife isn't here, Mr. Parenti?"

"My name is Lou, or Bittie," he said. "She's at my son's. I'm going to pick her up later. The party went on a little longer than we thought and——"

"And," Maureen said gently, "you didn't want her to be here when we talked."

He picked up his beer, nodding his head, and took a big drink. "Connie has a lot of feeling for you, sympathy, you know what I mean? That night, when I came home, she got hysterical, kept talking about how awful it must have been for you. Then when you . . . you know."

"When I had my breakdown," Maureen said without emotion.

Lou shrugged. "Right," he said, pouring more beer to keep his hands busy, though the glass was almost full. "Connie wouldn't stop thinking of it. Our kids are older than yours, but, you know how being a mother is?"

"I know," Maureen said, though she was sure she had never felt the kind of empathy for a stranger that Lou Parenti was describing.

"She's been after me since it happened to get out of the business or open a place in the suburbs. I'd been robbed three times before that night, and I've been hit six more since then. Last time I shot the guy, winged a dumb little Puerto Rican kid, sixteen. I don't know why I'm going on like this, but you know what I mean about Connie. So, now that that's over, what brings you here?"

Maureen wasn't sure how to begin. "Did you see the *Sun-Times* article or the interview with me on television?"

"The article," he said. "Neighbor saw the television, told us about it." He looked at her curiously and took another gulp of beer.

"Susan Breen," Maureen said, watching his eyes.

"Susan Breen," he repeated clearly, not recognizing anything in the name.

"She was behind the counter, the girl behind the counter the night it happened," Maureen explained.

Lou closed his eyes and put his hand to his forehead. "Right," he said. "Susie. God, I haven't thought about her in years. She quit a little after all that happened. I don't know what happened to her."

"She finished college, got a job at a television station, and was nearly beaten to death two nights ago," Maureen said, watching his face carefully.

At first, the news simply didn't get through, didn't register, didn't have any meaning. He looked at her as if she were mad, coming into his living room telling him about the violence that had fallen on someone he had long ago forgotten. "I'm sorry to hear that," he said, "but . . . hey, wait. She wasn't the one the other day, the one on television. Her boyfriend or something got killed the day before? That one?"

"Her boyfriend was Roger Simcox," Maureen went on. "He was in your stand the night my husband was murdered."

Lou fidgeted with his beer, put it down, picked it up again, and said, since she was saying nothing, "So? It seems kind of weird to me that they should know each other so close like that after all these years, but I've heard stranger things, some of them true. I've got——"

And then it hit him. He stopped, his mouth coming open slightly, and stared back at Maureen, who had sat up, folding her hands on her lap. "You're trying to say there's some connection between your husband's killing, the TV story on you, and what happened to them?" Maureen nodded. "And you're here——"

"To warn you," she said. "The story on me brought those killers back. One of them called me the night I did that television interview. He said they were coming for me. I think they're trying to kill all the witnesses."

"How many of us were there?" he asked, taking it all seriously for the first time.

"Seven still alive, counting my children. The easiest ones to find are my family, the old man, Mr. Brinkmann, and you."

"Why are you here and not the cops?" he asked.

"They don't believe it," she said. "They think it's just a coincidence, that Simcox and Susan Breen were killed by a jealous lover or a killer hired by his wife, that some harmless lunatic called to threaten me. What do you think?"

"I think," he said, standing up, "that I'm going to start carrying my gun. I think that if I see either one of those loonies who killed your old man, I'll shoot them in the face and worry about apologizing later. I think you just scared the hell out of me."

And, Maureen thought, he did look frightened, but he also looked determined and capable.

"Now you tell me something," he said, looking down at her, his voice suddenly gentle. "Why don't you look scared?"

"I am," she said. "Terrified. I just don't show it. I get a pain in my chest and I can't breathe and I have nightmares about the men who killed David, the men who smashed in our car window that night and tried to get me, to hurt my children. Mr. . . . Lou. I've learned to control it, but what's happened over the last week has . . . I am, to tell the truth, working hard to keep from letting go."

"Let go," he said with a shrug. "I'm letting go. I'm scared and goddamn mad. Hey, I don't remember that Susie kid very well. There've been maybe sixty kids like her working for me, most of them decent and going nowhere with their lives, kids from that neighborhood around Diversey, honest kids. Someone almost killed a kid like that. I'm mad. The one who almost killed her might be after me. I'm scared. It's simple."

"Not for me," Maureen said, getting up. "Just be careful. If I hear anything more, I'll let you know."

He took her offered hand. "You just came here to warn me?"

"Yes," she said.

"You want a gun?" he said, seriously and softly, as if someone might have suddenly started eavesdropping.

"No, thanks," she said. "I have a friend with a gun. Besides, I run fast as hell."

"For what it's worth to you," he said, opening the door and putting his cap back on his head, "I think about what happened that night a lot, maybe too much. A thing like that . . . In a way I hope you're wrong and those two guys are dead or on the moon or something. Another way, I hope they show up, walk through my door so I can have the satisfaction of ending their scummy lives. I'd probably piss in my pants, but believe me, I'd do it."

Maureen had a sudden vision of the younger Lou coming around the corner of his shop with a knife in hand. She saw the big killer throw something heavy at Lou, who didn't back away. She heard once again a sound she hadn't remembered she heard that night. It was the clanging of that heavy metal bar hitting the brick wall and clattering to the cement sidewalk. "I know you would," she said.

"You take care of yourself," he said, escorting her to her car and opening the door for her.

"Thanks, Lou," she said. "And tell your wife . . ."

"Connie."

"Tell Connie I said thanks."

"I'll tell her," he said, closing the door and backing away. "But do me a favor. If you find out something and you call here, don't tell her what it's about. I don't want her scared. I can be scared enough for both of us. Damn, you make your life selling chili dogs and wind up in the Wild West."

She looked at him once more in the light from the window of his house. It was fully dark now and crickets were chirping. He was bowlegged, probably from all those years of standing at the grill, and he didn't look all that young, but she was sure if anyone could handle what might be coming, it would be this man.

Maureen made a left turn at the next corner and then another left and went on till she hit Foster. She turned right and headed back toward Cicero, thinking, planning, juggling ideas. Her neck felt hot and gritty. She rubbed at it with a wad of Kleenex and reached for the radio, turned it on, and punched WGN, not remembering if the Cubs were at home or on the road. If they were home, the game was long over, since the Cubs were the lone holdouts against night baseball.

There was no game. "Extension 75" with Milt Rosenberg was on. She half listened to a discussion of Henry Kissinger and the Nixon administration. Two or three times she considered turning it off but gradually found that she could concentrate on what was being said.

When she hit Evanston, she wondered if it was too late to call old Mr. Brinkmann, whether Helen was right, that he was too old to frighten. She wondered whether, on the other hand, she should have gone to see the old man before seeing Lou Parenti. More guilt, she thought. She turned the radio off and planned the rest of her evening, half an hour with Nancy, if she was still awake, some discussion and a snack with Miles, if he wasn't already locked in his room, and a decision to be made about whether to invite Mike to stay. She didn't want him to think he was staying as protection. On the other hand, she didn't want him to stay thinking that it was his reward for being a surrogate father. On the other . . . no, she reminded herself, unless she drew on *Star Wars* imagery, there were only two hands. In truth, she didn't want to get into bed with Mike, not tonight. She wanted to go in the basement, the cool basement, and go through the entire routine she would use for the videotaping on Thursday . . . to exhaust herself. She looked forward to doing the routine, flowing into it to the sound of Mozart's No. 29 or No. 39.

When she turned down her street, she was sure that she would kindly, and with tact, send Mike home. He would understand. Mike always understood. For some reason, Mike's flawless understanding suddenly irritated her.

Normally she would simply have pulled into the driveway and left the car there, but Miles had taken to driving out to get a late-night Dairy Queen, and he had a hell of a time backing the car out. So Maureen carefully backed the car in. If Miles went out, he could pull it in and leave it. She backed into the driveway, turned off the lights and the engine, and then decided that she might be blocking the sidewalk. So she turned on the engine again and then the lights.

A van, its lights off, appeared in front of her, driving slowly down the one-way street. Her headlights hit it, and she saw two figures in the front as the driver stepped on the gas and moved out of her beams. One figure, leaning forward, had been average or even small, the other large, quite large, and Maureen was sure the large figure had looked directly at her. Then the van picked up speed and passed on.

She went into the house, forcing herself to walk slowly. Once inside, she double-locked the door and turned to accept the reassuring coolness of the air conditioner and the sight of Mike sitting shoeless on the brown, reclining chair in the living room with a book in front of him and his reading glasses on his nose.

"Hi," he said, looking up. "If I am going to do more baby-sitting for you, I'm going to start bringing my own books or give you some for trumped-up occasions. You haven't got much of a library, lady." He held up the copy of *The Golden Bough* that Maureen had bought almost twenty years earlier for a college class. "You could use some poetry in your life, Wonder Woman."

"Miles and Nancy," she said, stepping toward him. "Are they all right?"

He looked at her more seriously now and removed his glasses as he sat up. "Miles is in his room. Nancy is in bed. Jerry the halfback stole her heart, but she doesn't think he looks like John Travolta. The game wasn't much so we got an ice cream and came back early." He got out of the chair and took a few steps toward her, looking concerned. "What's wrong, Maureen?"

"I think I saw them."

"You saw who?" he asked, starting to reach out to support her. He stopped short, ready if she wanted him, but not offering more than she was willing to accept. It hadn't taken him long to recognize this aspect of their relationship. It was one of the things that made him comfortable for Maureen. It might be hard holding onto herself, but letting him enfold her might set her back a lifetime.

She motioned for him to sit down again, and she sat across from him on the brown sofa.

"I think I saw the two men who killed David," she said,

saying each word as carefully as she thought James Mason might have said them.

"Where?" Mike said, watching her face, his hands on his knees.

"Outside, just now. They drove by in a van with the lights off. I saw them in the headlights of my car. The big one just looked at me."

"I have a feeling you are not going to like my next question, but I'm asking it anyway," Mike said. "Are you *sure* it was them? You've been thinking about them, dwelling on them, and then two people drive past and you catch them in your headlights. This man, you're *sure* it was the same one?"

"Paulette next door said she saw a van with two men, an orange van driving around the neighborhood the other day," Maureen countered slowly, calmly.

"The van you saw, was it orange?"

"I don't know," Maureen answered. "It looked dark. There's more. A van was right behind me when I went to the television studio to talk to Susan Breen. It parked in the lot."

"And there were two men in it?" Mike was beginning to sound like Erika, that always reasonable Erika back at the institute.

"I'm not sure. A woman got out and came in with some story about being lost or something and—"

"Maureen," Mike said, reasonably, "you *could* be wrong."

"I could be wrong, but I don't think so," she said.

"One last question," Mike said, playing with his reading glasses. "If it was them and they have been around following you, why did they go after Simcox and Susan Breen? Why haven't they tried for you?"

"I don't *know*," Maureen said, closing her eyes, willing that throbbing in her chest not to come. "Maybe they're saving me for last."

"Come on, Maureen. . . ."

"All right," she said, opening her eyes again. "I just don't know. If the men in that van . . ."

"If?" asked Mike.

"They are," Maureen said. "Do you or do you not believe me?"

"Doesn't matter," said Mike, getting up again and walking to the window. He pulled the closed brown shade to one side and looked out at the street. "I don't see how we can take a chance on you being wrong. I think we've got to assume that they're there and feel better later if we're wrong."

"I'll settle for that," Maureen said.

"Besides," Mike went on, turning to her at the window, "I don't know anyone less likely to imagine things than you. They probably wrote 'Miss Level-Head' next to your high school picture."

This time Maureen got up, folded her arms in front of her, and smiled, but it was a humorless smile. "You didn't know me back then," she said. "Before my life changed. I was your typically disarranged and repressed American woman. Worse."

"You couldn't be." He grinned back. "There was only one archetype, and I married her. What do we do now? About them. Call the police?"

"Which police, the Evanston police? David was killed in Chicago. Simcox and Susan Breen were attacked in Chicago. Besides, they'd ask the same questions you asked and be one hell of a lot less sympathetic about my answers than you."

"So?" he asked.

"Helen Katz, I suppose," she said.

"She called," he said. "Left a number for you. It's by the phone in the kitchen."

Maureen took a few steps toward the phone but stopped when Mike called out.

"Maureen. When you're off that phone, I'd like you to

come back and sit with me on the sofa and let me put my arms around you. If it makes it easier to think you're doing it for me and not for you, that's fine. Because it is."

"We'll see," she said without looking back at him, and reached for the phone. The number was in Chicago, but she couldn't tell what part. It rang four times after she dialed, and a man answered.

"Helen Katz?" she asked.

"Just a second," said the man. There was a scrambling on the other end, and Helen came on.

"Yes?" she asked.

"It's Maureen. You called."

"One of those good news, bad news situations," Helen said. "Good news is that Susan Breen looks like she's going to live. It'll take a while to see if she'll have brain problems, but it looks good. Plastic surgery looks more than likely, but that's down the road."

"You saved her life, Helen," Maureen said.

"Maybe we *both* did, but there's no reason to celebrate. I haven't given you the bad news. The old man, Brinkmann."

Maureen blanched and turned to look at Mike, who was sitting back against the sofa, looking at her, his expression concerned. "Someone killed him," Maureen said with a cold shudder, her voice flat yet angry.

"Hell no," Helen said. "Weirdest damn thing. A few hours ago someone knocked on his door, said they were the police, wanted to talk to him about your husband's murder. The old man opened the door and saw someone there with a club in his hand. The old man didn't have his glasses on, couldn't see clearly, but that's what he said he saw, someone with a club in his hand."

"Well?"

"Well, that's it," sighed Helen. "Whoever it was stood there looking at him, whispered something, turned around, and went away. It doesn't make sense."

"But it does suggest a tie-in between what happened to Simcox and Susan Breen," Maureen urged. "Unless this is just another typical moment in the lives of Chicago citizens."

"It does cut into the odds," Helen agreed.

"Especially when I think I saw the Vanbeebers tonight," Maureen added dramatically.

"You saw them?"

Maureen went through her story again, and Helen listened silently.

"It's not enough to hang a warrant on," she said when Maureen had finished. "Maybe we can get something more. What time is it? It's not too late. How do you feel about my picking you up and both of us going to talk to the old man, try to get more out of him? You have someone to stay with Miles and Nancy?"

"Mike is here," she said, looking over at Mike, who nodded.

"It'll be easier and on the way if you pick me up, okay?" Helen said.

A flash of fear and anger touched Maureen. Hadn't she just said two killers were out there? Wasn't anyone taking her seriously? "Right, give me an address and be outside."

When Maureen put down the receiver, Mike held up *The Golden Bough* and said, "I'm up to taboos on intercourse with strangers. It's just getting interesting. You sure you want to go back out there tonight?"

"I'm sure," she said. "Just come outside till I'm in the car and on the way."

The moment was suddenly awkward. Maureen walked over to Mike and kissed him. She had meant it to be reassuring but wasn't sure she succeeded.

Outside, she walked slowly to the car, stopping her urge to dash and throw herself in. She locked the door and repressed the images from too many horror movies in which someone sat up suddenly in the rear seat. But she couldn't drive without looking.

There was no one there. She waved at Mike, who stood watching from the steps, and took off down the driveway, looking down the one-way street for a parked van, but there was none. She watched her rearview mirror carefully and drove slowly. There was almost no traffic on the side streets, and she was sure that no one was following her. When she hit Oakton and went toward the city, she felt a tug of uncertainty, a twinge that maybe, just maybe she had been wrong. Just some harmless people in a harmless van. Maybe.

Helen was waiting outside the apartment building for which she had given Maureen the address. She was wearing a black skirt and blouse and had her hair tied back. The familiar denim bag was over her shoulder, and she shifted it to the floor when she got into the car.

"Moving in with Rutgers 1970 is not proving to be such a good idea," was her first comment. "I got one night of respect and consideration followed by a day—today—of creeping assumptions about my time. He came close to complaining about my going out. I'm developing a theory about men. They're worth about two or three days at most."

"Very optimistic," Maureen said, relieved to have Helen next to her in the car.

"Who's talking about optimism?" she said, digging in her bag for something and pulling out a package of gum. "I'm talking about truth. Would you like four or five pieces of Juicy Fruit? I've been having this urge to go back to smoking since I walked out on Mojo, but I'm fighting it."

The conversation stayed light till they got to the apartment house where August Brinkmann lived. It was a massive condominium, a new building with the landscaping not even complete, one of two giant towers in a moat of mud, accessible only by a concrete strip of sidewalk.

"If he looks jumpy," Helen said, "we back off. Remember, he's old and sick."

Maureen nodded, following Helen into the lobby. They found the bank of buttons, and Helen pushed. "Yes?" came a male voice that did not sound old.

"Police," Helen answered.

"We already talked to the police," the male voice said.

"Something new came up," Helen shouted into the mesh speaker. "It's rather important. We won't take long."

In answer, the sound of a buzzer shot through the lobby. Maureen opened the inner door. One of the elevators was open and dark, being worked on or finished. They got into one of the others as a couple in their fifties stepped off and moved past them. On the way up, the two women said nothing, simply watched the numbers change. When 38 appeared on the panel, the elevator stopped, and the doors slid open smoothly.

They found the right apartment and Helen knocked, ignoring the white bell button on the door.

"Yes?" came a man's voice from inside.

"Police," she said, taking her wallet from her bag and holding it at her side as the door came open on a chain. She showed the badge to the man inside. He closed the door and loosened the chain as Helen whispered to Maureen, "Even I could snap a chain like that with a good run at the door."

"What do you want?" the man asked, backing away to let them in but looking at the two women suspiciously. He was somewhere over fifty, slightly overweight and wearing a dark suit and tie. His most prominent features were a large, pouting lower lip and thin, dark dyed hair flattened against his scalp.

"We just have a few questions to ask Mr. Brinkmann," Helen said. "It won't take long."

"The police were already here," the man said with irritation, walking into the small apartment. "I don't think they believed him. My father isn't the easiest person to get along with, but he's not senile."

They were standing in the living room, which seemed to be

the only full room in what looked like a studio apartment. It was large, and there was a bed in the corner covered by a spread designed to make it look like a lounge. The effect was a failure. There was a small kitchen alcove with a table big enough for three chairs. Seated at one of the chairs was an old man, the same old man who had witnessed David's murder.

To Maureen he looked far different from that man glimpsed once many years ago, but she now expected such changes. This man looked ancient. He was small, wearing thick glasses. His sparse white hair was wispy, and snowy strands of tufted hair protruded from his ears. He wore a clean, worn white shirt and slightly baggy trousers held up by suspenders. The apartment was far too warm, and the air conditioner in the window was, if not off, turned on very low.

"Mr. Brinkmann," Helen said. "I'm a police officer."

"That's what the other one said," the old man answered irritably. There was a single cookie on a plate in front of him, which he pushed away as if the cookie had asked him the offending question.

"The man who came to your door earlier tonight?" Helen prompted.

He turned to look at her as if she were an idiot, and took in Maureen. Something about her made him drop the look, and he stared at her as if trying to remember where he had seen that face before.

"Mr. Brinkmann," Helen went on. The man who had let them into the apartment had backed out of the conversation and moved to a chair in the living room to watch from a distance. "Can you tell us more about the man you saw?"

"I didn't say it was a man," the old man said with a clever smile. "I said someone came to my door and said 'police.' Might have been a woman with a deep voice. My hearing is almost as bad as my seeing. When the day comes that I can't taste food, I'm going to shoot myself."

"Pa," said the man from the living room. "You're not going to shoot yourself. Don't go around telling the police you're going to shoot yourself. You don't even have a gun."

"You can go into Ward's and buy a gun," the old man said.

"The person who came to the door," Helen went on, patiently glancing at Maureen. "What did he or she look like? Big, small, young, old. What was the person wearing?"

"I know what I wasn't wearing," the old man said. "I wasn't wearing my glasses. I had them right here on the table. The one at the door wasn't big, not small but not big. I think more young than old. It was a crazy."

"The club," Helen prompted.

The old man reached for a cookie and took a small bite, his face anticipating a bitter taste. Apparently, the cookie wasn't bitter. He took a second bite. "The person at my door had a club or something," he said. "I don't know."

"And he . . . the person said something to you?"

"Looked at me for a long time," said the old man. "Then said, 'You're an old man.' I know damn well I'm an old man. I don't need any crazy people coming to my door with clubs and telling me what I already know. Tomorrow another one will probably be by to let me know it's hot outside. I moved into this building because my son over there told me it would be safer than where I was living. You call that safer, people coming to your door with clubs?"

"No," Maureen said.

It was the first thing she had said, and the old man turned to her. A piece of cookie crumb clung to his lower lip. "I know you from where?" he said.

"I think we met briefly a long time ago," Maureen said.

"Before Elsa died?" he asked.

"Yes," Maureen said.

The old man looked down at the cookie and seemed to be thinking of something far removed from the present.

"Is there anything else you can tell us about the person who came to your door?" Helen said gently. "Clothes."

"'He wore clothes,'" the old man said. "That's a joke."

"A good one," said Helen with a small chuckle.

"I once met George Burns," the old man said. "People say I look a little like him."

"You do," Maureen said, though the man looked nothing like George Burns.

"You said 'he,'" Helen prompted. "'He wore clothes.' You're pretty sure it was a man, not a woman, then."

"If you asked me to bet my pension, I'd say I don't know. If you're just asking me, it was a man. What he was wearing, I don't remember."

Behind the man's thick lenses, Maureen thought she saw tears in his eyes. She reached out to touch Helen's arm, and the policewoman nodded, understanding.

"I think that will do it for now, Mr. Brinkmann," Helen said. "If anything more comes up, we'll be in touch. Meanwhile, don't open your door to strangers."

"You think this person is dangerous?" came the voice of the son from the living room.

"If he wanted to hurt your father, he could," Helen said, moving to the door. "I think it's nothing, just some drunk, but as a general rule, it's not a good idea to open your doors to strangers, even in a big place like this."

"I'll stay with him tomorrow," the son said, holding the door open for the two women. Maureen looked over his shoulder at the old man, who was prying a raisin or nut loose from the cookie in front of him.

"Probably a good idea," Helen said lightly, shifting her shoulder bag.

"To tell the truth," the man said as they stepped into the hallway, "I didn't think the police would give so much attention to a complaint like this from an old man. It makes you feel a little better about the police."

"Thanks," Helen said, with what Maureen could see was a false smile.

When the man closed the door behind them, Helen strode to the elevators and pressed the button. They didn't speak until the elevator came; they stepped in and the doors closed behind them.

"Well?" Maureen asked.

"It should tie in to Simcox and Breen, to your case," Helen said, clearly puzzled, "but why didn't he hit him? Because he saw he was an old man? The Vanbeebers don't seem like the kind to help old people across the street. I don't know. Maybe we are dealing with someone else, two someones, three different cases, a city gone crazy in the heat. Shit, give me a description of that van when we get downstairs, and I'll try to get it checked out."

Maureen drove Helen back to the apartment where she had picked her up, and Helen got out without enthusiasm.

"Sure you don't want to go out for a drink or coffee or come up?" Helen said.

"No, thanks," Maureen said. "You don't want to go up there, do you?"

"No," she said, "an artificial relationship takes too damn much work. I'll see you in the morning if you're still planning to run."

"Every morning," Maureen said.

Helen got out, closed the door behind her after pushing down the lock button, and took about ten long strides to the front door of the apartment building, her denim bag draped over her shoulder. Maureen waited till she was in and then headed home after stopping at an open Dunkin' Donuts on Howard and Western for a dozen muffins for the family breakfast.

It was slightly after midnight when she got back home. No

van came down the street behind her. Inside the house Mike was back in the recliner, book in hand, a cup of coffee on the table.

"Well?" he asked, getting up.

"As well as can be expected," she said. "Sorry I'm not much for jokes at my best."

"At your best you don't need jokes," he countered. "Miles came down looking for you. I told him where you went. I didn't mention the guy in the van. I think you better talk to him if he's still awake. He looked pretty shaken."

"He's still up," Maureen said, kicking off her shoes. "I'll go up. Would you like to stay around a while longer?"

He tilted his head to one side and gave her a quizzical look. "Meaning?"

"Meaning," she said, handing him the box of muffins, "I'd like to do a half hour or so in the exercise room and come up and find you here. Meaning you have a lot of reason and perfect right to walk out of here because I take you for granted."

"That's the way you look at it," he said, picking up his coffee cup and heading toward the kitchen. "The way I look at it is it's nice to be needed. And having sex occasionally for a change isn't too bad either."

"Well." She laughed. "You're honest."

"Honesty can lose you a ball game," he said. "My college football coach said that, a great man. Lost his job at the age of sixty for punching a sophomore tackle who wouldn't do ten laps in full uniform in weather pretty much like it's been today."

Maureen couldn't see him now as she started up the stairs toward Miles.

"Maybe you could skip the ten laps," he called. "Or at least let up and not put in a full half hour in the basement tonight."

"Maybe," she called back, knowing that she would have to get at least that much tonight if she was going to control the

—— 203 ——

threat in her chest, if she was going to breathe. "We'll talk about it when I get down."

She could hear him running the water in the kitchen, rinsing his coffee cup. The sound faded as she went up the stairs, blended with the voices of the television behind Miles's door.

"Miles," she called, knocking on the door.

"What?" he answered.

"Let's talk."

"I'm watching a movie," he said.

"Let's talk," she repeated.

For a moment she thought he wasn't going to open the door, but then she heard his bed creak and his footsteps as he padded across the hard wood in his stocking feet. Then the lock pulled back, and the door opened to let out the sound of the television.

Maureen looked into her son's eyes and then looked away. She wasn't sure, but she thought he might have been crying.

# 6

Cal was as happy as a rat in a graveyard, but Marty knew it wouldn't last long. Nothing lasted long for Cal. Parts, pieces of wire, fuses, all kinds of junk were spread out on his bed, staining the khaki blanket. It was early morning but so hot already that they had the fan on high. It only had two speeds, low and high. The television was on without the sound. Endorra the witch had just turned Darren into an ape. Marty didn't give a crap. He was just hot and bored.

"Needs a wire," Cal said, spitting on a little piece of metal and rubbing it on his already stained sleeve. "I can cut a piece off the lamp."

"Just be sure the lamp still works when you're done with it," Marty said, sitting back in the chair, which creaked under his weight. Darren's boss Larry came in and saw the ape, and Marty lifted up his foot to kick the television off.

"Kick it like that and you'll break it," Cal said, holding up a small wire cutter.

"Then you'll have something else to fix. How about not getting those little pieces of shit all over the floor?"

Marty had picked up the radio from one of the rooms down

the hall. They had been passing when they saw the door open and no one inside. Cal had nudged Marty and pulled the radio, tucking it under his shirt. They were back in their room around the corner before anyone showed up.

"Did him a favor," Cal said when they got back to the room. "Teach the son of a bitch not to leave his things laying around. Teach him to keep his door locked."

It turned out that the radio didn't work and wasn't much of a radio in the first place, but Cal had gotten to work on it when they got back in the room.

"We'll get her Thursday," Marty said, unbuttoning his shirt.

"Thursday," Cal repeated. "That's how many days?"

"Three," said Marty, "but we can do things before then. We can do things."

"The hot dog man," Cal hissed, searching the floor for his shoes. "The guy who came at us with a knife."

"Maybe so," Marty said with a smile, though he didn't give much of a damn for the hot dog man. Cal could have him. It was the woman he couldn't stop thinking about. It was her he *wanted*. He lay back and closed his eyes, listening to Cal playing with the radio and the sound of voices through the thin walls of the YMCA.

On Tuesday morning just before she finished breakfast, the phone call came. Maureen had been up at the usual time, run at the usual time, but without Helen, who had a sudden shift change and an appointment to see a lawyer about her divorce. Maureen didn't like admitting that she missed Helen on the run. The goal of the run, the theory of her whole regimen, was that one entered into the movement, not social contact. She tried to tell herself that it was really Helen's company before and after the run that she enjoyed, but she knew that wasn't completely true. The answer was simple. Without seeking it consciously, she had made what looked like her first potentially close friend since

David's murder, and it bothered her. One more person in the circle of her emotions meant one more person to worry about, feel for, be ready to lose.

The phone rang again, and Nancy said, "Hurry, Mom, we're gonna be late, and we're going to the beach on the buses. Hurry up."

"Hello," she said, dropping her big YMCA bag on the floor and putting one hand on her hip.

"Donnelly," came the voice. "Got a minute?"

"No more than that. I've got to get my daughter to summer camp."

"Simcox, Breen, Brinkmann," he said.

"How?"

"How did I find out? There's a little bar on lower Wacker, Billy Goats. You've heard of it?"

"I've heard of it," Maureen said, trying to think ahead, plan, head off what was coming.

"Well," Donnelly went on, "reporters go there and cops go there who like to share a bottle and a greasy burger and show how important they are by letting little pieces of information drop. You can pick up more information for the price of a couple of beers than you can with a bribe. But don't quote me on that. What do you know or what are you going to tell me?"

"I . . . all right. I think they might be here, the Vanbeebers. I think they might have killed Roger Simcox and attacked Susan Breen and gone after August Brinkmann. How's that for a story?"

"Fine," Donnelly said. "Maybe worth the bottom of page one, depending on what's going on in Lebanon. Are the police giving you protection?"

"Not particularly," Maureen said, looking at Nancy standing at the door, shifting from one leg to the other and pointing to her new wristwatch. "They're not sure the Vanbeebers are involved. Why don't you ask them about it?"

"You can be sure I will," he said. "I'm also going to talk to

—— 207 ——

the other witnesses if I can: Louis Parenti, the guy who owns Bittie's, and Simcox's wife, if I can find her. Funeral's this afternoon. She should be there."

"She should be," Maureen agreed.

"There was another witness," Donnelly went on, ignoring or missing her sarcasm. "A black man. Any idea how we can find him?"

"None," she said. "That's all I have to say, Mr. Donnelly."

"One last question. Off the record."

"Off the record," she said, motioning to Nancy that she would be off the phone in a second.

"Why are you answering my questions? Why are you talking to me?"

"I want those men caught," she said. "And I don't want that old man or Lou Parenti or Mrs. Simcox or me or my children hurt. I want everyone protected and the police moving every rock in five counties to find those killers."

"And," he said, "when did you decide this?"

"When you called a few minutes ago, Mr. Donnelly."

"Can we send someone out to take a few pictures?" he said.

"Good-bye, Mr. Donnelly," Maureen said, starting to hang up the phone.

"Wait. If you don't cooperate, we'll send someone out anyway, and then there'll be a scene, and we'll get the pictures, and they won't be nearly as good as if you cooperate."

"You're good at your job, Mr. Donnelly," she said. "You're a son of a bitch, but you are good. I'll give you that."

"I hear you're pretty good at your job yourself. Take care of yourself."

He hung up first, and his voice had made it clear that her words had not touched him. She, Nancy, Miles—all of them—were just a story. He was using them, and in honesty, Maureen decided, she was now using him.

"We are going to be late, Mother," Nancy said, near tears.

"If we miss the bus, I'll drive you to the beach myself."

Appeased, Nancy nodded, and Maureen urged her out the door, telling her that she would pick her up as usual, wondering if she should make some arrangement to get Miles out of the house. If things went well, there would probably be police watching all of them by the time the story came out the next morning. She also realized, as she started the car, that the press questions and calls wouldn't stop with Donnelly. They would all be after her. It was too late. In a way, Maureen felt as if she had taken another step against the Vanbeebers.

The next move was now theirs.

While she had been talking to Donnelly, the throbbing in her chest had begun threatening, and she feared that she wouldn't be able to take a deep breath.

"Mom," Nancy said from the back seat as they drove.

"What honey?"

"Are those men you were talking about on the phone, the ones you were telling Helen about, the ones who killed Daddy, are they going to kill us?"

Oh God, Maureen mouthed silently, looking into the rear-view mirror at her daughter, who sat with barrettes in her hair, wearing a blue-and-white dress. Nancy was clutching her ever-present Barbie and looking up at the back of her mother's head. She didn't look frightened, just enormously curious.

"No, they are not," Maureen said firmly. "The police are going to catch them soon. Try not to be afraid, Nancy. Someone will be with you all the time till they're caught, and I've been thinking of sending you and Miles out to Grandma Darla. How would that be?"

They were a few blocks from the community center, but Maureen was determined to finish the conversation even if it did mean driving Nancy to the beach.

"Would you like to come with us?" Nancy asked.

"No, I've got to help catch those men."

"Okay, Mom," Nancy said. "I'm not afraid during the day, only a little at night. And Mom?"

"Yes, baby."

"Miles is afraid too. Don't tell him, but I've heard him crying at night. If Miles is afraid, anyone would be afraid."

She pulled into a loading zone next to the center. The huge yellow bus was parked in front, children carrying towels standing in a line outside the closed doors.

"I talked to Miles about it last night," Maureen said, turning to look at Nancy. "They'll catch the men, and everything will be all right again."

"Miles says when Daddy died you went crazy and went away. Is that true?"

"It's true," Maureen said, praying that she could keep the tears from coming. "But I won't go crazy again, and I won't go away. I'm much stronger now."

"You are one tough broad," Nancy said.

"Where did you get that?"

"When I went to your class at the Y two weeks ago, that fat woman who pretended to like me said it when she thought I couldn't hear. Hey, I gotta go. Can we stop for Thirty-One Flavors after camp?"

"Sure," said Maureen. Nancy tucked her Barbie and her yellow towel under her arm, leaned over the seat to kiss her mother, and hurried out of the door, slamming it behind her.

Maureen's morning session in her studio went smoothly, though she never got fully into the routine. Two women stopped to talk to her when it was over, and one, a hard-working, well-preserved blond woman in her fifties, named Ann Townsend, invited her to bring her family over to her home on Sunday for swimming in her pool and a picnic. Maureen said she would think it over and let her know, but she knew she wouldn't go.

She had time before her one o'clock session to call Billy, who confirmed that the taping could be done outdoors at the lake and had to start no later than five if there was to be enough light, which meant she would have to use her YMCA class for the tape. There was also a chance that they couldn't get the whole tape done in one session, but the young woman who was setting it up, Jane Chong, said she would try.

She dug out the list of people in the afternoon class at the Y, Xeroxed it along with the phone numbers, and borrowed a felt marker to make a sign telling the group to meet in the park on Thursday. She Xeroxed the sign, drove the six blocks to the Y, and put it on the bulletin board in the lobby, where a couple of old men she had seen around the place were talking on a bench. She knew the men were longtime residents of the Y and had rooms upstairs. She had even known one of their names, that of the one with the bent back who carried the cane, but she had forgotten it.

She excused herself and reached over them, paying no attention to the complaint of the man with the cane. "I'm telling you," the man said, "you can't leave anything alone. Can you imagine stealing the damn radio right off the table when I was in the next room? People today . . ."

Maureen got back to the gym just in time for the one o'clock class. She announced the taping on Thursday, received enthusiastic agreement from everyone to appear, and handed each of them a Xeroxed reminder. In spite of everything, the memory of lost breath, the threat of throbbing in the chest, it went well. She was about half an hour into the routine; the class was perspiring, soaked in the early afternoon heat. They were doing her variation of jumping jacks, balancing on the balls of the feet. It was going well, and her eyes were unfocused until they looked through the door to the gym and saw a woman and a man with a portable television camera. It pulled her back.

And so it starts again, she said to herself, trying to ignore the man and woman, who waited patiently. Maureen finished the entire routine, though she got less out of it than she had wanted.

A few people wanted to talk after class, and she took her time dealing with them, showing them variations on movements, giving advice on an alternative movement to a stockbroker who was having trouble because of an old leg injury. Then Maureen turned and walked toward the camera, which the man held up and aimed at her. She suddenly became very conscious of her walk. What had always seemed natural and easy now seemed incredibly artificial with the camera turned toward her.

"You think you might ask permission before you do that?" she said.

"Turn it off, Art," the woman said, and then to Maureen, "We're from Channel Five. Can we talk to you for a few minutes?"

A few of the stragglers from her class were looking across the gym curiously and talking to each other.

"Let's go outside," Maureen said, stepping past the woman. She purposely hurried down the second-floor corridor to make it difficult for the woman and the cameraman to follow her. It was childish, she knew, but she couldn't resist giving them a slightly hard time in payment for intruding on her class.

She hurried, clutching a towel around her neck. Her hair was up in a sweatband, and she moved across the lobby floor, heading for the outside. A gray-haired man in need of a shave stepped out of her way as she opened the door. He looks like one of them, she said to herself. Everyone looks like one of them. She had sudden and distinct self-doubts about the whole thing, about being so certain that the Vanbeebers were here, had done these things, that the man she had seen in the van was the big one who had killed David; but it was too late. She had talked to Donnelly and was about to talk to Channel 5 and who knows how many other channels and radio stations before the day was over.

"Let's do it here," she said, stepping into the sun and leaning against the bicycle rack in front of the building.

"Right," the woman said. "We've got to hurry to make the six o'clock, so let's go, Art."

Maureen watched the woman turn to the cameraman, straighten her hair, and hold up the microphone. A second man, a little one she hadn't seen before, suddenly appeared behind Art the cameraman with a pair of earphones and a tape recorder slung around his neck.

The reporter, suddenly turning intensely serious, softly said, "A bizarre turn of events has taken place in the case of the couple attacked in the last few days in the Lincoln Park area by someone apparently carrying a club. It seems possible, in fact likely, that the attack was prompted by an eight-year-old murder, the murder of Maureen Dietz's husband."

With this the woman turned and held the microphone out to Maureen's face and said, "Can you tell us how this all came about, Mrs. Dietz?"

# 7

Packing for Nancy and Miles took longer than it normally would have. Miles packed his own things, arguing with Maureen through the whole procedure that he did not want to run and hide.

"First they kill my father. Then they make me run and hide," he said, throwing an unfolded shirt into one of the battered, medium-sized suitcases, the origin of which eluded Maureen.

"We're talking about a few days," she said, picking up the shirt, a green pullover with an orange diagonal stripe down the front. She folded it neatly and put it in, only to have him throw another shirt on top of it. "Let's just say you'll be taking care of your sister."

"You say it," Miles said angrily, looking around the room for any other necessities. "The people responsible for my father's death shouldn't be making me run. They're the ones who should be running, and they should be tracked down and beaten to death the way my father was beaten. I'm not going." He stopped suddenly and pounded his right fist down on his dresser.

"Maureen," came Helen's voice from downstairs. "Can you come down here?"

"Miles," Maureen said. "I've got to keep working. I've got to be at least reasonably visible so the police have a chance to catch them. You can't help. You really can't help any way but going to Mike's for a few days."

"And if they're not caught in a few days?" he asked.

"We'll talk about it then," she said. "I've got to get downstairs and see what Helen wants."

Miles clenched his teeth, adjusted his glasses as he often did when thinking, and looked around his room. The room was small and usually a mess. His bed was parked as close to the TV set as possible, but the television set was more like a command post with a video recorder, video game box, and cable attached. Odd boxes and plastic containers sat on almost every available inch of counter space. A pair of pants usually lay draped over the one comfortable chair in the room, an overstuffed monstrosity donated by Maureen's uncle.

"If they're not caught," Miles said, "you'll try shipping us off to Grandma in California. And we'll hide there. Damn it. I've got friends living on their own. I mean they have their own apartments. Their mothers don't tell them what to do."

"Maureen," Helen called up again.

"I'm coming," Maureen shouted. "Miles, please."

"If you'd just accept my help," he said, stepping toward her with his arms out and achieving just the opposite effect of the one he sought. Instead of looking solid and mature, he looked like a little boy again. "You'd be surprised at what I can do, Mom, how much I can help if you'll just let me."

"We'll talk about it downstairs," she said, reaching over to touch him, but he backed away from her outstretched hand.

When she got to the living room, Nancy was sitting next to Mike on the sofa, talking. She didn't look happy either. Her complaint had been that she would miss camp. Mike was talking to her about the things they could do at his house.

"Mom," Nancy called as Maureen came into the room, "Mike says we can eat out every night at his house, every night."

"Sounds good to me," Maureen said, smiling at her and then at Mike, who shrugged. Helen was standing to one side near the window. She wore a no-nonsense brown dress and a frown. So far the morning had been tense with Helen, from the moment Maureen insisted that she was going to make her morning run till the phone calls began to slow down.

Helen had explained the situation the night before when she came running over after the six o'clock newscast on Channel 5 and just about the same time the early editions of the next day's *Sun-Times* were available.

The deal, prodded by Maureen's latest contact with the press, had been negotiated between Helen's superiors in Chicago and the Evanston police. Helen was, along with others outside, assigned to Maureen Dietz, at least for the foreseeable future. "Lieutenant Jacobs thinks I set this whole thing up," she explained. "He thinks I'm trying to make a reputation using you so I can push for a promotion. But he's caught between the tube and the printed page."

"I'm sorry," Maureen had said as they'd jogged more slowly than they had for days. The heat was getting worse. It was now the ninth straight day with temperatures over ninety.

"Sorry?" Helen had panted. "I didn't plan it, but if we catch them and I get promoted, I won't issue any complaints. Truth is, Jacobs has been on the force six months less than me. I should have been the lieutenant and he should be worrying about keeping me happy. Now let's shut up and run."

Helen had fielded most of the later incoming calls while Mike concentrated on Nancy. Most were from radio stations, and Helen had the okay to say Maureen wasn't available. There was enough publicity out now. If something was going to come of it, no more was needed.

"Van's been found," Helen said quietly, taking Maureen's arm and leading her away from Mike and Nancy after an incoming call. "In Rogers Park on Damen near Lunt. Orange, 1979 Ford with Cole Electric written on the side."

"Now they believe me?"

"Well," said Helen. "It proves there's an orange van, but it doesn't prove the Vanbeebers were driving it. Registration's being checked now. It had no plates. We've got someone watching it in case they come back, but if they removed the plates, I doubt they're planning to."

Maureen had not mentioned the van to Donnelly at the newspaper or to any of the television people. The police had hoped that it might be the link that would lead them to the Vanbeebers, but so far it hadn't done so.

"So, what's next?" Maureen said, ignoring the phone that was now ringing a few feet from them.

"A check on cars stolen in the last twenty-four hours," said Helen. "If they dumped the van, they may have picked up another car. Maureen, the chances are this publicity is going to send them running. Let me get that."

Helen reached over and picked up the phone, saying, "Yes?" And then she listened, quietly nodding before saying, "Thanks," and hanging up. "The van was purchased in Phoenix, Arizona, two years ago," she said. "Used his real name. Registration is in the name of Martin Vanbeeber. They're working on it."

"So," said Maureen, breathing deeply. "There's no doubt now, is there?"

"No doubt," Helen said.

Nancy and Miles left with Mike about twenty minutes later. Nancy seemed to be taking it as a vacation. She carried her own small suitcase in one hand and a Barbie in the other. Miles, on the other hand, looked sullen, and wouldn't meet her eyes.

"I'll call you later," Maureen said as they went out the door.

"Take care of yourself, Mom," Miles finally called back.

Maureen moved to the window to watch them leave, but they didn't right away. After Miles and Nancy were in the car, Mike came running back to the house, jingling his keys in his hand.

"Forget something?" Maureen said as he came in.

"I'm coming back tonight," he said.

The phone rang again, and Helen moved to get it.

"Helen's here," Maureen said. "I'd rather have you stay with the kids."

"I'm not hiring on as a baby-sitter," Mike said. "You know I like the kids, and I'll see to it that they're all right, but if I'm going to be responsible for taking care of this family, I'm going to start making some decisions. It may not be the best time to bring it up, but let's have no more orders to good old Mike. Instead of orders, let's make it joint discussions. I've smiled a lot and done what I was told because I didn't want to lose you, but it stops, right now. I think I'd rather be lonely, good-natured Mike again than keep things going the way they are. You've been spending a lot of time and energy in the last few days trying to put a dead husband's memory away. Maybe, just maybe, you're caught in the past because you don't want to deal with the future, with me." And out the door he went.

Helen hung up the phone and was coming into the room. "What was that about?"

"Mike just raised the ante again," Maureen sighed. "And I don't think he's bluffing. He just picked a hell of a time to do it."

"What's a good time?" Helen said.

The phone rang two more times before they got out of the house. Once it was Billy, who had seen the television interview.

"You could have told me," Billy said, sounding more like a disappointed father than an offended business relation.

"I'm sorry, Billy," she said. "A lot has been going on. Is this going to cancel the taping?"

"You want to cancel the taping?"

"You want to answer me with an answer instead of a question?"

"I'm sorry," Billy said slowly. "I talked to the health club people. They want the tape now more than ever. If you want it straight, they think they've got a bargain now, a potential national celebrity who came back from adversity through exercise. They want the tape as fast as possible. Frankly, I think they are planning to exploit you."

"So what should we do?" Maureen asked.

"My advice is, let them exploit. So are we taping or are we taping?"

"We're taping," she said. "We'll talk about the exploiting some other time."

Helen had done the driving while Maureen sat and listened to the policewoman give the details about her coming divorce and her adventures with the assistant state's attorney. "I told him last night that I was moving into your house on assignment," she said. "When we catch the Vanbeebers, I am not going back to his place. I don't know where I'm going, but it is not back to him and not back to Mojo. I'll get my own place, which is what I should have done ten years ago. You know, I've never lived alone? I married Mojo Bruckner when I was still living with my parents."

"I never lived alone either," said Maureen. "Maybe there's a profundity here that's escaping us, or is it simply a minor coincidence?"

Maureen had expected that her late-morning session would be plagued by reporters and that the people in her class would either not show up or would be too voyeuristically inclined about her case to make the class work. She had been pleasantly wrong on each count. There were no reporters. All of the twenty-two people in class showed up, and they seemed to put forth an extra effort to make the class work. The strain of feeling their support cut into Maureen's ability to enjoy the workout fully, but it was better than she had anticipated. It was starting to worry her, though, that it was getting more and more difficult to practice what she preached.

The afternoon session at the Niles Community Center had not gone quite as well. Carla Lahue had begun by waddling over to Maureen, putting her hand on her arm, and cooing, "Are you all right? Is there anything we can do to help you?"

What you can do, thought Maureen, is not act as if I were suddenly hopeless. "No," she said, looking at Helen, who leaned against the wall, her denim bag at her feet. "Let's just start our workout."

For the rest of the session, Carla strained, grunted, and moaned, suffering every second to the music of Bach and Vivaldi and looking at Maureen with baleful eyes that made it difficult to concentrate.

"How," Maureen said to Helen later as they drove back toward Evanston, "am I supposed to conduct a session when every time I open my eyes I know Mother Hubbard will be looking at me as if I'd swallowed the last bone?"

"The woman reminds me of my mother." Helen laughed with a touch of bitterness. "Very Jewish. Very protective. Very concerned. But somehow she always made me feel that every ounce of sympathy she gave me took a few months of her life. Whatever I suffered, she suffered for me and a little more. I think I became a cop to get back at her, to say, 'Mom, if you really want suffering, wait'll you see what I've got for you.' I didn't marry a Jewish professional. I became a cop. And do you know what she did?"

"How would I know what she did?" said Maureen.

"Divorced my father and married an Italian bartender. She lives in Palo Alto and her name's Sophie Danuto. How do you like that? I keep the family name and my mother becomes a Danuto. The last time I talked to her, which was about four years ago, she was thinking of becoming a Catholic."

"Is that a sad story or what?" Maureen said. "I want to give you the right response here, but I don't have a clue. . . ."

"It's sad and it's funny," Helen said. "Why can't something be both at the same time? In fact, most Jewish jokes, of which I may be one, are sad and funny at the same time. Hell, maybe I should make another try with Mojo. Maybe I wanted us to fail. What do you think?"

"I think it's none of my damn business. But I also think you change your mind awfully fast about a lot of things."

When they got back to the house, Helen went in first, checked the rooms out, and, without asking permission, turned on the air conditioner. Maureen had gone to her room to change and came back to hear the living room machine pumping.

"I turned it on, all right?" Helen said, kicking her shoes off.

"I saw. It's fine," Maureen said. "The shoes?"

"The shoes, right," Helen answered, getting up. "Maybe we can make a compromise. I'll be a little neater if you get just a touch less neat. You know, let the dishes go for an hour, skip an hour of exercise."

"Can't," said Maureen. Her plan was to call the kids and talk to Mike, try to persuade him not to come over. He had to understand that she needed to control. It was one thing she was sure of. No matter what happened, she had to be in control.

The doorbell rang. "I'll get it," Maureen called as Helen settled in a living room chair.

"Check first," Helen called.

Maureen didn't think that the Vanbeebers would simply walk up to the front door at five-thirty on a Wednesday afternoon, but she humored Helen and peeked through the curtains as the bell rang again.

It wasn't the Vanbeebers. At first she couldn't be sure of who the man was. His back was partly turned, but she could see that he was dressed in an old, dark suit, a suit much too heavy for the weather and much too old for the neighborhood. He rang again and turned his head to the window, and their eyes met.

His face hadn't changed greatly. The eyes were brown and filled with sympathy, the chin well shaved and strong. He was older, but it was the same face, and Maureen hurried to open the door.

"Hello," she said.

"Miz Dietz," he said. "You won't remember me . . ."

"I remember you," she said, reaching out to open the door wider so he could enter. "Please come in."

He hesitated only for an instant, and then the black man who had comforted her eight years ago on the night David died stepped into her house.

"This is my friend Helen Katz," Maureen said, leading the man into the living room. "Helen this is——"

"A friend," said the man, looking around the room to see if anyone else might be present. He did not seem to Maureen to be nervous or frightened. He did not even appear to be in any great hurry, but he did make it clear that he planned to proceed at his own pace.

"Well, Mr. . . ." Maureen tried again. The black man simply smiled back at her. "Well, what can I do for you?" Maureen finally said, looking over at Helen, who nodded to show that she knew who this man was.

"A little," he said. "Not very much, but I think maybe I can do something for you. Is there someplace we can talk private? I mean no offense," he said to Helen.

Helen put up her hands to indicate that she took none.

Instead she leaned back on the sofa and reached for the iced tea she had poured.

Maureen led the way downstairs to the workout room and turned on the lights. The man walked behind her lightly and slowly. When the fluorescents finished pinging, he looked around at the mats, the weight equipment, the wall charts, and then at Maureen.

"You've changed some," he said.

"I've changed a lot," Maureen said. "Would you like to sit down?"

"I think maybe you haven't changed quite so much as you think, Mrs. Dietz. Last time I saw you, your eyes weren't much different than they are now. How's the boy?"

"The boy?" Maureen asked, leaning against the wall.

"The little boy in the car that night. I never saw a look like that on a child. Truth to tell, when I read that you went to the mental hospital, I thought the boy might be going too. The baby now, she just seemed normal scared. You see, I recall that night pretty well too." The man suddenly looked tired, as if he had dug into his memory to pluck something out and the operation had been costly.

"Can I get you a drink?" Maureen said, stepping forward.

"A cold glass of water would do me fine," he said. "I don't remember when it was as hot as this."

"I'll be right back," Maureen said, going up the stairs.

Helen looked at her and whispered, "Well?"

Maureen whispered back, "Nothing yet."

She got a large glass, removed two cubes from the plastic tray in the freezer, dropped them into the glass, and filled it with water. When she got back down to the exercise room, the black man was sitting on the edge of the weight bench. His old suit jacket was open but still on. He reached out and accepted the glass. Maureen said nothing as the man drank deeply, took a breath, and then finished the water before handing the glass back to Maureen, the cubes still solid.

"Would you like another?" Maureen said.

He shook his head no. "I'd be obliged if after we talk you do your best to keep the police lady from stopping me," he said.

"She's . . ." Maureen began, and then, looking at the man's eyes, held back on the lie. "I'll do my best."

"Good," he sighed. "I'm sixty-two and in good condition, but I've got touches of the arthritis, and I don't feature the idea of running down the street in this weather. I came here to ask you to stop looking for me, to have the police stop looking for me. If those men are caught, I am not going to testify against them."

A moment earlier, she had been sure the man would say the exact opposite, but he had calmly come in, accepted a drink of water, and announced that he would not help get the men who had killed her husband.

"They're killers," she said. "If we don't testify against them, they'll go out and kill others."

"They surely will," he nodded in agreement. "There's no forgetting those two. I'm sure they'd kill me dead if they knew who I was and where I was. That's one reason I'm not telling you who I am and where I'm going."

"So you came here to tell me you're frightened and you want to be left alone?" Maureen said, and she knew that there was more than just a touch of contempt in her voice. She folded her hands in front of her and looked down at him coldly. When he had come through the door upstairs, she had remembered the feeling all those years ago, a sense of the man's sympathy, confidence. An ideal father, she had once thought in remembering him, whoever he is, he is an ideal father.

"I'm not frightened all that much," the man said. "I've faced up to devils since I was a kid. Truth be told, miss, I was more than a devil myself. The police get my name, look me up, and they're gonna find that I've got a record. It was a long, long time ago, but it was bad enough and I got no pride in it. Some defense attorney get me on the stand and trots out the time I did for assault with intent, and my testimony won't be worth much to you. Won't look too good in the place I work either. They don't know about my record, and I'm far too old to try starting again. Problem here is this is a white crime, white people involved. It'll be all over the newspapers and television."

"I understand," Maureen said. "I'll show you how to get out the back door without seeing Sergeant Katz. If you'll follow me . . ."

The man was still sitting, shaking his head. "No, missus, you don't understand," he said, sitting up straight and rebuttoning his jacket. "If you testify, I testify, the whole of the County of Cook testifies, there's still a chance that those two'll be on the street. I've seen it happen. Maybe bail'll be set. Maybe someone will make a mistake, and they'll walk away clean from a trial, or they'll get a smart lawyer who'll make a deal, and they'll do a little prime time and be out on the street in three, four, six years. Six years I hope to be still going, and I know you do. That boy and girl of yours will be around too. Are you following where I'm leading?"

"Yes," Maureen sighed.

"Only way to beat people like that is to stay out of their way or make sure they're not around to get in yours." He paused, licked his lower lip, and watched her face. "I've seen people like that. I see them every day, and I used to have to share space with them. You don't let them see you, or you kill them."

"What?"

"I said what I said, Mrs. Dietz." With this he stood up. "Your talking to the TV and the newspapers flushed me. That's the truth. I couldn't stay shadowed and not doing something. It's not my way. I want to meet my maker justified."

"And you can do that telling one person to take another's life?" she asked, raising her voice.

"I couldn't face God's Sunday unless I did tell you to do it if the chance comes," he said. "Get yourself a gun, and if they come within daylight of you, start shooting, and don't stop till they're dead. No jury on Lord's earth going to convict you for it."

"I can't just . . . just do that," she said. "You're telling me to—"

"To do what I'd do to protect myself and my family," he said. "I'm not asking you to do it. I'm telling you what I would do. I could have told you this on the phone, but I wanted to do it face-to-face. Tell the truth, I wanted to see what you looked like now, and I was hoping to see the kids. I'd like a different memory of them than the one I'm carrying."

"Thank you," Maureen said. "Now I think you can leave."

"What I just told you is plain sense," he said, taking a step toward her. "When I came in, I said I might be able to help. If the time and chance come, I'll be willing to take it on myself to kill those two. If I knew where they were right now, I'd drive over to them and do it and pray for their souls on Sunday."

"That," said Maureen with a nervous laugh, "would be murder."

"It rightly would, to the law," he said. "I don't know for sure how God would see it, but I'd be willing to take my chances."

He put out his hand, and Maureen thought he was trying to touch her, comfort her. She didn't know why, but she put out her hand to him. Those warm eyes were on her. She felt something touch her hand and looked down. It was a piece of paper, a blue printed receipt from the drugstore. She turned it over, and there was a telephone number on it.

"That's a number where you can leave a message for me if you've a mind to," he explained. "Man who answers won't be

—— 226 ——

me. It'll be a friend who wouldn't tell where to find me if the police promised to pluck out his eyes, which wouldn't matter much to him because he's blind. Just tell him you want Stubbs to call you."

Maureen put her hand to her forehead, closed her eyes briefly, and then opened them to look at the man. "Mr. Stubbs—"

"That's not my name."

"Whatever your name is then, I'll respect your wishes."

"Now if we can get the rest of the world to do the same for each other, we'll have gone a long way." He smiled for the first time, good white teeth, and in spite of herself, Maureen smiled back.

"I'll show you how to get out through the back," she said, stepping in front of him and starting up the stairs.

"If you don't mind, missus," he said, following her, "I'd rather go out the front door."

"All done?" said Helen cheerfully as they came up and the black man headed for the front door with Maureen at his side. "That didn't take long."

"I didn't have that much to say," he said, looking at her. "Now I've got to get on home. I've got a family and a dinner waiting."

"You have far to go?" Helen said brightly.

The man looked at Maureen with a smile. "Depends on what a person thinks far is," he countered. "Bye, Mrs. Dietz. Take care of yourself and the children."

And out the door he went. Maureen looked over at Helen, expecting the policewoman to leap up and go after him, but she took a sip from her tea and looked at Maureen.

"Well?" she said.

"He knew you were the police," Maureen began, going to the window and pulling back the curtain to watch the man. He walked slowly down the sidewalk.

"And I knew he had done time," Helen said. "Who is he and what did he say?"

Maureen didn't answer at first. She watched the man disappear behind the bushes near the corner and then, as he turned the corner, she could see glimpses of him through the leaves in the late-afternoon light. He wasn't heading for the bus stop, so, she concluded, he must have a car parked nearby, but not near enough so that it could be seen from the house.

When she was sure the man was gone, Maureen turned to Helen and told her what the man had said. At the end of her account, Maureen looked at the other woman, waiting for the counterarguments.

"He has a point," Helen said instead. "But if you ever tell anyone I say so, I'll call you a liar. Mo, if one of those two walked up to the door right now and rang the bell, I'd open it wide and put a bullet or two right in his face, even if he was carrying a Bible in one hand and a rabbi in the other."

The doorbell rang, and Helen almost dropped her glass. It rang again, and they exchanged looks. If fate was testing her, Helen was ready. She leaped out of the chair in her stocking feet, went to her denim bag in the corner, and pulled out the gun that Maureen had seen before. Helen nodded toward the door, and Maureen moved, almost hoping that it would be the Vanbeebers, that Helen would step forward and shoot them and end the dreams, but it wasn't them.

"It's Mike," Maureen announced, looking through the plate-glass window of the front door. Helen put her pistol away and went back to the sofa, where she sat cross-legged, her feet tucked under her.

"Hi," Mike said, coming in.

"Hi," Maureen said, taking his hand.

Mike was wearing clean slacks, a red knit shirt with short sleeves, and new shoes that looked like Hush Puppies. Maureen closed the door behind him, and he greeted Helen.

"Mike," Maureen said, "I've been through a lot, and I don't think I'm up to a really serious discussion about you and me and the future."

"How about a movie?" he said.

"What about the big talk you wanted?"

"It can wait," he said. "I just fed your kids enough Double Cheese with Bacon to keep them sick for a week. They're watching a movie in my place, and they don't need anything. Why don't you give them a call and pick out a show. I'll even let you two pay without arguing."

"Pay your own way," Maureen said, smiling.

"Speak for yourself," Helen said. "If Big Mike wants to pay for me, I'll accept it as protection money. I've got enough confidence in my image not to worry about who pays for who. Besides, I'm a cop, and I can't afford to worry about financial independence. I make my stand on more important issues."

"Such as?" Mike said, showing his big teeth and chuckling.

"Such as you are both putting on one hell of a lousy show to try to keep me from fear and depression," Maureen put in. "You are, however, succeeding. Give me fifteen minutes to call the kids and do a short routine in the basement. And then?"

*"Tender Mercies,"* said Mike.

*"Jaws 3-D,"* Maureen responded. "I guess the tiebreaker's yours, Helen."

"I was going to vote for *WarGames,*" she said, "but I'm not paying. I'll go with the man paying the bills. Besides, I can't get those damn glasses to stay on over my own glasses."

Maureen made the call from downstairs, and Miles answered. Above her in the living room she could hear Mike and Helen talking, but she couldn't make out what they were saying. The glass of the black man who had just left was still on the counter near the phone. The cubes were melting and Maureen picked up the glass and swished them around as she talked.

"How are things over there?" she said.

"Fine," Miles answered. She could imagine him pushing his glasses back on his nose and standing with a hand under his armpit as he talked, shifting from one leg to the other.

"You still mad at me?" she said.

"Yeah, if you want the truth."

"But you still love me, right?"

"I guess," he said.

"You know."

"All right. I know. You want to talk to Princess Daisy?"

"In a minute. Miles, do you remember a man, a black man on the night your father died?"

There was a long silence, and Miles finally broke it. "The one you told the television people about and the *Sun-Times?*"

"Yes," she said.

"I remember him," Miles said so quietly that she almost didn't hear him. "Why?"

"I talked to him," she said. "He wanted to know how you are. He remembers you. I told him you were fine, that Nancy was fine."

"So, why are you telling me?" he asked. "Is he going to help get those guys or what?"

"Or what?" Maureen said. "I'll tell you more when I see you. Let me talk to Nancy. I'll call you tomorrow morning."

"Not too early," he said. "I plan to watch a midnight horror movie, *The 3-D House of Representatives.*"

"Okay," she answered.

"That was a joke, Mom," he sighed. "Remember we heard it on 'Second City TV'?"

"Sorry," she answered, trying to put a laugh in the word. "I'm not too good at picking up jokes these days."

"I'll get the kid."

Time was moving, and Maureen wanted to get at least a short routine in before she went out with Mike and Helen, but she made her voice patient and unhurried as Nancy came on, complaining about her stomach.

"I ate too much, Mom," she said. "Mike bought me too much, and I didn't want to waste it."

"I'll tell him to give you less food, Nancy," she said.

"I might throw up," Nancy threatened. "I think you should come over here."

I've heard that one before, Maureen thought, but she answered very slowly, "If you do throw up, Miles will know what to do. I'll tell him how to reach me, and I'll get there in fifteen minutes, but you've got to give me a promise." Mike and Helen had stopped talking upstairs, and Maureen could hear only the electric hum of the air conditioner.

"What's the promise?"

"That you won't stick your finger or anything else down your throat to make yourself throw up the way you did on Halloween when I went out."

"I promise," Nancy said. "Mom, you think I'm lying?"

"No, love, I think you're lonely for me. I miss you too. Kiss Miles for me and good night."

"Miles won't let me kiss him," she said. "You know that. I'll hug him though. Good night."

The after-screening consensus was three to nothing against *Jaws 3-D*. They were having coffee at Swensen's Ice Cream Factory after the show. Maureen had given Miles the number at the theater and told the manager where she was sitting and that she was a doctor. When they got to the ice cream shop, she called Miles, who said that Nancy was asleep and without a stomach ache.

"What did you see?" he asked.

"*Jaws 3-D*, a must miss," she answered. "Good 3-D though."

"I'm watching something," he said. "Talk to you tomorrow."

Conversation over coffee was steered away from the Vanbeebers and the investigation. Maureen didn't tell Mike about the black man. She hadn't decided what she thought of the man's visit. It was an event that had to be worked out without words and conscious thoughts.

When they got back to the house, Helen insisted on going in first again and checking each room. "The truth is," she said, coming back into the living room where Mike and Maureen were waiting, "a patrol from Evanston is checking up on the house. My guess is we'll get twenty-four-hour service for a few days, but there are other ways to get in here. Well, I'm tired. I'm going upstairs to get ready for bed. Thanks for the show and the 3-D glasses, Mike."

"My pleasure," he said, waving to her as she moved up and out of sight. "That was a discreet exit in case you want to invite me upstairs."

Maureen moved into his arms and gave him a quick hug, and then she stepped back again to look up at his face. It was wide, strong, and far too open.

"It was a good evening," she said. "I needed it, but I'm not ready for—"

"Who's talking about sex?" he said. "I'm fifty years old. I'm not looking for sex every day like a kid who's just found out he can use it for something besides peeing. We can just lie in each other's arms and feel we're not alone. That's a good feeling, isn't it?"

"It's a good feeling," she admitted. "But each of us is alone most of the time."

"So we have to stay away from coming close to other people, from feeling, because we can't have it all the time?" he asked.

"Something like that," she agreed. "You knew I had problems when you got involved with me, Coach."

"I'll go home and have a snack with Miles, if he's still up," Mike said, giving in and stepping back. "Maureen, that offer in San Diego looks pretty sure. I got a call today. I'm thinking about it. If I go, I don't want to go alone."

"Come on upstairs for a while," she said, "and we'll talk."

It was evident on Thursday morning that Helen did not want to run three miles, two miles, or even around the block. There was some question of whether she even wanted to get out of bed, but she called, "Be right with you," when Maureen knocked at Nancy's door at six-thirty.

Maureen was well into her warm-up on the front lawn when Helen staggered out in white shorts and a bulky sweatshirt.

"Kind of hot for this early in the morning," she said, sitting on the lawn with a yawn.

"Supposed to go up to almost a hundred," Maureen said, standing to stretch backward, her face to the clear sky. "Why don't you skip running the park."

"I'm coming," Helen said, getting up awkwardly. "I'm not supposed to leave you alone, remember? However, I am considering driving around the park."

Maureen spread her arms and began doing trunk twists, right to left. "I'm going twice around the lake and back," she said.

"What would happen to you if you took a day off? One day," Helen said, holding up a finger.

"I wouldn't like it," Maureen admitted, stopping. "Let's go."

"Let's go," Helen said with a shrug, removing a white sweatband from the pocket of her shorts and placing it on her head. "If you can do it, I can fake it."

Helen took off first, and Maureen considered the bulge at the back of her sweatshirt. It was, she decided, a gun, which explained why the policewoman was wearing a bulky sweatshirt.

When they got back, Maureen called Mike's house. There was no answer. "Probably left to take Nancy to camp already," Maureen said, accepting a large glass of orange juice from Helen. "Can't imagine Miles getting up early though."

She woke Billy with her next call. "Everything is set for this afternoon," he said. "I'll be there. You sure your class will be there?"

"Enough for the taping," she said. "See you later."

After they had showered and changed, Helen called in to her precinct. Nothing much had changed. Susan Breen was still alive. Roger Simcox's funeral had been held without incident or the appearance of suspects, and there had been no luck in trying to tie recently stolen cars to the Vanbeebers. They decided to take Helen's car, and as they walked to it on the street, an Evanston patrol car cruised slowly past the house. The driver watched them go to the car and then pulled ahead.

From that point on, the day went badly. She had agreed to do a special introductory session at the Ridge Park Community House in Chicago. Sessions like this drew people to the center and introduced them to Maureen, who might pick them up as regulars at her studio. They got to the center slightly before ten and were greeted by its director, known to Maureen only as Chico. Chico looked like a tabletop telephone: broad shoulders, big bottom, and a bald head. He wore a whistle around his neck and was forever blowing it to warn kids off equipment, away from the building, and for no great reason at all.

"Calling the session off this morning," he said as Maureen and Helen came into the gym, which served also as a meeting room and makeshift theater. "No air-conditioning."

"We don't need air-conditioning," Maureen protested, dropping her bags.

"What can I tell you, babe?" Chico said. "First three people in your class came about ten minutes back, and I sent them home. I don't want heart attacks."

"I help prevent heart attacks, not give them—and Chico, don't call me 'babe,' remember?"

"Whatever," he said, with an annoyed shrug. He started to put the whistle to his mouth absently and then let it drop. "Be that as it may," he picked up, "I sent them home, and I'm going into my office and sit with the air conditioner. You two want to join me? I'll ice up some tea."

Maureen felt the anger tingle from her feet through her body. It wasn't his right to call off her class. He had no idea of what she was about, what she was doing. She looked to Helen for sympathy, but canceling the class obviously did not strike the policewoman as crisis material.

"If anyone shows up in the next ten minutes," Maureen said to Chico, "I'm going ahead with the class."

Chico looked around the gym in exasperation before turning back to Maureen. "Look, I don't want to give you more trouble than you've already got . . . but I'm responsible here. Four people died of the heat a couple of days ago."

"They were in an old people's home, and the air-conditioning went out," Maureen argued, angry that she was dealing with him at his own level, a level at which he had some expertise.

"See," he said triumphantly. "Air-conditioning went out. Don't give me trouble, ba . . . Mo . . ."

"Mrs. Dietz," she said.

"Mrs. Dietz," Chico said. "Let's go to my office and cool off. We'll do the session next week."

"You," she said, "are going to call every one of the thirty-seven people who signed up for this session and tell them that we're having a session next Tuesday, no extra charge."

"Thirty-three," he corrected. "Four people dropped out during the week and asked for their money back. I've got to check the pool, and then I'm going to my office. Do I have to lock the door here or what?"

"Or what," Maureen said, picking up her bag. She turned and walked to the door with Helen right behind.

"Don't be mad," Chico called. "Hey . . ."

"If he blows that whistle at me," Maureen hissed at Helen, "I'm going back there and shove it up his nearest open orifice."

"Hey," he called as they went through the gym door and headed down the corridor. "How about being a little reasonable?"

When they were back in the car, Maureen looked at her watch and said, "Damn."

"Can I say something?" Helen said, starting the car.

"That means, whatever you have to say, it won't be supportive, right?"

"The man wasn't all wrong," Helen said. "You're running your own marathon. You can't blame people if they don't always want to go along."

They decided to go back to the house, where Maureen discovered that her car was gone. A note on the front door said, "Mom, I took the car for the day. Mike said he'll call you later. Nancy thinks she has a cold. Miles."

Maureen and Helen talked for a few hours, just talked, and though Maureen had the urge to go into the basement to catch up on the morning workout she had missed, she controlled it and even enjoyed Helen's rambling autobiography.

"So, what do you think?" Helen said when the day had worn into afternoon. She had fielded and turned away several phone calls, and it was getting close to time to leave again.

"I think a tough routine in the park will make up for this morning."

"Ever think of starting your own army?" Helen said. "Don't answer, I'm afraid you'll say yes."

They arrived about twenty minutes early. The crew of students from Northwestern was already there and Jane Chong, looking serious and younger than her twenty-four years, came up to them and was introduced to Helen. She wore her hair cut short and was wearing jeans and a T-shirt that said LET'S PLANT SOME TREES.

"We're using three cameras," she explained. "One on you, one moving from a long shot into a section of the group, and one moving from one individual to another."

"Stay on the same individual till each exercise is complete," Maureen said. "That was the only problem I could see on the last tape."

"Right," agreed the young woman, in an accent not of China but of New York City. "Made it hard to cut, but I think we've got it down now. I've got a better camera operator on that this time. Mr. Stultz said no sound, that you'd do a voice-over later, but I brought out the sound equipment just in case."

Maureen looked at the Northwestern students in a clearing between two trees. They were setting up equipment professionally. Beyond them she could see the lake, still and warm.

"Can we just do sound on the opening?" Maureen said. "Then cut it off?"

"Sure," said Jane Chong. "I'll set it up." And off she went, writing something on the pad of paper on her clipboard.

Members of the class began to show up, but they trickled in slowly, very slowly. Billy arrived at two-thirty and looked nervously at his watch.

"We can't do it with six people," he said, throwing his golf ball in the air. "And Jane says we've got to start soon, or we're going to lose the light."

"Give it five more minutes," Maureen said. She had already limbered up.

"What the hell," Helen said. "I'll fill in."

Five minutes later four more members of the class showed up. The only thing that went right in the taping was Maureen's opening comments.

"I want you to watch me," she said, remembering not to

turn toward the directional microphone aimed at her by a skinny boy with short yellow hair and a ring in his left ear. "Just do what I do. Don't count and don't think about how long we've been exercising or how much we have left to do. If your thoughts wander and move from anything except the exercise, bring them back. Just see me, and do what I do. After a while, you'll be able to change to another routine when I simply give a key word such as 'butterfly' or 'spider out.' If something distracts you, hum a single note to yourself, not a song but a single note, and listen to the note while you watch me. Let's begin."

The introduction was made for the cameras and audio equipment, not for the class, which was into its tenth week of the program. Maureen punched the button on her cassette player, and Mozart lightly filled the air. The routine went well for all of two minutes, till a gang of boys on bicycles, all around ten or eleven, drove right through the group, laughing. Jane called "cut" and Maureen stopped a routine just as she was going into it. Ten minutes later the heat took out one of the cameras, and a brief conference was held among Jane, Maureen, and Billy. Through it all Jane Chong remained calm and had a variety of suggestions. The best she could do with this was to take the camera she was using to concentrate on long shots and switch it to one-shots of class members. "We'll have to go back and pick up long shots, do a part of each routine after we're done."

"Fake it?" Maureen said.

"Maureen," Billy said gently. "This is a videotape of an exercise routine, not the filming of the Bible."

"I don't like it," she said, biting her lower lip.

"But you'll do it?" Billy said.

Her sigh was enormous as she looked over the class. Several of the less hearty and less committed members were clearly wilting. The hope of real concentration for the tape was gone. Now all that was possible was the act.

"I'll do it," she said.

After another hour, Bobby Stashki, his gray sweat suit dripping wet, announced during a break for camera problems that he had to leave for a business appointment. Brenda Bayston heard his apologetic statement and quickly chimed in, saying she too had to leave. This led to another change of production plans for the unflappable Jane Chong. Billy had long since departed.

"I'm with you to the end," Helen said, puffing out air and mopping her face with a towel plucked from her bag.

"I'll get by with a little help from my friends," Maureen whispered, moving past her to give the remaining class members a pep talk before taping resumed.

Just when it looked as if they were going to reach the end, the kids on the bikes returned. Maureen could hear them coming, could see them from the corner of her eye, though she didn't want to turn her head while the camera was on her.

"A bunch of crazies," shouted one kid, barreling through the middle of the class with two others right behind him. The kid in front was white and freckled. Helen threw a tired left leg toward him, and he swayed away from her, barely retaining his balance. The two other kids, both black, veered away from her and sped after the freckle-faced one.

"You come back here again," Helen shouted, "and I'll rip your tires and throw those damn bikes in the lake."

The kid farthest back turned, grinned, and gave her the finger.

"Once more from the start of that last exercise," Jane Chong said, stepping in calmly. "We're almost there."

Whatever Billy was paying her, Maureen thought, it couldn't be enough, not nearly enough. The woman should be directing "60 Minutes" or an invasion of Nicaragua.

When Maureen finally finished the last routine, the sun was dangerously low behind the trees.

"That's it," called Jane Chong. The four students who were with her professionally and quietly began packing the equipment.

"We lost a lot of light at the end," she said, "but that might work out to our advantage. I'll cut in a couple of shots of the sunset."

"Whatever," Maureen said with a wave of her hand. Helen was lying exhausted on her back, and the members of the class were coming to say good-bye and accept Maureen's thanks.

"It must be ninety-five or a hundred," one woman said. Her face was fire engine red. The woman tried to smile, lifted her hand slightly, and staggered away.

Five minutes later, Helen got to her feet and slung her bag over her shoulder. "I've had enough exercise for the decade," she said, shuffling behind Maureen toward her car. "If you go down in that basement tonight there is a serious possibility that I'll have you straitjacketed."

"No more exercise today," Maureen said, sliding into the passenger seat. "Let's stop back at the Y for a shower and then go out for a sandwich."

"You go to the Y for a shower," Helen said. "I'll sit right in this car with the air conditioner on and dream of milk shakes. I'm not worried about body odor, just survival."

When they pulled in front of the Y, Helen spotted a parking space and backed in.

"I won't be long," Maureen said.

"Take your time," Helen answered, putting her head back and closing her eyes as she groped for the air conditioner. "But don't take all night. I don't want the *African Queen* to overheat."

The sun was down when Maureen went through the main door and walked slowly past the open door of the lounge. She was vaguely aware of some men inside, watching a blaring television.

"Closing up," the man at the outer desk said. "No one's in there."

"I'll just take a quick shower," she told him. "I'll lock up when I'm done."

The man, who knew her, nodded and said, "Suit yourself. I'm off in five minutes."

There was a night light in the woman's locker room. She flipped on the overhead, went to her small locker, turned the combination, opened it, and pulled out the change of clothes she kept there. She stripped, feeling the moisture on her body and tingling in the hair between her legs. A cool breeze, brief but pleasant, came from a slightly open window and rippled over her. She tiptoed to the shower room off the locker area, turned on one of the lights, put her towel, soap, and shampoo down, and turned on the shower. The water thudded warm and hard against her. She let it hit her shoulders, her back, her neck, and then turned to let it bounce between her breasts and down between her legs. God it felt good. If the pool had been open she would have gone through the far door of the shower room and plunged in naked, but she was . . . And then she heard it.

The sound came from the locker room or possibly from the outside, through the slightly open window. With the water on she couldn't be sure. She glanced toward the door to the locker room and then went back to soaping herself. The second sound was louder, the clanking of metal on metal. She rinsed herself quickly and turned off the water.

"Someone there?" she called. "Helen?"

There was no answer. She toweled herself rapidly, keeping her eyes on the door. It couldn't be anything to worry about. No one had followed them from the park. Helen had been watching. No one knew she was coming to the Y for a shower. The awful irony might be that it could be some rapist who had nothing to do with the Vanbeebers. It was more likely her imagination working with a creaking locker and a faint breeze.

Pull yourself together, she told herself, and then she heard it again. There was no doubt about it this time. The sound came from the locker room. It's nothing, she told herself, nothing, but she walked slowly to the pool door, away from the locker room. It was open.

Moonlight through the high windows hit the water, which lapped gently in the darkness. The moon itself could be seen, fragmented and quite beautiful, in the pool. Maureen looked around the pool and up to the empty balcony. She moved slowly, her towel wrapped around her. The door to the pool office was open, and she walked, barefoot, and paused at the inner door that led to the rear of the locker room. If someone was there, she would be behind him. She opened the door slowly, carefully, willing it to be quiet, and it obeyed. The shower in the locker room was running. The lights were out, and she tried to remember whether she had turned them off when she went into the shower. She didn't think she had, but that wasn't necessarily anything to worry about. A janitor or staff member might simply have come down, seen the lights on, and turned them off . . . but they would have heard the shower running, would have looked in there and turned it off.

The locker room was darker than the pool, which had a bank of windows. The locker room had only two small, nearly opaque windows on the far side of the room away from her. Maureen stood for a minute, letting her eyes adjust to the lack of light, trying to breathe deeply and quietly. She saw nothing and moved slowly back to her locker in the corner. She got her T-shirt and shorts on and was about to put on her shoes when the voice came out of the darkness.

"Now you can just take them right back off again."

She stood up from the bench, holding her shoe in her hand, straining into the darkness. God, God, God, no, she said, but she said it to herself.

He stepped forward out of the darkness, and a vague glow of light from one of the windows touched his face. There was no doubt, and it was no dream. It was him, the smaller of the two men who had killed David. His steely gray hair stood up on his head, and his buttoned, striped short-sleeved shirt sagged with dark sweat.

"Take them off," he said, "and I won't hurt you."

He took another step forward. She had always thought of him, remembered him, as a small man, but standing fifteen feet away she could see that he wasn't small. She had gauged him in terms of his partner, his cousin, his fellow monster. This man was slightly bigger than Maureen, and though his face looked flushed, his shoulders were taut and sinewy.

There was only one way to go. Maureen threw her shoe at the face emerging from the darkness and ran for the door to the gym without looking to see if she had hit him. She heard the shoe hit a locker and the first footsteps of the man coming after her.

She took the stairs upward two at a time, stubbing her toes, trying not to think of his hands reaching out to grab her, pull her back into his darkness. When she hit the gym level, she pushed on the door. It was locked. She pushed her weight onto the corridor door to the gym offices. It too was locked. There was only one place to go. The man lunged for her, panting as he hit the top of the stairs, and she went up the next flight of metal steps, knowing that there was only the track over the gym and the handball courts in front of her. There was no exit.

# 8

Calvin was gone, but where the hell had he gone this time? Marty had left him sitting in the lounge watching television after their own TV had died. Then Marty had left, promising to be back in an hour with a bottle and the final steps in the plan. It was hard, since Marty had purposely not stolen a car or let Cal steal one. When the time came for them to have fun—if it came—they would steal a car in the middle of the night, put their own Missouri plates on it, and drive four or five hundred miles away from Chicago before they dumped it.

But where the hell was Calvin?

A fat black man in the lounge was chewing on a cigar and watching the White Sox with his fat hands folded over his belly. "You see a guy in here," Marty asked him, "about so high, short gray hair, wearing a striped shirt?"

The man shook his head without really listening, and Marty put his right hand on the man's shoulder and squeezed. The man's mouth went open in surprise, and the cigar tumbled out onto his lap. "Hey, what?" the man cried.

"You seen the guy I'm talking about?"

"I didn't see no guy," the black man said, trying to push Marty's hand away, but Marty just squeezed harder.

"Hey," called an old man in glasses sitting closer to the television. "Let Sam alone or I'll tell the desk. I saw your friend leave about maybe ten minutes back, just before the sixth inning."

Marty let the black man go and turned to face the old man, who lifted his metal cane. "You come near me and I'll bust this off your fucking head," he shouted.

"No need to scream, old man," Marty said, backing away, not wanting to attract attention. "I just want to find my friend and give him some medicine." He patted the fifth of cheap whiskey in his pocket.

"Your friend is a crazy nut," the old man yelled. "A crazy nut. Woman runs by and he takes off like a . . . a crazy nut."

"A woman?" Marty repeated, trying to take in what he had heard.

"That's what I said," the old man called, feeling bolder now that Marty was backing away. "She went running past the desk, and he went after her. Instead of bothering us, you should be chasing your ass after your crazy friend before he gets into real trouble." The old man was up now and taken by his own demon. "There's too many goddamn crazy animals like you two," he shouted. "Can't go anywhere no more without you, people like you, hurting, pushing, taking other people's radios."

How the hell did he know about the radio? Marty thought, but he didn't have time to think about it. He glanced at the black man, who sat still, rubbing his shoulder where Marty had squeezed him. The man looked down at his cigar. Marty was sure he was far too fat to bend down and pick it up.

"I'll be back, old man," Marty said.

"I'll be waiting," the old man shouted, white flecks appearing on his lips. "I'll be waiting with this cane and my gun, you big shit."

Marty went through the lounge door and passed a thin black man with a suit and mustache. The man, Marty knew, was the night manager.

"Guy in there acting nuts," Marty said to the man, who looked at him suspiciously. "Must be the damned heat."

The man went past Marty into the lounge, and Marty took off into the darkness of the corridor leading to the gym.

The door to the overhead track was open. Maureen went in, dashed down the banked track, and began running. She wasn't used to running barefoot on the track, and it felt strangely soft and warm under her. The windows on the far side of the small track let in both streetlamp light and a thin layer of moonlight.

She could hear the man running behind her. She could see that the windows were closed. There was no time to open them and scream. Even if she did, they were on the third floor level and were facing the parking lot.

When the footsteps behind her seemed not as close, she slowed down and looked over her shoulder. He had stopped, trying to catch his breath. He looked ghostly white as his chest heaved.

She halted when she was on the far side of the track, away from him, and they looked across the unfathomable darkness of the gym below them. He leaned forward on the steel railing, and she did the same. She looked down toward the gym floor, but with the lights out she could see nothing. It was a bottomless well, and they were standing on its rim.

"If you don't stop, you bitch," he panted, "I'm gonna hurt you when I catch you. I'm gonna hurt you the way you deserve after what you did to us."

"What I did?"

"We minded our own business," he said, his voice echoing

off the walls. "We didn't hurt you. That husband of yours boned up, put it to us. He asked for it. We did it in self-defense, and you fucking well know it."

"Bastard!" she shouted. "You insane murdering bastard."

The man pushed away from the railing and took off, going in the opposite direction. Maureen was shaking with fear and anger and found herself almost hypnotized. It took a remarkable effort to force her trembling legs to move. She realized that he had stopped again. She also realized what he had done. He had placed himself in front of the only door to the track.

"I'll get you now, bitch lady," he said. "Marty's gonna come looking for me, and we'll have you circled. So you just stand there and wait."

She djdn't know if he was bluffing or telling the truth.

"Just stand there, lady. Stand there and I'll look at you, and we'll just wait for Marty. You know what you did to Marty? You and all of them? We were back in California not bothering any-one, and you started this."

While he was talking, hidden in the corner except for his legs, which were touched by the light from outside, she heard a sound below them, deep below from the locker room. She strained her eyes into the darkness to see if the madman had heard it too. She couldn't tell. She had to do something, had to act before that second figure appeared through the door to trap her. A scream would do no good. It would only echo off the thick concrete walls and point to where she hid.

She backed slowly to the wall, up the incline of the track, her bare toes pushing to keep her from slipping. A slight breeze from behind indicated that a window was open a crack. Another sound came from below and was coming closer. She sucked in at her stomach and turned her back on the man around the oval. Her hands went up and pushed at the window. It stuck on one side, and she heard the footsteps of the man coming around the track. She forced herself to stop, realigned the window, and threw it open, expecting to feel his hands grabbing her ankles. She made a massive effort and pushed herself through the window.

There was a narrow ledge outside, about three feet wide, with a drop straight down to the cement parking lot. The plan came without much thought, but it came. She lay back, the gravel of the ledge scratching into her back through her thin shirt. She lay with her head over the ledge and her feet pointing at the darkness of the open window. Above her, the nearly full moon was covered by a slowly moving cloud, and Maureen thought it looked quite beautiful. She could hear the man scrambling through the window. First his fingers curled over the edge in the faint moonlight, and then his head appeared. He looked out, not seeing her, and then his eyes turned downward. Their eyes met, and his eyes went down her body as he started to pull himself through the window.

A voice came from deep behind the man. It was a warning and a moan. "Calvin," it said. "Calvin, what the hell . . . ?"

And then she kicked. With both feet, her back pushing against the gravel and with all the strength she had put into her body over the past eight years, she kicked at the man who was wedging his way through the window toward her. She kicked, and her bare feet caught his bristly neck and hit him in the face. She could feel breaking teeth and saliva on her heels as he gave a wild, animal cry and tumbled backwards away from the window. She watched him tumble back down the incline, his mouth bloody in the white light from the street. His balance was gone and, startled, he groped backwards to stop himself, but his back hit the low railing, and he fell into the dark well of the gym floor. She heard the body hit and a voice in the darkness groan, "Calvin."

Without brushing herself off, she scrambled back through the window and moved down to the railing. She could see nothing below, nothing.

"I see you," said a voice from the darkness below. "I see you. And you are dead. You are dead. Calvin was my family. He was my family. Do you know what that means?"

"David was my husband," she said, trying to penetrate the black below.

"David?" came the dazed voice.

"The man you murdered eight years ago," she cried. Tears were on her cheeks, tears of rage. Her fists were pounding against the railing. "His name was David."

The lights suddenly flashed on. They came on like a wave as someone flipped the switches. The darkness below her was gone, and there were two figures on the floor where she had been conducting classes for almost eight years. One was a headless man lying awkwardly. She looked again and saw that he was not headless but that his neck was broken, his head twisted back underneath him.

Standing at the entrance to the gym below, looking up at her, was the big man, the man in her dreams. They looked at each other in silence, and something strange happened. The big man with the mustache looked frightened. He took a step back, glanced over at his fallen cousin, and choked back a sob.

"I'm coming for you," he shouted, and his voice seemed to echo and echo through the gym. "I'm coming."

He turned, and Maureen saw that someone was standing in the doorway, blocking his way. The figure stepped forward and pointed a gun at the big man, who took a step back into the gym.

"Are you all right, Mo?" Helen called without looking up.

"I'm—" she said, and the big man lunged forward as Helen fired. The shot cracked and rattled the windows behind Maureen. The man's neck turned wet red, and he pushed at Helen, sending her back into the hallway below. He went after her, and Maureen could hear grunting and the sound of something tumbling down the stairs.

"Helen," she shouted, starting to run toward the door of

the track, the door that would lead to the big man and the policewoman.

Maureen bolted through the door leading from the track and hit the light switch. As she went hurrying down the stairs, she only partly formed an idea of what she would do if the big man appeared before her. She could leap down at him, trying to knock him backwards, off-balance. She tried not to think of what the leap would do to her. All she knew was that something had happened to Helen, and she wasn't going to simply stand on the track and wait for help. There was no one there when she reached the alcove outside the now-lighted gym. Before she could stop herself, she slipped on a stream of blood. From this position, his bloody face was turned toward her, his eyes open and fixed on Maureen.

She turned to the darkened steps leading down and flipped the light switch. Two small bulbs down the stairway popped on, and at the bottom she could see the crumpled form. Helen wasn't moving. She took the stairs two at a time, holding the railing.

"Helen," she called, but there was no answer and no sign of life until she kneeled next to her. The policewoman's head was awkwardly leaning back against the wall, and she seemed to be sitting impossibly on her right leg. She was breathing heavily, but she was breathing.

"Helen," she repeated softly, touching her head and looking around at the door to the locker room.

"Broken," Helen said, and then her eyes came open, fluttered, and looked up the stairs. Maureen turned her head quickly to see what was there, but there was nothing.

"I'm getting help," Maureen said. "I'll be back in a few seconds."

Helen's answer was to close her eyes again. Maureen could see no blood, but that wasn't necessarily good news. She opened the door to the locker room and plunged into the darkness, expecting more terror. Nothing clutched or touched her, and she ran across the floor and to the stairs. When she reached the upper door she pushed, sending it back with a thud. She had to hold her hands out to keep the door from hitting her as it bounced back. There was no one at the locker room desk, so she ran past it, past the darkened cafeteria and to the main desk, where the night manager was on duty.

"Help," she panted. "There's a—"

He looked up at her. He held a stack of white index cards, and they fluttered in his hands.

"A man's dead in the gym, policewoman is hurt. Get help. There's a killer in there."

She could see it in his eyes. She had seen it eight years ago in hospital aides, former friends. He thought she was mad. There was a mirror next to the desk, and she looked at herself. She looked mad. Her hair was wild, her T-shirt filthy with slinging dirt and gravel, and her feet bruised and tinted with blood.

"Take it easy," he said, and over his shoulder he called, "Karen. Come out here now will you, quick."

"I'm not insane," Maureen insisted. "Get on the phone. Call an ambulance—the police—and for God's sake come and help me. She's hurt."

From the office behind the desk, a thin, pretty black woman emerged, looked at Maureen and then at the manager, who said, "I'm going with the lady. You call the police and an ambulance."

He leapt over the counter, looked at Maureen again with some doubt, and said, "Show me."

As she padded down the hall, she could hear the woman named Karen making the phone call. They followed the faint bloody footprints Maureen had left, and she realized that the blood on her feet was not Helen's or the dead man's but that of the big man.

The next hour was a collage: Helen saying things that didn't make sense; the police taking Maureen to the police station a few blocks away and asking her questions; more people showing up; and a man who she assumed was a doctor giving her two pink-and-white capsules, which she reluctantly took.

The police station was small, clean, and uncrowded. It reminded her more of the town hall of a prosperous suburb than a place where people dealt with crime.

"Mrs. Dietz," a man wearing a tieless suit said gently. He had a Karl Malden nose. "Where did Sergeant Katz shoot this man? What part of the anatomy? We'd like to have some idea of how badly he's injured."

"Neck or shoulder. I couldn't tell for sure. It was across the gym, and it happened fast. He just leapt at her. How is Helen?"

"Hospital says it's too soon to tell for sure, but it looks like her right leg is broken in two places, her right shoulder is dislocated, and she has a concussion. You say she went down that whole flight of stairs?" The man shook his head incredulously. "She must be in pretty damn good shape to live through that."

"She's getting there," Maureen said. Someone had retrieved her clothes from the locker at the Y, and she had cleaned up and changed in the woman's room at the police station. She accepted the coffee the policeman handed her and drank it. It tasted familiar and pleasant.

"Mrs. Dietz," the man said gently. "How are you feeling? I mean how are you taking it? You want us to call some friends, family?"

Maureen took a sip of the coffee from the white mug and considered the question. All in all she wasn't doing badly. There was no pressure in her chest, and she was breathing normally. And then she realized that the big man was still out there, and she remembered what he had said. "Not bad, but I'll feel much better when you find him."

The man reached up to his neck as if to adjust a tie, but there was none there. "Can't see that he can get far," he said, looking toward the darkness out of the window. "He and his cousin had a room at the Y. It doesn't look like he went back to the room after he was shot. Suitcases, some personal things are still there. He's not from this area and probably doesn't have any friends he can go to. He's shot in a very visible place. We'll find him."

"May I use the phone?" she asked, and he pointed to it.

"My name's Cornish," he said, stepping to the door. "By the way, I'm a Chicago homicide investigator, and I've worked with Helen Katz. I knew Barelli. We'll find Vanbeeber. Since this happened in Evanston, the Evanston police are going to want to talk to you some more. You up to it?"

"I'm up to it." She nodded, starting to dial, and he stepped out of the room to give her privacy.

When she looked at her watch, she expected it to be two or three in the morning. It was just past eleven. The phone rang four times before Mike answered.

"Mike?"

"Yeah, Maureen? Are you all right? You sound—"

"I know," she cut in. "I'll tell you all about it. Are Nancy and Miles there? Are they all right?"

"They're fine," he said. "Nancy's asleep. Miles should be back any minute. He went back to your house in the car to pick up his stereo."

"He's not supposed to go back there," she said, looking at the door, ready to shout for the policeman, who had just left.

"Maureen," Mike said. "He is seventeen years old, and I'm not his father. He doesn't take orders very well. He promised to pick up his friend Mark and to wait in front of the house in the car till the police come by on their check, then to ask them to go in with him. He promised."

"And you believed him?"

"I didn't have a hell of a lot of choice, Maureen," Mike said with some impatience, a Mike she had rarely heard. "I could have sat on him or held him in a hammerlock. He's not a fool. I can't see him doing something stupid and dangerous."

"Stay with Nancy," Maureen said and hung up as Mike blubbered out, "Maureen, what the—"

She stood up, walked to the door, and opened it. A group of men including Cornish were standing around talking. One of them, a young man in uniform, was laughing. Maureen looked at him as if he were a strange alien presence. How could anyone laugh after what had happened? But, she remembered, it hadn't happened to him, and that made all the difference.

"I've got to get home," she said.

"I'll give you a ride just as soon—" Cornish began, and held up a cigarette to show that he wanted to finish.

"Now," she insisted. "My son might have gone back there."

Cornish nodded, put his cigarette out in an old-fashioned porcelain plate on the nearby desk, and said, "Let's go."

They drove in silence except for Maureen giving him directions and him calmly saying, "Okay." Ten minutes later they pulled into the driveway. Her car wasn't there.

"I was wrong," she said. "I thought my son was here. He had my car. He must have picked up what he came for and gone back. Thanks for the ride anyway." She started to get out, and Cornish leaned over to keep her from closing the door.

"Might not be a good idea to stay here tonight," he said.

"I'm not," she said, putting her hand to her forehead. "I'm not thinking too well. Look, just wait here a second and I'll go in and get a few things I need."

"I'll come in with you," he said, starting to open his door.

"It'll take me two minutes," she said, motioning for him to stay. "I'll check the house and wave to you from the window over there. If there's anything suspicious, I'll come out. If I don't appear in the window in about a minute, you come in. I'll leave the door open. I really don't like the idea of thinking that I need a keeper."

"Suit yourself," he said, and turned on the car radio, which was preset to WJJD. Frankie Laine roared out "Mule Train," and Maureen walked up the stone steps to the front door. She fished out her key, went in through the second door, and turned on the light in the living room. Everything was in place and quiet. She went into the kitchen, turned on the light, and checked the basement. Then she went to the window, waved at Cornish, and indicated with two fingers that she would be out that quickly.

She was on the second floor landing when she was aware of something. It wasn't something out of place, but something she hadn't expected, and then she knew what it was. The door to Miles's room, at the top of the little flight of wooden stairs leading upward, was closed, and a crack of light came from under the door. It was unusual for Miles to forget and leave the light on, even if he had just picked up some stereo equipment and was hurrying with his friend Mark to get out.

She pulled herself up the stairs, opened the door, saw nothing, and reached for the light switch. He grabbed her wrist. The hand was huge and sweating. It pulled her in and spun her around. As she fell backwards, she put her hands behind her and hit the wall. Her right hand grasped for something to stop her fall and came away with a drawing Miles had done years ago of Mr. Spock. It had been Scotch-taped to the wall, and now it clung to her hand.

She sat on the floor, looking up at him, trying to decide, to feel, to scream for help, to get to the door behind him. He stood, large, weaving back and forth. His left shoulder was soaked with blood.

"Where's Miles?" she said, starting to pull herself up by the edge of the desk. She tried to let the drawing drop from her hand, but the Scotch tape clung, and she had to shake it loose.

"Miles?" he said.

"My son," she went on, working to keep tears of rage and fear back.

"Lady, I don't care about your kid or anyone. Don't you feature that? I don't care about your kids or anyone else. I know what all this shit is about this witness killing. You and the police faked it to keep the papers and TV after us. Cal and I had that figured. I never gave a shit about those witnesses. Hell, I wouldn't know where to find them. You," he said, staggering forward, "you've got to stop being on me. You called me back to it. You been calling me back night and day. You witched me. Now you've killed Calvin. I knew it, should have known it, first time I saw those eyes looking at me like right now. I don't know if it was a curse or . . . but I've got to close those eyes. I may die for it, but I've got to make them stop looking at me."

She wondered how long she had been in the room, when Cornish would check, come running, but she had learned not only this night but in her life that time could move so slowly that it didn't seem to move at all. They might have been there for only a few seconds. She wanted to stall but couldn't think of anything to do.

"Wait," she said as he moved toward her, blocking her off between the desk and Miles's bed. But he didn't wait. He lumbered forward and their eyes met. She bent down, picked up the National Football League wastebasket, and threw it at him, but he pushed it away and reached for her.

"It's got to be," he said. "Me, Cal and me, never in our lives went looking for trouble. Never." He was inches from her. She could smell his breath and blood, and she had the feeling that he was pleading with her, pleading for understanding before he killed her. His eyes were wet with tears. For an instant she did have the insane desire to forgive him; to close her eyes, forgive him, and let go. She had been through enough. It never stopped, never.

"Just step out the way, missus," came a voice from behind them.

Marty Vanbeeber didn't turn around to the sound. He

reached forward for Maureen's neck, but she dropped to her knees and pushed herself behind Miles's desk. The big man was reacting slowly, probably in a fog from the loss of blood. He had a perplexed look on his face, as if she had simply disappeared.

"Behind the desk," said the voice from the doorway, and Maureen pushed herself farther behind the desk. Only then did Martin Vanbeeber turn around to see who was giving orders, changing his plan.

"I remember you," Martin said, pointing a finger at the black man, who was no longer wearing the suit he had worn the day before when he visited Maureen. Instead he was in overalls that looked very much like those he had worn eight years earlier. The rifle in his hand was pointed at Vanbeeber's chest, and the two were no more than six feet apart.

"I got no fight with you," Marty Vanbeeber bellowed, tears coming from his eyes. "It's between me and her."

"No," said the black man. "Never was just between you and the lady. We were all part of it."

Maureen knew what was going to happen next, and she wanted to shout "No!" but she couldn't. She could only watch from behind the desk as the black man pulled the trigger and a screaming noise filled the room, the noise of bullet and dying man.

Vanbeeber staggered back, looked over at Maureen, trying to say something, and reached down in a vague attempt to find the hole the black man had just put into his stomach.

She watched him from behind the desk, and she knew that she had seen this before. The big man toppled forward, and she had to pull herself up to see him on the floor. He looked back at her with fear in his eyes.

She stood up now and looked around Miles's room. It was covered with blood: the bed, his papers, the television, the wooden floor. Then she looked at the black man.

"No other way," he said. "I've been waiting on him for three days now."

Below in the house she could hear glass breaking. "It's the police," she said.

"It's all right," the man said calmly, putting the rifle down next to the wall. "I'll just step into the light, put my hands up so they don't do nothing dangerous, and we'll explain things."

The door broke below and footsteps crunched on glass. "Mrs. Dietz?" Cornish shouted.

"Up here," she said. "Everything's all right. Don't shoot." Then Maureen said to the black man as she looked down at the body, "Did you hear what he said? He said he didn't kill Simcox, he and the other one didn't attack Susan Breen. How could . . . ?" And she stopped as she looked into his eyes. He knew something he didn't want to put into words, something that had now become a terrible possibility.

"No," she said. "You didn't just come here to wait for Vanbeeber."

"No, ma'am," he said. "I'm glad he came, but no, ma'am. I came to tell you . . . something I think you just figured out for yourself."

Cornish stepped into the room now, his pistol aiming at the black man's chest.

"He saved my life," Maureen said. "He"—she pointed to the body—"was waiting for me."

"Okay, then," said Cornish, his gun still out. "Then just put your arms down easy while I make a call, Mr. . . . ."

"Robichaux," the black man said, dropping his hands gently to his side as he turned to Maureen and added, "I wouldn't have shot anybody but one of those two who killed your husband, Mrs. Dietz. I'd like you to believe that."

"I believe it, Mr. Robichaux."

Cornish was dialing a number on Miles's phone with his

free hand. He looked down at the body and seemed satisfied that the man was dead.

"I didn't hear anything the big man said," Robichaux added in a whisper so low that Maureen wasn't sure she heard him, "but you'd best find your boy."

"Thank you," she said, and for the last time she looked down at the bloody body of Martin Vanbeeber, and she knew the nightmare was not over.

"I'm going downstairs," she said to Cornish, who, still on the phone, nodded, giving orders, information to someone on the other end. Robichaux had moved to Miles's bed and sat down.

When she got to the living room she was suddenly aware of the heat, that terrible heat. It came through the window Cornish had broken, filled her lungs, brought tears to her eyes. She went out the door, turned, and ran into the darkness toward the alley. She ran into the alley and down. Normally, she would have been aware of shadows, doorways in the alley this late at night, but that older fear seemed almost comic to her. She ran on, made a right turn, and hurried toward the park, where she knew there was a phone near the baseball field.

She found the phone, dug out a quarter, and dropped it in. Three young men wandered across the street and past her, wondering what a good-looker was doing out alone this late, whether she was looking for three guys. She gave them a look of searing anger as the phone rang, and one of the young men said, "She's a nut, boy," and the three wandered away.

"Hello," Mike said.

"It's me, Mike," she answered. "I need your help. Don't ask me anything. Just get in your car and pick me up at the corner of Main and Dodge as fast as you can."

"You want me to wake Nancy?"

"No, leave her a note. Let her sleep. She's safe now."

And before he could ask her what she meant, she hung up, and waited for him to appear.

A warm breeze announced the arrival of Mike, who pulled up at the corner. Maureen pushed away a long strand of hair that clung moistly to her forehead and got into the car.

Instead of starting the car, Mike looked at her, one hand on the wheel. Traffic at the intersection was light. The two gas stations across from the park on opposite corners were closed, but the Texaco sign turned lazily in the air. Maureen looked at it and then at Mike.

"You look awful, Maureen," he said gently. "What's—"

"I think we have to hurry," she cut in, reaching over to touch his hand. Her palm was perspiring, and the back of his hand was moist. "I might be wrong or we might be too late, but we've got to hurry." She told him where to drive, and he took off toward the expressway.

"The Vanbeebers are both dead," she said, putting her arm out the window to catch a breeze that didn't exist. "And Helen is in the hospital."

"And?" he encouraged. "What happened?"

She told him as they drove past the darkened, set-back factories on Oakton and beyond the intersection near the expressway at Touhy and Cicero, where late-night restaurants and all-night gas stations were neon bright.

When they got on the expressway heading south at fifty, the wind hit her face, warm but not moving. She could feel the beads of perspiration on her upper lip vibrate and tickle. She wanted to close her eyes, but she kept them open.

"They didn't kill Simcox," she said after a while. "They didn't attack Susan Breen. All they wanted was me."

"So who did kill Simcox?" Mike said, glancing at her. His voice was low and gentle, and she had the impression that he was humoring her, that he thought she was sinking back into some long-past madness awakened by the nightmare of the last few hours.

She put her head down and closed her eyes. She could feel her thin shirt sticking to the back of the warm car seat. The scratches on her back from the gravel on the YMCA roof stung, but she welcomed the stinging as they pulled off the Kennedy into an area of the city she had avoided for many years. They made a left turn, and Maureen took a deep breath as they drove under the dark viaduct that marked the fringe of the forbidden circle. Something in her from the past told her to reach over, scream at Mike to turn around and get out, but something greater was in control, and she folded her hands in her lap as they drove down Diversey.

"There are only three witnesses left to David's murder, not counting me, Miles, and Nancy," she said, looking straight ahead. "The one who killed Simcox, attacked Susan Breen. He can't find Robichaux. Simcox's widow must be surrounded by the police. He could have gotten the old man, Brinkmann, and didn't. That leaves only one witness."

"Maureen," Mike said, reaching over to put his right hand on her leg. "There's nothing going on here. It's all in your mind. Come back to my place and I'll call the police. I've got a better idea. We'll stop at the Gold Coin for coffee, and we'll split a pecan roll. What do you say? We'll talk it all through."

Maureen didn't answer. She put her right hand to her chest, waiting for the throb as she passed familiar corners, buildings. Had that McDonald's been there before? Yes, maybe? That grocery store. It looked old, battered; a hand-printed sign in the window said they had Krakus hams.

"All right," Mike said with a deep sigh.

"Humor me," she said finally. "If there's nothing there, we'll go. I don't want to be right, Mike. God, I don't want to be right about this."

"About what?" he said. They were stopped for a red light. "What the hell are we talking about?"

"There it is," was her answer. She nodded forward. He

looked, but since he was unfamiliar with the street, there was nothing to see but a string of dark stores and distant lights.

Three blocks farther and they were there. He almost drove past it. For some reason she had assumed he would know where to turn. It was as if, for a whisper of time, he was David, and they were driving to Bittie's for a hot dog, and the kids were in the back seat and time had changed its mind.

"There," she said. "Turn left."

He turned quickly, crossing the street, and pulled into the parking lot. There were only two other cars in the lot, and Mike pulled next to the one he recognized. "What's that doing here?" he said, pointing to the car on the right.

Maureen didn't answer. Her head was light, floating in the same approximate space where David had parked, and she looked across through the window of Bittie's. The little castle hadn't changed much. There was no Elmer Fudd painted on the window. It was clear and clean. The counter was new, at least different from the one she remembered, and something else had changed, the color of the walls? Something. She had expected some radical difference, some indication of the passage of the years, but there was so little, so little. She wanted to get out, run inside, but she couldn't move. All she could do was look at them through the window. There was Lou behind the counter, white-aproned, chewing something—gum, food. There was no girl taking orders, but there were two customers. The one being waited on was a grossly fat woman with gray hair. She was wearing a blue dress with little white flowers. Behind her stood the person she had hoped would not be there. He was carrying a paper bag at his side, and it looked as if there was something heavy in it.

"Maureen?" Mike said, looking at her. She forced herself to look back at him and saw the disbelief in his eyes. "No," he said.

She didn't answer but reached out to open the door. Her hand touched something fluttery, a flying insect that had landed for a moment, only to be accidentally crushed by her hand. She wiped the sticky palm on her shorts as she got out, slammed the door, and hurried across the small parking lot with Mike behind.

"I want to go in alone," she said.

"No," he said.

She turned to face him. They were standing just about where David had been killed, standing on his memory, his ghost, his mark on them. "Yes," she said firmly. She met his eyes as she stood there with fists clenched at her sides, trying to keep her body from trembling. Beyond Mike the night heat rose from the lot, a shimmering two-foot band above the ground, adding to the dreaminess of the moment.

Mike's face went from determination to anger to defeat. He threw up his hands and took a step back to sit on the hood of his car with his arms folded.

"I'll be watching," he said.

"Thank you, Mike," Maureen answered and turned to go around the corner and to the door of Bittie's. The fat woman was just coming out, breathing heavily and looking into the white paper bag she was carrying to be sure her order was right. The smell of hot dog wafted from the bag to Maureen and added to her memories of the last August night she had been here. And then she went in.

Lou looked over at her, pausing in the order he was taking from the only other customer in the place. The customer's back was turned to her.

"Hey, Mrs. Dietz," Lou said, surprised. "What brings you here?"

Miles turned suddenly to face her, his eyes wide, surprised. She looked at him and made clear in the look that she understood everything, and Miles closed his eyes.

"What's wrong?" Lou said. "You in some trouble?"

He started to come around the counter, a look of concern for her on his face, but she kept walking toward Miles, her hand out. Miles wiped his glistening cheek, adjusted his glasses, and tried to shake his head no, but her hand remained out.

"You know this kid?" Lou said, uncertain about what was happening.

"He's my son," she said, and Miles handed her the paper bag. It was heavy but not bulky.

"All right," Lou said, looking at them. "But what's going on?"

"I told him to meet me here and order some hot dogs," she said. "A friend of ours is in the car. Mike is in the car, Miles."

Miles glanced through the window at Mike, who sat against the hood and looked back at him.

"I wanted to come here," she said, her eyes fixed on her son, "to tell you that the Vanbeebers are both dead. You won't have to worry about them anymore. We won't have to worry about them." She took Miles's hand.

"Hey," Lou said, sitting on one of the stools at the counter. "That's great news." The air conditioner hummed above them.

"They're dead, Miles," she said. He nodded.

"Let's celebrate," Lou said, getting up and clapping his hands. "What'll it be? It's on me." He moved back behind the counter and looked at them, waiting for their order.

"I think we'll come back another night," she said, walking Miles to the door.

"Well, that's the way you want it," Lou called. "You got a raincheck. Any time. Bring your friend and your little girl. Anything you want, anything."

She looked over at him and saw the relief in his craggy face. He didn't know and would never know how close he had come to being Miles's third victim.

When they got outside, she held tightly to Miles's hand and walked around Bittie's, feeling the weight of the bag in her other hand and the sudden return to sighing, heavy heat.

"It was here," Miles said as they moved across the small lot. "My father was killed right here. I remember it, Mom."

"I know, baby," she said.

Mike pushed himself from the car, but Maureen motioned him back, and he sat back with his hands bracing himself.

Miles looked around, at Bittie's, at the lot, at the street. "I thought it was bigger, a lot bigger. But it's just a little place."

"You were just a little boy," she said. "Let's get in the car."

She guided Miles to her Omega, the car he had driven to Bittie's, helped him into the passenger seat, and dropped the paper bag into the back seat. It thudded heavily on the floor. She hadn't looked inside but imagined a tire iron, a metal bar.

"We'll meet at your place," she said to Mike.

"I'm sorry, Maureen," Mike said, taking her in his massive arms, hugging her.

She could smell him, sticky and humid. It felt good, and she imagined herself falling suddenly asleep, imagined him picking her up in his arms, tucking her into his car, and driving her home like an exhausted child. She pushed away. "Okay," she said.

"Okay," he repeated, and she got into her car, closed the door, and looked at Miles, whose head was down.

"Your glasses are falling," she said, reaching over to help him as she had when he was a child. She brushed his hair back. She turned the ignition and looked over her shoulder to back up. Mike was already turning down Diversey. As she followed him, she looked back in her rearview mirror at the retreating hot dog stand. The little castle grew smaller and smaller and then disappeared.

"They're dead?" Miles said, not looking at her. Night shadows rippled on his face from the street lights they were passing.

"They're dead," she said. "Miles? Why did you do it?"

She thought she knew, but she had to hear it from him, had to be sure, had to make him share it, let it out.

"They let my father die," he said, his voice catching. "They could have come out, helped him, saved him, but they let him die. They just stood there watching while those two beat him to death. I hated them. You just went crazy. You left me. You left

— 265 —

Nancy. You didn't give us a chance to . . . We couldn't go crazy. But I remember it all."

They were just turning onto the expressway to head north. Mike was far ahead in the surprisingly heavy late-night traffic.

"Simcox," she said.

"When we saw him at Barnaby's, I followed him," Miles said. He was biting his lower lip, trying to keep together. She wanted to pull over, hold him, but he might shatter. She looked straight ahead. "I followed him to her apartment."

"Susan Breen's," Maureen said, her hands wet and slipping on the steering wheel she was clinging to.

Miles nodded. "He wasn't married to her," Miles said. "That's the kind of people they were. They didn't care about anyone, just themselves. I waited for him, the next morning, and I went back for her that next night. I was supposed to be at the movie with Mark, but I didn't go. I knew you wouldn't ask me about the movie. You never do. You're too busy running, exercising."

"Miles, I—" she began and then went quiet.

"She let me in. I told her I was your son, and she let me in," he said.

Maureen remembered the blood, the savage attack on Susan Breen and shuddered. "And the old man?" she asked.

"I was going to do it," Miles said, "but he opened the door and he was so old. He must have been old when my father was killed. He was too old to have helped him. He didn't deserve to be hurt. The others did. They deserved to die, the way my father did. But he was too old to help."

"I see," Maureen said, forcing herself to be calm. "I wasn't too old. I could have helped your father, but I didn't. Why didn't you want to hurt me?"

"I could have helped him," Miles said softly to himself. "I've thought of that so many times. I could have helped him, gotten out of the car, gotten their attention, given Dad a chance."

"Miles, you were nine years old. You were a frightened

little nine-year-old boy. And those people were frightened. I was frightened. If you can't blame me, you can't blame them. You can't blame yourself."

They didn't speak for the rest of the ride to Mike's house. Maureen considered turning on the radio. She tried to decide what to do, whom to turn to, but it wasn't coming. When they pulled in front of Mike's townhouse, his car was already parked and he was inside. She unbuckled her seat belt and turned to Miles, who looked up at her with moist eyes. His glasses were dirty. When they got inside she'd take them to the sink, clean them, give them back. They'd have a drink of Coke or root beer and talk, but after the talk a decision would have to be made.

"What are we going to do?" Miles asked.

"I'm not sure," she said.

"I'll go to jail," he said. "I deserve to go to jail. I deserve to be killed."

"Because you didn't help your father when you were nine?"

He looked out the window toward the house. The street was quiet, and the crickets were going mad.

"Let's go in," she said. As they walked up the path, she put her arm around his shoulder and pulled him close. It was awkward. Miles was slightly larger than she was and he was dazed, but he accepted her comfort and leaned against her as they went up the path.

It struck her that her son was right. When David had died, she had let go, dropped to the bottom of despair, and then climbed out slowly, painfully, not always successfully. But Miles had not gone mad, had not shown it. He had distorted and tried to deal with the situation. It had been buried alive and waiting inside him for the day Roger Simcox happened to see her at a restaurant, the day Helen Katz brought Barelli's file on the Vanbeebers back, reopened the memory of that night.

For Miles it was a delayed reaction. She knocked gently at the door to Mike's, and then reached over to touch Miles's burning cheek. Miles had waited eight years for his madness to come, for that guilt inside him to come out. Now he could begin to climb out, begin the horrible, grasping pull back to reality. She could help him. She had made the trip, had the dream, felt the pain. She could lead him.

Mike opened the door, and she could see the look of controlled concern on his face. "Hi, Miles," he said. "Let's have some Coke and talk in the kitchen."

As far as the police were concerned, the Vanbeebers had killed Simcox and attacked Susan Breen. Only the three of them and Robichaux knew that wasn't the truth, and Robichaux was not going to talk. That left the decision to Maureen and Miles. Maybe they could get away with it, but if they did, Miles could never get help. There was no choice.

It was a little after one in the morning when she called the police. She had checked on Nancy, who was sleeping gently, her thumb in her mouth, and then made the call. Cornish wasn't in but she left her number. He called back in less than five minutes.

"Mrs. Dietz," he said, obviously trying to control himself, "where are you and what the hell happened to you?"

She was in Mike's living room. The phone was stretched as far as it could go so she could sit holding Miles's hand on the brown shaggy sofa. Mike had straightened the place, which didn't need straightening. There were touches, remnants of Mike's family in each room: a photograph of two girls—his daughters—a set of decidedly non-masculine drapes, bright wall hangings.

"Mr. Cornish," she said. "I've got to see you alone, now."

"Mrs. Dietz," he said with a sigh. "I'm now into my second straight eight-hour shift, well into it. I'm sitting here in an air-conditioned office. The only thing waiting for me at home is a small window fan and a lot of old newspapers on the floor. Let's talk."

# 9

The heat wave broke three days before Labor Day. Maureen was driving home from Taylorville when the rain began, not the rain of the previous weeks, heavy and penetrating, but a clear rain, popping dust from the pavement as she headed up I-57. The weatherman out of an Effingham radio station said a Canadian low had been hovering for a week or more, seemed to be waiting and watching, and then moved down, decided that the summer punishment was now over.

Miles had been in a good mood, talking about the possibility of starting school a year late, trying not to be specific about when he might be getting out of the hospital. Dr. Wyngartner had promised nothing but said that if Miles continued to cooperate and improve, there was no reason why he shouldn't start spending weekends at home. He could even foresee the day not too far in the future when Miles would be able to come home and resume his life with a regular program of psychiatric treatment as an outpatient in Evanston Hospital.

Since Miles was still a juvenile, would be for another month, the judge who had met with Maureen's attorney and the state's attorney's representative agreed to handle the situation quietly. Maureen and Miles had agreed to a voluntary commitment to the mental hospital in Taylorville.

In the three weeks he had been there, she had visited him three times, never talking directly about Simcox. Maureen had been told that Dr. Wyngartner would deal with that and let her know what to say and do when Miles came home. This time, however, Miles had asked about Susan Breen.

"She's getting out of the hospital next week," Maureen had said, watching him closely.

"That's good," he said, nodding and looking down at the books she had brought him, both collections of light pieces: one by Robert Benchley, the other by Art Buchwald.

"She's looking much better," Maureen continued, not sure of how far to go but knowing that Miles was asking for something. "The doctors say she should look almost exactly the way she did before and can get back to work by as early as November."

"Does she . . . she know?"

"She knows, Miles. I had to tell her."

"I want her to know," he said, and she stiffened, watching his eyes for an unrepentant hardness, but it wasn't there. Even though she knew it was true, knew it had all happened, she couldn't visualize Miles—her Miles or even the shadow part of Miles—stalking through the night with a baseball bat. When she tried to imagine it, she was filled with a sense of sorrow that wouldn't let the scenes form. "I'm going to have to talk with her, to tell her . . . I'm sorry, Mom. I'm really sorry."

They had been sitting outside on the wooden porch. Patients and staff came in and out on the lawn, and a few people were playing catch with a McDonald's beach ball. The heat had not yet broken so they moved slowly, languidly, as if playing were a chore. The place reminded Maureen of her stay in the University of Illinois Hospital. It was similar, yet it was different. There was more light and hope here, partly because there was more money here. The cost was tremendous, and she would have to work doubly hard to pay for it, especially if Roger Simcox's widow did decide to sue, a possibility that Maureen had been told was genuine. It was a weight and a threat that she would have to live with, the possibility of the suit, of the whole story becoming public. Her lawyer, a friend of Helen's, had said that the greatest deterrent to the suit would be the fact that Roger Simcox was killed coming from the apartment of a young woman he had spent the night with. Mrs. Simcox had just been subjected to that publicity and, he reasoned, would not be likely to want to face it again, but one never knew.

The rain kept coming, but the sky never went completely dark. Maureen opened her window all the way and let the drops hit her arm, swirl against her face and body. She could carry the weight of Mrs. Simcox' possible suit. She had carried much more for a long time.

The highway was long, straight, and boring, but Maureen felt clean, cool, and light. She wasn't quite sure why.

When she got home late in the afternoon, Helen was sitting in the recliner with her foot propped up on one of Nancy's low wooden chairs. When she had first come from the hospital, Helen had agonized her way into the recliner one afternoon when no one was home and leaned back to rest her massive cast on the footrest. She found, ten minutes later when she needed a toilet, that she couldn't get out of the chair. Since then she had used the small chair.

"How is he?" Helen greeted.

"Good, really good," Maureen said, opening the windows in the living room. A cool breeze shot through against her face as she moved to each one and told Helen what had happened. Then she turned off the air conditioner.

"I got Nancy to camp this morning and picked her up," Helen said. "It took about twenty minutes to wedge myself into the car and a near-collision with a parked car to adjust to stepping on the gas and brake with my left foot. It's amazing what you can adjust to and how fast."

"Amazing," Maureen agreed.

Helen was wearing a tentlike green shift and looked like a little girl playing dress-up in her mother's clothes.

"That dress looks great with the cast," Maureen said.

"I'm thinking of painting the cast green to match it," Helen said. "Nancy volunteered to paint it."

"Mom, Mommy," Nancy called, running down the stairs. "Did you bring me anything?"

She was wearing a red T-shirt and a blue skirt she loved, though the zipper had long since passed into the land of dysfunction. Maureen reached down to catch the rush of her daughter and lifted her from the ground. No doubt, Nancy was getting heavier, growing.

"Juicy Fruit," Maureen said, kissing her hair. "In my bag, and an extra one for Paulette."

Nancy scrambled down and went for the purse, calling over her shoulder, "How's Miles?"

"Fine," she said, and that sense of sorrow pushed away the image of her son. "He'll be coming home for visits soon and might be back to stay in a month or two. His headaches are getting better, much better."

"I told Paulette Miles was getting an operation on his head."

"He's not getting an operation on his head," Maureen said.

Nancy looked disappointed, pocketed the gum, and said, "What time is dinner?"

"In about an hour," Helen answered.

"What're we having?" Nancy said, starting up the stairs.

"Junk," said Helen.

"Great," shouted Nancy. "Can Paulette have dinner with us? We love junk."

"Sure," Maureen said, "we've got plenty of junk."

Nancy disappeared up the stairs, shouting back, "I love you, Mom. I got to see the end of 'Spiderman.'" And she was gone. The door to her room snapped shut.

"Billy brought the tape," Helen said. "Over on the table."

Maureen walked over, picked up the tape, and turned it over. If it was reasonably good, there might be more money, money she would now need. "And?" Maureen said.

"And," Helen said, putting down the *New Yorker* magazine she was holding. "Mike called from San Diego to ask how things were. He said he was sorry to miss you and would call tonight."

"To tell me that he's decided to move to California to be near his daughters and that he has a job as a football coach, gym teacher, camp counselor, book reviewer." She stopped and shrugged.

"He ran, Mo, face it. They tend to do that," Helen said.

Maureen looked down at the tape, trying to decide whether she was relieved, disappointed, or hurt that Mike made some quick decisions since that night three weeks ago. A little of everything, she decided, but she knew she wasn't angry. She would miss his comfort and reliability, but she hadn't been ready for him. There had been something she had to learn, had to face before she could be really close to a man again. She was sure she would be ready the next time.

"I'm going up to look at the tape," she said, starting up the stairs. "Can I get you anything first?"

"A beer," Helen said. "A light beer. I bought a few bottles."

Maureen went to the refrigerator, opened a bottle of Michelob Light, and poured it into a tall glass. Then she brought it to Helen, saying, "For the winner."

Helen nodded and took the glass.

"You're going to put on a few pounds sitting around downing that stuff and getting no exercise," Maureen said, looking down.

"You're probably right, Mother. That's why I'm drinking

light beer. I'll let you punish me into shape when the cast comes off. Right now I've got to spend all my energy distracting myself so I don't even begin to think that it might itch. Shit, I shouldn't have said that." She put her beer down, pulled up the green shift, and tried to insert her finger into the cast.

"I think I'll pass this part," Maureen said and, tape in hand, went upstairs.

They hadn't really talked about Helen being a permanent resident, but it looked as if it might be a long-term thing until Helen decided to take a chance on another man or the Chicago police decided she shouldn't have an Evanston address. No one had promised anything, but Helen had picked up from visitors from the department, particularly Cornish, that she was in line for a promotion when she got back to duty.

Maureen went past her daughter's closed door and heard the theme music from "Spiderman" vibrating. She paused for a moment and then started up to Miles's room, where the video recorder was attached to his television set. She had cleaned the room herself when she came back to the house the day after Robichaux shot Martin Vanbeeber. She had scrubbed away the blood that could be scrubbed away and thrown out the bedspread and various other pieces that could simply be thrown out. She had arranged to have the broken window downstairs repaired and had forced herself to spend time in the room, to convince herself that it was just a room, not a dark vault of horrible memories where Miles had hidden and brooded and planned, and where a man had died. She had gone through that with Bittie's. She didn't want it to happen again.

As she went through the door, the light of the late-afternoon sun came brightly through the window. She leaned over Miles's bed to open the window and let in some of the fresh, cooling air, and then she turned to the video recorder.

She paused, testing herself. She remembered Martin Vanbeeber lying there, remembered the blood, his eyes. She touched her chest, listened to her breathing, but felt nothing. It seemed to be gone. She had had none of the symptoms since that night. What she did have now was a memory about Robichaux.

The police had arrested him, charged him with several dozen felonies and misdemeanors. Only a series of lies from Maureen had managed to gain him his freedom. The central lie was that she and Robichaux were old friends, a statement Cornish and the other detective who questioned her clearly did not believe. Robichaux had agreed to watch the house, she said, to protect her and her family after she had asked him to do so. She had, she said, not had full faith in the police to protect her and in fact, she had been proven right. He had saved her.

There were holes, contradictions, inconsistencies in her story, but Robichaux refused to say anything other than that the police should ask Mrs. Dietz. So they had asked her and eventually given up. The man had shot someone who had killed her husband, threatened to kill her. There didn't seem to be any doubt about that, and the police had other things on their minds, other murderers still roaming loose. After three days, they gave up.

The newspapers and television weren't as troubled by the situation. In an increasingly black city with a black mayor, the story of a black man saving the life of a suburban white woman was one hell of a great fairy tale. Robichaux, who had wanted to be forgotten, had become a front-page hero. There was no probing beyond this fairy tale, no thought that the Vanbeebers might not have done all the killing. It was still a fragile situation, but so be it. Things could be worse, much worse.

Maureen turned on the television, flipped to Channel 3, pushed the video recorder power button and the button to turn the machine from TV to VCR. Then she pushed play and sat back to watch.

There she was, that first image. She heard her own sincere

voice, saw her own serious, intense face, and listened to her words, as if it were someone else speaking.

"The object of a good exercise program, a good workout, is to reach a state in which you almost feel yourself hovering above, out of body, watching as your body and mind lose the boundary line between them. When this happens, you go beyond strain, beyond pain. Exercising ceases to be a dreaded and necessary chore and becomes, instead, a form of relaxation. If you exercise to stay alive a little longer or to look a little better, you're only a small step on the way. The goal is to exercise because you feel good—right—doing it, because it makes you unashamed, proud of your body and mind."

It sounded a bit too philosophical and maybe even a bit pretentious, though it had not when she said it. That bothered her less than the woman she saw doing the routine. The words had been fine, but the woman on the screen, the diminished Maureen, didn't seem to be enjoying what she was doing. No doubt about it. She sat watching herself and realized that there was no joy in the routine. It worked, but there was something— life—missing from it. She had been preaching and acting out escape. Exercise had been a retreat, a diving into a sanctuary.

She laughed once out loud and shook her head. Someone had told her that a long time ago, Erika at the Illinois State Psychiatric Hospital. Maureen had agreed with her, said it was possible, thought it was possible, but it held no meaning. The analysis had been without pulse.

It had taken her eight years. It had taken her horror, but she had experienced it, and only through experiencing it did it have any real meaning. She moved to Miles's desk quickly, opened a drawer, and pulled out a pad of paper. There were changes to make. The opening of the tape would have to be redone, rewritten.

She jotted furiously, words, ideas that she hoped would make sense later, and then she looked up at the television screen.

Jane Chong had inserted a shot of the sunset over the beach. Maureen looked at it in fascination. It had been a long time since she had looked outward, out of herself at something as massive and simple as a sunset. She felt like crying for Miles and for Mike and for herself. Instead she watched the end of the tape, pushed the stop button; and then, as the tape rewound, she called Billy.

"I just saw the tape," she said when he came on.

"Looks great," he said. "That Chong kid is——"

"I want to make some changes," she said.

"We don't need changes." He chuckled. "The health center board saw it yesterday. They love it. They're talking about you doing television spots, like Victoria Princeton——"

"Principal," Maureen corrected. "The tape needs some changes, a new introduction. I can live with the routine. I've lived with it a long time."

Billy's sigh was enormous, exaggerated. "I thought you told me you need money. Was I wrong or did you tell me that? You know how much we can make if you do their commercials? It could lead to more, too. You're not a bad-looking woman."

"Congratulations, Billy. You managed to be both sexist and insulting with a single compliment. If you want me to do television commercials, I'll do television commercials, but the tape needs a few changes. Please, Billy, don't fight me."

"You're not being fought," he said, giving in. "I'll give them a call, tell them you've got an idea for making it even better. It is going to be better, right?"

"Much better," she said, lying back on Miles's bed. She hadn't worked out what she was going to say, but she was sure it would be better, at least for her.

"I'll call the Chong kid," Billy said. "We'll set it up as soon as we can. I'm going for tomorrow."

"Tomorrow looks good to me," Maureen said. "Good-bye, Billy."

She hung up, retrieved the tape, and left the room. Nancy

was still in her room as Maureen hurried down the stairs to find Helen in the kitchen, comically balancing at the refrigerator on her heavily cast leg.

"Let's see," Helen said. "Generic macaroni-and-cheese leftovers, a little two-day-old tuna salad, three old slices of frozen pizza, no known brand of origin, and Kool-Aid. Is that junk or is that junk?"

"It's junk," Maureen agreed, putting down the tape.

"How's the tape?" Helen asked, holding on to the counter near the refrigerator and pulling out an aluminum foil–covered bowl, which probably contained the tuna salad.

"Not bad," Maureen said. "Needs a few changes."

"It'll take me about twenty minutes to put all this together," Helen said, examining the odds and ends she had placed on the kitchen table. "I can take a little longer. You drove all day, and you must be going out of your mind from not running. Do your three miles, and everything will be on the table when you get back. All the junk you can eat."

Maureen pushed the refrigerator door closed, reached for the cold pieces of pizza, and said, "I think I'll skip the run today. I don't think I really need it."